The Spider

By the same author

DEATH CARE

COLDER THAN THE GRAVE

CRIPPLEHEAD

GIGOLO

DARK ANGEL

KISS AND KILL

THE DOLL DOCTOR

INNOCENT BLOOD

The Spider

Raymond Haigh

ROBERT HALE · LONDON

© Raymond Haigh 2010
First published in Great Britain 2010

ISBN 978-0-7090-9165-3

Robert Hale Limited
Clerkenwell House
Clerkenwell Green
London EC1R 0HT

www.halebooks.com

2 4 6 8 10 9 7 5 3 1

Typeset in 11/15pt Janson
Printed in Great Britain by the
MPG Books Group, Bodmin and King's Lynn

PROLOGUE

I t was a large room. Linen blinds, drawn down three tall windows, shut out the glare of the autumn sun and the dim light had a restful quality. Books lined the window-facing wall, their covers and bindings relieving the drabness of blue-grey shelves and walls and carpet. There were no pens or papers on the desk beside the far wall, just a solitary black telephone.

A bespectacled man, thin and slightly stooping, rose from a chair beside a brown-leather couch.

'Dr Uberman?' Samantha's high heels rocked a little as she crossed the thick carpet towards him.

He reached for her hand and held it. 'And you are Miss Quest. Please …' he gestured towards the couch. She sat down and he reclaimed his comfortable-looking chair. 'I gather that when you made this appointment you advised my receptionist that you wish to submit to analysis. Analysis can be a long and time-consuming process. May I ask why you feel the need for it?

'My state of mind.' Samantha laid her clutch bag on her lap and crossed her legs.

Dr Uberman chuckled softly. 'All of my patients come to me because of their state of mind, Miss Quest. Can you be a little more specific?' He made a steeple with his fingers, pressed them against his chin and began to study the young woman more closely. Black hair with a deep fringe framed a pale face, out of which burned eyes that were large and of a particularly vivid green. He only half-heard her husky voice saying, 'Fear, anxiety, ennui, sleeplessness.' Intrigued by her appearance, he was watching her crimson lips shape the words. She'd said ennui, not depression. Apart from that there was nothing particularly unusual. Suddenly aware that she was no longer speaking, he cleared his throat and said, 'This insomnia, is it very severe?'

'I suppose so. And when I do sleep I'm troubled by dreams; disturbing dreams, and recently there's one that recurs, almost nightly.'

'Is it always the same?'

'The same, but gradually unfolding, as if something is being revealed to me. And when I wake, I feel exhausted, robbed of all vitality.'

Dr Uberman drew his fingertips from his chin and picked up a notebook. 'Our first session is going to be rather short, so, if I may, I'd like to ask you some general questions about yourself. Then perhaps you could recount this dream? Are you happy with that, Miss Quest?'

'Of course.'

'Do you wish to remain seated, or would you rather stretch out on the couch?'

Samantha glanced towards pillows protected by a paper towel. 'I think I'd prefer to lie down.' She kicked off her black-and-white shoes, swung her legs up and reclined back. Her short-sleeved dress had a dramatic black-and-white zigzag pattern. It looked elegant and expensive, rather like the creations Dr Uberman saw on the pages of the fashion magazines his wife was so fond of. When she arranged her skirt over her legs, her black-and-white bag fell with a thud to the floor.

Dr Uberman rose and picked it up. His fingertips traced a large, hard shape, and the weight of the bag surprised him. He laid it beside her, then pushed his chair closer to the desk. When he sat down again, the end of the couch blocked his view of his beguiling new patient; important if he was to remain alert and focused.

Opening his notebook and uncapping his pen, he said, 'Tell me your full name, Miss Quest.'

'Samantha Judith Quest.'

'Shall I address you as Samantha, or Miss Quest?'

'Samantha or Sam,' the husky voice whispered. 'Intimates call me Sam, and I imagine this is going to get pretty intimate.'

'And your age?'

'Thirty-two.'

'Any serious illnesses?'

'None.'

'Your general health is good?'

'Yes, always.'

'Have you ever been married?'

'I'm a widow. I've resumed my maiden name.'

'How long have you been widowed?'

'Nine years and nine months.'

'May I ask how your husband died?'

'He was shot by a sniper. He was a doctor, attending a patient on a kibbutz near the Gaza Strip.'

'Does his death still distress you?'

'Every day that passes the feeling of loss becomes more intense, the anger and hatred continue to smoulder.'

'Anger and hatred?'

'For arrogant men; murderers who abandon reason and use violence to impose their ideologies on others.'

'Do you have children?'

'No.'

'Would you like to?'

'No.'

'Your father: is he still alive?'

'He died when I was twelve: a heart attack.'

'May I ask his name?'

'Jacob Kwestrovitch. He changed it to Quest when he emigrated to Israel. He was a Russian Jew.'

'Are you a Jew?'

'Jewishness is transferred along the maternal line. My mother was an Irish Catholic, Teresa O'Farrell, so I am not a Jew, but I have strong sympathies.'

'You are a Catholic?'

'I was baptized by the Bishop of Dublin and confirmed by the Patriarch of Jerusalem.'

'Do you still practise your faith?'

'No.'

'You have lost it?'

'No. It might be better for me if I had.'

Dr Uberman noted the remark in his small, neat handwriting, then underlined it. Not now, he decided. This was something to return to later. 'And your mother...?'

'She died when I was eight. Cancer.'

'So,' Dr Uberman glanced back through his notes, 'you were orphaned from the age of twelve. Who cared for you?'

'My half-sister, Rachel, she was my father's daughter by his first marriage, and her husband, Isaac. They were kind and loving parents to me.'

'You still see them?'

'They're dead; murdered in Berlin. Terrorist bomb, left on a bus. They were on their way to the synagogue: my half-sister, her husband, their little girl, were all killed. Isaac had just taken up a lecturing post at the university.'

'You said you experience fear and anxiety. When do you have these feelings?'

'Usually in the small hours, when I wake from sleep.'

'Are you alone at these times?'

'Yes.'

'Have you had any relationships since your husband's death?'

'Sexual relationships?'

'Yes, sexual relationships.'

'No.'

'Do you have any close friends?'

'I have a friend who cooks and cleans for me; takes care of my clothes, attends to domestic matters.'

'She acts as a housekeeper?'

'He: it's a man. And he's more than a housekeeper.'

'But no more than a friend?'

'A very special friend. I love him.'

Confused now, Dr Uberman placed three question marks in the margin of his notes. 'Does he return your love?'

'How can one ever know if one is favoured by another's love? He's kind, protective, caring; sensitive to my moods, very tender and gentle. He allows me to be myself.'

'You confide in him?'

'I lie to him.'

'Do you find him physically attractive?'

'Extremely. He's a male model. He's very handsome.'

'Would you like a sexual relationship with him?'

'He's homosexual, Doctor. He has absolutely no interest in me as a woman.'

She'd said homosexual, not gay; and she'd avoided his question. Dr Uberman made a note, then asked, 'You're quite sure of that?'

'A woman can always tell. But we're very intimate.'

'You mean you enjoy a cerebral kind of intimacy?'

'Yes, and also a physical intimacy. In some ways we're probably more intimate than many married couples.'

'I do not understand. Please explain.'

'He's interested in the clothes I wear. Sometimes he helps me choose them; he suggested this dress and bag and shoes for my visit to you. He hand-washes and irons my silk blouses and under-wear, takes things to the dry-cleaners for me. Occasionally he'll run my bath, bring drinks through and sit and talk to me while I bathe. And he cuts and styles my hair. He owns and manages a rather exclusive hairdressing salon: modelling's a precarious profession, particularly for a man.'

'Have you ever seen him naked?'

'Not completely, and then only in magazine photographs.'

Dr Uberman wrote: *Has frustrated desire for a sexual relationship with male friend triggered seduction behaviour, or is gay man a mother substitute?* He turned to a fresh page. 'Does he have male lovers?'

'A procession of them. His sexuality and his good looks have made his life difficult.'

'Do you feel jealous of these men, these male lovers?'

There was gentle laughter. 'Not jealousy, Doctor, only sadness for the pain they cause him.'

He reached down the side of his chair, picked up a file and opened it. 'You live in a place called Barfield. Where is that?'

'It's a nondescript little town in South Yorkshire.'

'Why do you choose to live in a nondescript little town?'

Because it's just that, Samantha reflected, a backwater place. No one knows me, I'm lost, hidden. Old enemies, men who would wish to harm me, are not likely to look for me there. She said, 'It's a quiet place. I like it. And it has good rail and motorway links.'

'You've journeyed a long way to see me.'

'I have another appointment, a business meeting, later this morning.'

'May I ask the nature of your business?'

'Fashion: I'm a buyer. I travel extensively.' She'd anticipated the question and prepared an innocuous answer.

'Your appointment is in London?'

'Tanford; a small market town about twenty miles south of the City.'

'Then I think we should end your first session, or you won't keep your appointment.'

'End it? But I haven't recounted the dream.'

'It's after eleven. You can tell me about the dream during our next session.'

Samantha sat up, swung her feet to the floor and groped for her shoes. She heard a movement behind her, and a beam of sunlight crept across the room as a blind rattled upwards. The brighter light exposed the doctor's thinning hair, the thick lenses in his spectacles, the creases in his dark-blue suit.

Rounding the couch, he watched her stand and pick up her bag. She had small hands with slender fingers and nails the colour of blood. There was something intriguing, almost disturbing, about his new patient. What, he wondered, would his analysis uncover. 'Miss Forster will make another appointment if you wish to continue,' he said.

'Continue?' Samantha laughed huskily. 'I hadn't realized we'd begun.'

'On the contrary, the background details are crucial. Without them it would be impossible for me to put the things you tell me in context. You've given me a great deal to think about.' He held out a hand; felt, for an instant, the soft warmth of her fingers, then led her to the door and opened it. He stood aside while she stepped out into the reception area.

Miss Forster, her greying hair neatly styled, clinical in her white coat, looked up from a keyboard and gazed at them over blue-rimmed spectacles. She smiled.

'Bernice, could you make another appointment for Miss Quest?' He glanced at Samantha. 'Early next week?' Samantha nodded. 'Until next week, then, Miss Quest.'

Back in his consulting room, Dr Uberman retrieved his note-book and carried it over to the desk. He sat for a while, tapping his teeth with his pen and gazing over at the offices and consulting rooms on the other side of Harley Street. Suddenly leaning forward, he wrote: *Childhood, adolescent and early-adult traumas: death, loss, dislocation, loneliness. Are fear and guilt being induced by abandonment of religious practice? Patient seems intelligent, confident, composed and very self-controlled. (Problems when we move on to free association?). Sexuality sublimated – in what? Or has trauma made her frigid?*

The woman's fragrance still lingered in the room, restrained yet provocative. He recalled her fashionable dress and bag and shoes. Her appearance was clearly a thing of considerable importance to her. Why? The answer to that question could be revealing. And those eyes and the blood-red mouth and fingernails. He shuddered. There was something unnerving, something strangely compelling, about her eyes and mouth. It was as if they might devour you.

ONE

Samantha tugged at a white porcelain knob and let it snap back into the pilaster. Somewhere in the vastness of the place a bell would be ringing. Stepping away from the door, she glanced up at the house. A rather impressive example of nine-teenth-century mock baronial, it sported square bays, an oriel and a couple of turrets, all crowned by crenellated parapets. Rain-water pipes crept over its grey stones and rose, like black veins, to hoppers set beneath a riot of slated roofs.

A movement behind one of the upper windows caught her eye. Samantha focused her gaze on a pale face, half-hidden behind curtains. The woman was scowling down at her through tiny panes of glass that distorted her features, but her expression was clearly distressed; anguished even. When the woman realized she'd been seen, she disappeared from view.

The heavy door opened and a sallow-faced young woman frowned out at her.

Samantha smiled. 'Quest: Lord Conway's expecting me.'

Surprised eyes flicked over Samantha's black-and-white dress and bag and Sergio Rossi shoes. 'Please, come inside. Lord Conway instructed me to take you straight through to him.'

Polish, Samantha mused, as she crossed the threshold. Pink clips held the maid's short brown hair away from her face. Her grey dress had long sleeves; her white apron was small and plain. As Samantha followed her across a stone-flagged hall, she glimpsed the woman who'd watched her from the high window. She was standing in the shadows at the turn of an impressive flight of stairs. Her expression was venomous.

The maid led her through an archway and down a carpeted corridor. She walked with short, brisk little steps, her calves plump beneath black stockings, her rather large feet laced into highly polished black shoes.

'You come from Gdansk?' Samantha asked.

The girl turned. 'You speak Polish! And how do you know I come from Gdansk?'

'I spent some time there, in the shipyards. Your dialect's unmistakable, even when you're speaking English.'

'You worked in the shipyards?' Shocked, the girl looked Samantha over again.

Samantha laughed. 'Don't worry. The ships won't sink. I didn't do any welding.'

Pausing beside an oak door panelled in the Jacobean style, the maid tapped gently. At a muffled command to enter, she led Samantha inside.

'Samantha Quest, sir. You said he … she had to be brought to you immediately.'

'So I did, Anna. Thank you, you're very kind.'

The girl beamed and her sallow face became almost pretty. Stepping back into the corridor, she closed the door.

Samantha advanced across a Persian rug towards the old man behind the desk. He was staring at her, eyes wide, his big features slack with surprise.

'You're a woman, dammit! Thought Sam Quest was a man. You sounded a bit like a man on the phone.'

'Do I look like a man?'

Suddenly remembering the courtesies, he rose to his feet, ran a finger along a bristling moustache, and held out a hand. 'Not in the least. Never seen a woman who looked less like a man. It's the name, and the husky voice over the telephone, rather confusing.'

Crimson lips parted in a smile. 'Others have made the same mistake, Lord Conway.' Samantha slid her hand into his wrinkled old paw.

He held it while he studied her face, then bold eyes slid down to the shadows between folds of silk that formed the bodice of her dress. She tugged her hand free.

'Sit down, sit down.' He gestured towards a low-backed leather chair. Samantha settled herself into it and crossed her legs. Blue eyes, watery, like melting ice, captured every movement.

She allowed her smile to widen. 'Do you still wish to discuss your problems with me, Lord Conway, or does my being a woman change things?' She settled her clutch bag on her lap.

He lifted his gaze from her legs to her face and cleared his throat. 'Is it miss or missus?'

'Miss.'

'I'm sorry, Miss Quest. You're something of a surprise. Marcus hadn't time to talk when we met at the club; he just said Sam Quest, and gave me your number. And the husky voice down the telephone ...'

'Don't worry about it. Am I still eligible?'

'Of course. Rather delicate matter. Might be better, your being a woman.' His hair was white, but it hadn't thinned. It made his long face and impressive beak of a nose appear even more florid. Captivated old eyes were wandering over her again.

'A delicate matter?' Samantha prompted.

He collected his straying thoughts. 'Family business. Rather embarrassing. Don't quite know how to begin. Your being a woman doesn't make talking about it any easier; there are things I could say more openly to a man.'

'You can't shock me, Lord Conway. And all families have difficulties. Why not tell me what the problem is, then take it from there?'

He sank back in his chair. 'Daughter-in-law and my grand-daughter have disappeared.'

'Abducted or just gone away?'

'Gone away. Left the family home about a week ago. Not seen or heard from them since.'

'You've contacted the police?'

He nodded. 'Not helpful. Must say, I'm rather disappointed in old Maitland.'

'Old Maitland?'

'Chief Constable. Thought he was a friend of mine. Refused to help. I'm pretty sure he knows where they are, but he wouldn't say a word.'

Samantha frowned. 'I'm not following you, Lord Conway. Why wouldn't he—'

'Maitland was being cautious; trying to protect the girl when there's absolutely no need for it.' Embarrassed now, the old man looked down at the desk. 'She had an affair. My son came home; found her with her lover in the bedroom. James gave the blighter a thrashing. Went too far and killed him. I did what I could behind the scenes, but he got eight years for manslaughter. Might have been a good deal longer if it hadn't been for his barrister.' He glanced up, bushy white eyebrows arched. He was waiting for a comment.

'The provocation was extreme,' Samantha murmured huskily.

He nodded, satisfied he had her sympathy.

'And how does this tie in with your daughter-in-law disappearing?'

'James is coming home. Done almost four years. Model prisoner; selected for early release. Gets out of Doncaster jail on Monday.'

'She's moved away because she's afraid?'

Lord Conway nodded. 'Order for his release was confirmed about six weeks ago. The police must have warned her. That's why Maitland was so cagey.' His blue eyes held Samantha's for a while, then he said, 'She's no reason to be afraid: a gentleman never harms a woman, no matter what she's done. At the trial, James's barrister asked her if he'd ever hit her or treated her badly. She said he'd been a good husband who'd never harmed her, then started weeping buckets. Judge adjourned the trial so she could compose herself. Whole thing was a terrible ordeal for the girl. James's barrister made her look very cheap. Had to, I suppose, but it was a bad business.'

He fell silent again, then his voice became softer, his gaze distant, as he said, 'Something similar happened when I was in my teens; my father's brother and his wife. Father took me into the library and told me to be particularly kind to my Aunt Harriet. He said, "Always remember, my boy, it's never the lady's fault."' Lord Conway sighed, pursed moist purple lips, then went on, 'Times have changed, Miss Quest, and James might not be as magnanimous as that, but I'm sure he wouldn't harm her.'

Samantha studied the old man. Tall and broad-shouldered, the sagging flesh around his throat was almost hidden by a yellow paisley cravat. His red sweater sported a golfing logo. The fine head of white hair, the bristling moustache, gave him an aura of authority, imparted a vitality, that belied his years.

Uncomfortable in the silence, embarrassed by his revelations, he suddenly changed the subject. 'Known Marcus long?'

'He was my Section Head for a number of years.'

Lord Conway nodded. 'He told me you'd worked with him; said you were the very best, came with his highest recommendation. We served together, in the Guards; Household Cavalry. He's a gentleman through and through. Fine horseman, splendid polo player. Ridden to hounds with him and his wife many times. Have you met Charlotte?'

Samantha shook her head. 'I've not had the pleasure.'

'Great girl. Bishop's daughter. Breeds sheep. Handles a horse better than a man; she's got the thighs for it.'

Samantha suppressed a smile.

Glancing down at the desk again, he muttered, 'God, I miss the Regiment: harnesses jangling, hoofs clip-clopping, scarlet tunics, sunlight gleaming on helmets and breastplates.' He held up huge withered hands. 'And I can't play golf any more. Arthritis. Can't hold a club. Now Helen's gone and taken Jennifer. What's left for me?'

'Did you see your daughter-in-law often?'

'Called two or three times a week. Persuaded her to stay on in the marital home; not get divorced. I helped financially, of course. Paid Jennifer's school fees and dealt with the big items.'

'You persuaded her not to divorce your son?'

'Perhaps persuaded's a bit strong. Just advised her to think twice about it. And I always treated her and Jennifer as if nothing had happened. I really liked the girl. We hit it off. We were good chums. And we've all done things we regret, dammit. And James did kill the poor beggar: honour satisfied and all that. I'm still hoping they'll get together again; that James will swallow his pride and think about what's best for Jennifer.'

'Your son didn't sue for a divorce?'

Lord Conway shook his head. 'His mother's visited him in jail, every week, never missed. He's not once mentioned Helen or Jennifer; just refused to talk about the marriage. Elizabeth thinks bursting in on his wife like that, killing the man, being locked up in jail, has done something to him, changed him, made him hard and cold and distant. She says he's not her son any more.'

'You didn't visit him?'

'Couldn't cope with it. Couldn't deal with the shame. Searches, sniffing dogs, the humiliation of it all.'

'Your wife: has she kept in touch with Helen?'

'Elizabeth took it very badly. As far as she's concerned, Helen's ruined her son's life and blighted ours. But she's never been what you'd call welcoming.' He grinned ruefully. 'Is any girl good enough for a mother's son?'

'Has Helen become involved with anyone else?'

'I've seen no sign of it, and Jennifer's never mentioned anything like that when we've been alone together.'

18

Samantha slowly uncrossed and crossed her legs while she reflected on what Lord Conway had said. The tip of his tongue slid across his upper lip and watery old eyes lingered on her knees. Sighing, he brushed a crooked finger, first one way, then the other, along his moustache.

'Does Helen have any family?'

'No one close. Father died before she married James. Mother died a couple of years ago. No brothers or sisters. No one she could go to.'

'How about money? I know you said you've helped, but if she's left the marital home …'

'Helen got a good price for her mother's house. It wasn't far from here; bit lower down the hill. Bought it for a song years ago, tad run down, but it's the location that matters. She should have enough money to live on for quite a while if she's careful.'

'What about your granddaughter's school? Have you checked there?'

The old man nodded. 'Headmistress complained she hadn't been given much notice that Jennifer was going to be taken away. James's early release could have caught Helen on the hop.'

'And the headmistress didn't know where your granddaughter was moving to?'

'Said she didn't, and I believed her. If Helen's running away because she's afraid, she wouldn't tell her the name of Jennifer's new school.'

'And you want me to find them?'

He nodded. Sad, anxious eyes searched her face. His bottom lip was quivering.

'And what do you want me to do if I locate her? Just give you the address so you can make a surprise call, or ask her whether or not she wants to make contact?'

He sniffed. 'Better ask her. That would be the gentlemanly thing. And tell her she's perfectly safe. I wouldn't let anyone hurt her.'

'What if she still says no.'

He shrugged. 'Just give her and Jennifer my love. Tell them I miss them dreadfully, and if there's anything I can do to help all they have to do is call. At least I'd know they're alive and well, and she might let you act as a go-between.'

'It's not the sort of case I'd normally take, Lord Conway, and I'm expensive. When I accept a job, I charge for a full week, whether it takes a week or not. After that I charge by the hour, plus expenses.' She gave him details of the weekly and hourly rates, then said, 'You could engage someone local who'd do the job for far less.'

'Marcus gave me his word you're the best; quick, efficient, discreet. That's what I want. Above all, I want the discretion. Suffered too much shame and embarrassment already. Couldn't bear any more.'

He glanced around the oak-panelled room with its massive fireplace, at the thick rugs and leather armchairs, the golfing trophies, the mounted sword, the silver helmet with its horsehair plume resting on top of what was probably a drinks cabinet. Then he gazed out through the bay window, over grounds where red and gold leaves were being blown across wide lawns.

His eyes met hers again. 'I'm not without means, Miss Quest, and I want to know they're safe and well. And if I'm able to see them again ...' He stared down at his hands and sniffed. 'God, I do miss them.'

'Do you have any photographs?'

Glancing up, he said, 'Knew you'd ask,' then slid open a drawer, took out a manilla envelope and laid it on her side of the desk.

Samantha crossed over and picked it up. While she studied the images, fascinated eyes studied the shapes beneath her dress. She turned a photograph of a laughing girl in a T-shirt and jeans towards him. 'This is recent, I suppose?'

'This summer. Helen took it. We drove down to Brighton for the day.'

'And this one?' She held up a photograph of a woman in a black evening gown. A tall heavily built man, elegant in a dinner jacket, was standing with his arm around her. They were both smiling.

'Helen and James. Rotary Club dinner and dance. It was taken about a week before the break-up. Helen's not changed much. Lost some weight, wearing her hair shorter, that's all.'

Samantha studied the photograph. The son was a younger, dark-haired, clean-shaven replica of his father. The black evening gown the woman was wearing had been cut to display an emphatic figure. Tall for a woman, close to being plump, her blonde hair had been pinned up and her dangling earrings and necklace looked expensive. The photographer had artfully captured an impression of wealth and status and contented togetherness.

Samantha returned to the image of the daughter: long blond hair, tied with a ribbon; bright, happy, open-faced; her breasts and hips were straining against a skimpy T-shirt and tight jeans. Samantha glanced up. 'Jennifer's very much like her mother.'

Lord Conway nodded. 'Grew up so quickly. Skinny schoolgirl one year, young woman the next. Very bonny. Sweet nature, too. I do miss them. God, how I miss them.'

'Did Helen take things from the house when she left?'

'Clothes, jewellery, bedding, a few items of furniture small enough to get in the back of a car. I went there most days for more than a week, stayed a few hours, but she never turned up.'

'Do you have a key?'

He reached into his trouser pocket, produced a bunch of keys, selected one and began to slide it from the ring. 'Front door,' he said. 'Back's always bolted. Code for the security thing is seven eight five six.' He handed her the key.

Samantha smiled down at him. 'Seven eights are fifty six.'

'By Jove, you're right!' He laughed. 'Never realized that before.'

'How long can I keep the key?'

'Long as you want. There's another in the desk somewhere.'

Samantha returned to her chair, slid the photographs back in the envelope and tucked the envelope beneath the gun in her bag. 'The address of the house,' she said, 'and the name of your grand-daughter's old school?'

He gave her the details. She noted them down.

'Have you had lunch?' he asked. 'I could ask Magda to rustle something up. We could—'

Samantha gave the old man a radiant smile. 'Got to press on, Lord Conway. I have other business.' She rose to her feet.

'Must you?' Sighing, he heaved himself out of his chair, rounded the desk and pressed a button beside the ceiling-high fireplace. 'When do you think you'll have some news for me?'

'Give me forty-eight hours. I should have found her by then. If I've not, she might be difficult to trace and we'd better have another talk.'

He nodded, saw her gazing at the golfing trophies ranged around the room. 'You play golf?' His face had brightened.

'The game's a complete mystery to me, Lord Conway.'

There was a faint tapping on the door. They were shaking hands as the young woman in the grey dress and white apron entered the study.

'Miss Quest's leaving, Anna. Would you show her out?'

The maid led her back to the entrance and waited until Samantha had climbed into her car before closing the door. Samantha keyed the ignition, felt the Ferrari Modena rumble into life, then let out the clutch. Seconds later she was braking hard. A tall slender woman had emerged from the shrubbery in a swirl of leaves. She approached the car, the stiff breeze tugging at her green dress. Samantha lowered the sidelight.

'You brazen hussy! How dare you visit my home in broad daylight? Don't you have any thought for me at all?' Under the heavy make-up, her still beautiful face was white and trembling with rage. It was the woman who'd watched her from the window and from the bend in the stairs.

'And you are?' Samantha asked.

'You know very well who I am, you shameless little tart. How can you be so insensitive, coming here, bold as brass, defiling my home, doing things with my husband while I'm ...' Her face crumpled. Tears began to smudge her mascara.

'There's been some mistake,' Samantha said softly. 'My name's Quest; Samantha Quest. Your husband's just engaged me to find your daughter-in-law and granddaughter.'

The woman covered her face with her hands. 'Oh God, what have I done? I'm sorry, so very sorry. I thought you were visiting my husband for—'

'Come inside the car, Lady Conway.'

'But I ... God, I feel so ashamed.'

Samantha pushed the passenger door open. 'Get into the car. We need to talk, and we can't do it out here. We'll find somewhere to have coffee.'

Hands cupped over her face to hide her shame, the grey-haired woman rounded the bonnet, sank into the low seat and lifted her legs into the car. She slammed the door, then tugged the hem of her dress over her knees. 'I'm so sorry, Miss ... What did you say you're name was?'

'Quest; Samantha Quest.' Leaves swirled as they swept down the drive and swung out into the deserted road.

TWO

Lady Conway perched on the edge of her chair, grey hair a trifle windblown, back straight, hands folded across her skirt, her slender legs and brown brogue country shoes neatly pressed together. More composed now, she had about her a look of forlorn dignity.

'Coffee won't be long.' Samantha settled herself into a chair on the opposite side of the low table. 'Barman's going to bring it over.'

The older woman managed a bleak little smile. 'I'm sorry,' she said. 'So very sorry. Your hair and make-up, the exquisite dress; I thought …'

'Your husband invites women to the house?'

'When I'm away. I began to suspect it months ago, then Anna found an article of underwear. I knew for sure then. Magda put them on my dressing-table. When I asked her what they were doing there, she said, "Anna found them when she was making the beds. I think they're yours, madam." She knew they weren't mine, of course. She was letting me know what had been going on while I'd been at my sister's.'

'Anna's the Polish maid?'

Lady Conway nodded. 'And Magda's the cook and housekeeper. They're mother and daughter. Last night I told Fergus I was going to leave early and spend the day in London, but Dobson took the car so I couldn't get to the station. When I saw you ringing the bell

24

I thought Fergus had taken his chance and told some agency to send a woman round.'

'Dobson?'

'Jack Dobson: he's the chauffeur and handyman. The burglar alarm was ringing at our son's house and the neighbours phoned to complain. Last night's high winds must have set it off. Don't know why we fit the things. No one phones the police or goes to the house to check. Dobson had to drive over and reset it.'

'And your husband uses an escort agency?' Samantha held her gaze.

Lady Conway flinched. Dear God, such penetrating eyes. So searching and probing. She stiffened her shoulders. 'Some place in the West End. It's unbelievably expensive, especially when they stay all day or overnight. He pays by card. I've seen his bank statements. And he did say he was engaging a man to find Helen and Jennifer.'

'I'm sure that was a genuine mistake.'

'Your voice is husky, Miss Quest, but it's unmistakably female.'

The white-coated barman approached the table and served their Gaelic coffees from a tray. Samantha smiled her thanks, then turned back to Lady Conway. 'And how do you feel about my being engaged to find them?'

'Can't say I'm very happy about it. The truth is, I never really took to the girl, and all she's brought us is heartache and misery.' She picked up one of the cups, sipped at it, then closed her eyes. 'This is heavenly. You've been very kind. I can't tell you how ashamed I feel, behaving like that.'

'Forget it,' Samantha murmured. 'I understand.'

Sighing, Lady Conway opened her eyes and said, 'Helen was engaged to someone when James became involved with her. A boy called Woodward, a solicitor; he's a partner in his father's firm now. If she'd had any scruples she'd have fobbed James off, at least until she'd ended the engagement. That put me on my guard. I mean, what sort of girl accepts advances from a man while she's engaged to someone else?' She took another sip at her coffee. 'Fergus didn't see it. Sentimental old fool doted on the girl from the very start. Anything female sets his whiskers twitching, and Helen is rather attractive in a fleshy kind of way.' She licked cream from her upper lip. 'Young women have no sense of commitment these days, that's the trouble. They soon become bored and start looking for diversions.'

'How old is Jennifer?'

'Sixteen; soon be seventeen.'

Samantha smiled. 'You look much too young to have a sixteen-year-old granddaughter.'

Lady Conway let out a trill of laughter. 'You're being very sweet to me, Miss Quest. I was married at seventeen, a mother when I was eighteen.'

'All the same …'

Laughter erupted again. 'Coming from such a beautiful and elegant young woman, that's a compliment I'll treasure.'

'Mutual admiration,' Samantha said, and her husky laughter mingled with Lady Conway's falsetto trills.

Lady Conway drained her cup and slid it on to the table. 'That was more than pleasant. Thank you.' The warm whisky had restored some colour to her cheeks.

'Have mine,' Samantha offered. 'It's not been touched.'

'I couldn't.'

'I'm driving and I shouldn't. It would be best if you drank it.' She pushed the cup towards her, then reclined back in her chair and watched Lady Conway take it and lift it to her lips. The alcohol had relaxed her, but so far she hadn't said anything that was particularly useful. She had to keep her talking.

Lady Conway sighed and sipped at the coffee. 'Fergus – that's my husband – cut such a dash in his uniform. I was Jennifer's age when I first saw him. I went weak at the knees. A couple of years later I was a mother and I'd had to grow up. It was then I realized he was all swagger and no brains. He's a romantic old fool, obsessed with the opposite sex. He used to pick up women at the golf club. Crept off in the afternoons for his little trysts.' She laughed bitterly. 'Most of them were supposed to be my friends! He can be so charming, and he's very particular about his appearance. But the arthritis in his hands put a stop to the golf and he started paying for sexual favours. Perhaps charm wasn't enough to win the day any more. I mean, what woman would want his wizened old paw sliding up her thigh?'

'You seem quite philosophical about it.'

'Philosophical! I can be philosophical when I'm sitting here talking to you, but when the maid found some other woman's knickers in my bed, when I was confronting him about his sordid little liaisons at the golf club, I wasn't philosophical.'

'You've never considered divorce?'

'Often, Miss Quest. But reason always prevails. Fergus is eighteen years older. Why should I settle for less than half when I can have it all if I'm patient. And he can be very sweet, and he's stupidly kind. The Polish maid adores him. Thank God she's plain; thank God her mother watches her like a hawk.'

'Your son and his wife; has there ever been any talk of a divorce?'

'James refuses to discuss the marriage. He seems to want to block it out of his mind. I've tried to steer the conversation round to it, but he just changes the subject and talks about the business.'

'The business?'

'Conway Electrical. Fergus inherited it from his father. Had to resign his commission in the Guards when his father died so he could take over the running of the firm. Made an utter mess of it. All he was good for was strutting around in his uniform and galloping along beside the Queen's carriage.' She laughed. 'Stands to attention in front of the telly when she makes her Christmas speech. Can you believe it? James gradually took over after university – he did engineering at Imperial College – put the firm back on its feet, won a lot of military contracts. It was James's hard work that got Fergus the peerage. They said it was for services to industry, but I think it was for some big donations to political parties.'

Lady Conway gave Samantha a bleak look. The effects of the alcohol seemed to be wearing off. Sighing, she said, 'James has become very hard and bitter. He's not the son I used to know. Mothers suffer for their children, Miss Quest. Giving birth is only the beginning. You can't imagine how humiliating it was, visiting him in prison.'

Samantha gave her an understanding smile. The conversation had yielded no useful information. 'Shall I drive you home, Lady Conway?'

'Would you? It's been so pleasant, talking to you like this, but I ought to get back.' Her voice brightened. 'Three more days, then I'll have him home. Dobson's taking me to collect him from Doncaster jail on Thursday.' She rose to her feet and they began to drift through the empty lounge, strolling towards reception and the entrance. 'When will you start searching?'

'Tomorrow, probably.'

'I'm not happy about it. Passions have run high, Miss Quest. My son killed a man, four years of his life have been taken away. The situation's very fraught. Finding her could open up a great big can of worms. It could destroy us all.'

Samantha held the car door while Lady Conway lowered herself into the seat. 'Don't you want to see your granddaughter again? Don't you miss her?'

Bright eyes swept up and held Samantha in a chilling stare. 'The less said about that, the better. Fergus is a sentimental old fool and all James can think about is business and football. But I'm not blinded by a pretty face.'

Samantha slammed the door, rounded the car and slid behind the wheel. 'Your husband's engaged me, Lady Conway. I've got to do the job.'

'Then would you at least keep me informed. Fergus knows how I feel about the girl, and he might not tell me anything.'

'Of course,' Samantha said. 'What's your mobile number?'

The woman recited it; Samantha noted it down.

'Our conversation back there,' Lady Conway went on, 'we talked about very intimate things. I hope—'

Samantha roused the Ferrari into life, drowning out the words. Raising her voice above the roar of the revving engine, she said, 'My discretion's absolute, Lady Conway,' then eased the car out on to the road and made it snarl as they raced back to the house called High Gables.

James Conway lay on his bunk, watching the afternoon light fade beyond the high window. Three more days, then he'd be free; there'd be no more of the stink of cheap deodorant and over-cooked food. He'd have the regulation farewell chat with the governor, they'd give him the few possessions he'd brought in, then two guards would walk him to the pedestrian door in the high gates and let him out. His mother had said she'd come with Dobson to collect him. The prison officer had told him 10.30. He made a mental note to phone her and let her know the time.

He heard the distant sound of keys jangling against metal, doors opening, feet tramping along the corridor outside his cell.

Four wasted years. It had been a living death, and all because of that sly little slut. Before the first year was over, he'd begun to feel sorry for the poor bastard he'd killed. He'd told the chaplain, told the governor, and the parole board had taken his remorse into account when they'd agreed his early release.

And his feelings were real, not feigned. Helen would have encouraged the man, led him on, just as he'd been led on. The man's wife had written to him, told him she understood why he'd done what he'd done, that she bore him no ill will for killing her husband. She'd said she was finding it easier to come to terms with his death than with his infidelity, even though her son and daughter had been so distressed she thought they'd never get over it.

They'd never get over it! What about him, after watching her

husband's pimply arse thrusting away between Helen's lily-white thighs while she whimpered and moaned? The sight and sound of it still haunted him. Psychological castration. His four celibate years hadn't been a problem. Whenever his thoughts turned to sex, that vision of rumpled sheets and his wife and her lover stifled all desire.

The bitch was going to pay. Problem was, he couldn't decide how to make her. He daren't touch her; daren't even harass her. He was going to be on parole. One slip and he'd be back in here, or somewhere worse, serving another four years, maybe longer. He couldn't bear that. He'd already spent four years doing little else but think about Helen and the marriage, going over how they'd met; their brief, lust-fuelled courtship; the instant pregnancy, Jennifer's birth. Giving birth and caring for a baby hadn't changed Helen. Her appetite for sex hadn't waned.

During her last visit, his mother had told him Helen had left Tanford. The slut knew he was coming out. He was a violent offender, so the police would have warned her. The bitch was afraid. She was probably very afraid. His lips stretched into a humourless smile. He liked that. He relished the thought of her being afraid.

There was a question. A profoundly important question. When he had the answer to it his feelings about Helen would clarify. He'd know then how big a price she had to pay. But whatever he decided, he'd have to find some means of making her suffer that wouldn't leave him exposed to the law.

Keys crashed against metal, the lock grated and the heavy door swung open. The sound of shuffling feet and men's voices was suddenly louder. 'Come on, Conway. Exercise hour. Let's be 'aving yer.'

James rose from his bunk. Just three days now and he'd be back behind the desk in his big office, Ella taking dictation, arranging meetings, sorting his diary, while he ran the family firm. His nightmare would be over. Helen's was about to begin.

Marcus Soames frowned down at the intercepts spread out on his desk. They made no sense. Afflicted by the endless repetition of human conversation, they seemed to be utterly without meaning. A sudden gust of wind lashed rain against the windows. The room had darkened. He switched on the desk lamp, then returned to the typewritten sheets, looking for patterns, grateful that others, more skilled, would be searching for secrets beneath the banality.

A forceful knock on the door startled him. He glanced up, saw a tall woman, her iron-grey hair tied back with a black ribbon, step into the room.

'God, I'm glad you're still here, Marcus. Have you got anything to drink in the office?' She strode towards the desk. The pencil skirt of her navy-blue suit was creased, but her white blouse looked pristine. She wore the outfit like a uniform. While she'd headed the department her style of dress had never changed.

'I could put a gin and tonic together, ma'am.' He slid open the deep bottom drawer of the desk and lifted out bottles and a couple of glasses. 'How did it go?'

'Bloody awful. Politicians! Give you a verbal flaying and when you respond with a few home truths they've suddenly got skins like peaches.' Loretta Fallon dropped her briefcase and sank into the visitor's chair.

Marcus poured tonic on the gin and handed her one of the glasses.

She sipped at it gratefully. 'Government's taking this banking problem very seriously. Some group's been hacking in on a random basis; tampering with accounts.'

'Diverting funds?'

'Thirteen million. Monies scheduled for transfer to banks in Pakistan. Not a lot in the grand scheme of things, but it's the breach in security that's upsetting the bankers, and the politicians are very edgy after the big bail-out. I'll let you read the report to

31

the Cabinet sub-committee. It's all in there. So far it's only British and Asian that's suffered actual loss. Industry's trying to keep it quiet; they're concerned about customer confidence.'

Marcus studied Loretta. Her colour was high, her cool grey eyes unusually bright. They'd really ruffled her this afternoon. 'Could be drug payments intended for Afghanistan. British and Asian are a favourite conduit.' Changing the subject, he nodded at the papers strewn across his desk. 'Security threat seems to be increasing. Been a big rise in suspect e-mail and phone traffic. It's the usual gibberish. Fowler's team's trying to make some sense of it.'

Refusing to be distracted, Loretta added, 'They want us to act.' She sipped at her glass.

'Who? The banks or the government?'

'Both. PM said he wouldn't tolerate another banking crisis.'

Marcus laughed softly. 'He might have to. And what has British and Asian had to say about it? Surely it can regulate its own security?'

'Their experts are mystified. They've increased the level of encryption, they keep making changes to passwords, making them more complex, but there's still a problem. They're beginning to wonder whether it's an inside job.'

'Could it be an inside job if more than one bank's having trouble?'

Lorreta shrugged. 'They claim they're the only bank to have suffered actual loss. Anyway, the PM wants us to get involved.'

'How involved?'

'Directly involved; put someone in.' She studied Marcus over the rim of her glass. A broad-shouldered, big-framed man, he was becoming heavy in middle-age, but he still carried himself well. He seemed unusually preoccupied. Or could it be that it was late and he was tired?

'Bit strapped at the moment, ma'am. Don't think there's anyone we could allocate at short notice.'

Loretta drained her glass. 'Pity Quest's gone.'

'She's seeing an analyst.'

'Christ, that's all we need. Quest on a psychiatrist's couch. The things she knows! How long has this been going on?'

'First appointment was this morning. Dr Heinze Uberman, Harley Street.'

'How—'

'Been monitoring her calls on a random basis, ever since she left the service. We picked up the call she made to Uberman's receptionist. I put the consulting rooms under surveillance this morning. She kept the appointment.'

'This is more than worrying, Marcus.'

'Quest's astute, ma'am, and she's as much to fear from careless talk as we have. Another drink?'

'Are you travelling home tonight?'

Marcus shook his head. 'Charlotte's visiting her mother in Kilbride, the girls are away at university, so I'm staying at the club.'

'Then I will have another. Some new cars were delivered to the pool yesterday: Mini Coopers. Book one out and drive me home. You can stay over – unless you'd prefer to spend the night at your club.'

'I'd be delighted to drive you home, ma'am.' He reached for her glass, poured out a generous measure of gin then splashed in the tonic.

'I hope you're going to stop calling me ma'am.'

He smiled. 'When we've left the building, ma'am.'

Laughing, Loretta took the glass. The discretion of the perfect gentleman. She'd made a prudent choice. He'd never compromise her. The only drawback was, he made love as if he were riding a horse to hounds. She peed red-hot needles for a week after it. But she needed a distraction after that battering from the Cabinet committee. She took a long pull at her drink. 'So, what are we going to do about Quest's visits to Dr Uberman? Is he British?'

'Born and bred. Had him checked out when Quest made the appointment. His real name's Brian Stoddard. Heinze Uberman's the name he practises under; any self-respecting Harley Street analyst needs a German name. I gather he's highly regarded. I'll get copies of his case notes on Quest and we'll monitor the situation. If it becomes worrying, I'll take action.'

He gazed at Loretta. Although no longer young, she was shapely and slender, and her cool grey eyes and rather angular features radiated intelligence. He found her aura of authority enormously attractive. The alcohol seemed to have calmed her. He decided that this was the moment to make his suggestion. Shaping his features in a thoughtful frown, he said, 'Why don't we put Quest in?'

'Into the banks?'

He nodded.

'She's no longer a servant of the Crown, and you keep telling me she won't come back.'

'I might tempt her with a short-term contract; the sort of thing we're using for consultants. Three months with an option to renew. We could reinstate her passes, supply her with an encrypted phone.'

'Does she know anything about banking security?'

'The banks have already got clever people looking at that, ma'am, and if that's the extent of the problem, they'll deal with it. On the other hand, if it's something to do with traffickers and terrorists diverting drug money, Quest's the woman for the job. She's feared and respected. She could be our cat amongst the pigeons. If we can persuade her to go into the bank, and if these groups are involved, they'll show their hand and we'll discover who we're dealing with.'

'You'd tell Quest this?'

'I think not, ma'am. If I did, she'd say no. She's become bothered about recognition and retribution. That's the main reason why she wanted out of the service; had a long run, probably thought her luck wouldn't last much longer if she continued to expose herself to the dangers. I'd tell her it was banking fraud, possibly an inside job.'

Loretta gave him an uncertain look.

'It's the only way I could get her to go in. Once she was in, she'd have to cope with any threat the job posed. And we'd have her back in the organization while she's undergoing analysis with Uberman. We could be generous with the short-term contract, and you'd be able to tell the PM you've taken urgent and drastic measures.'

'Don't think he'd be very pleased to learn Quest was back; she knows too many of his dark little secrets.'

'He might not like it, but he'd have to accept you'd done all you could to respond to the committee's concern.' Marcus gave her one of his slow smiles. 'Two birds with one stone, ma'am?' He made his voice coaxing.

A sitting duck and a stool-pigeon, Loretta mused. 'Very well, Marcus. I hope this isn't the gin talking, but go ahead; see if you can persuade Quest to take it on.' She rose to her feet.

Marcus switched off the desk lamp. The wind had stripped most of the leaves from the trees in front of Thames House and they could see the lights of London glittering beyond the river. He'd got the decision he wanted. All he had to do now was persuade Quest to take the job. He picked up Loretta's briefcase and followed her to the door.

'Keep a tight hold on things, Marcus. Quest knows far too much about the great and the good. If she slides over the edge she might not realize what she's saying to that analyst.'

THREE

Samantha hid the Ferrari in a cul-de-sac and walked the hundred yards back to the house. Set behind an area of lawn and some mature trees, Helen Conway's former home was, even by the standards of the area, rather grand. Built from biscuit-coloured bricks, its frontage was wide and symmetrical, and stone columns supported a pedimented canopy that sheltered an impressive front door. Grey and yellow lichen spotted the brown-tiled roofs over the house and detached triple garage.

The gates had been pegged back. Samantha gathered her raincoat around her and tied the belt before heading down the driveway. Not expecting to linger on in Tanford, she hadn't packed a change of clothes and her black-and-white dress wasn't meant for chilly autumn mornings.

A sudden breeze scattered a pile of leaves as she stepped beneath the porch. She rang the bell, then peered through rippled glass in a window beside the door. No one answered and there were no signs of movement in the hall. She listened for a while to birds twittering in the shrubs that marked the boundaries of the plot, then found the key Lord Conway had given her, unlocked the door and stepped inside. The alarm controller was mounted near an unframed mirror set above a telephone table. She keyed in the code, then relocked the door.

Mail had piled up on a mat. Ignoring circulars, she picked up the three envelopes that looked as if they might contain real correspondence and tore them open: a letter to Jennifer Conway regarding overdue library books, a reminder to Helen that a car service was due, and an electoral registration form; nothing that mentioned her new address. She slid the letters back in the envelopes, scattered them amongst the junk mail behind the door and began her search of the house.

A dog-legged and surprisingly ordinary flight of stairs rose to the first floor. Samantha climbed it, crossed a landing and entered the master bedroom. It had an abandoned look. A king-size bed was standing askew in the middle of the floor. Its mattress had been removed, exposing wooden slats and a supporting frame. An ivory-coloured headboard, decorated with gilded scrolls and garlands, linked a pair of bedside tables. Samantha checked the drawers; found hair grips, an earring, a rolled up pair of tights and an empty perfume bottle in one; a cheap wristwatch, indigestion tablets, and till receipts for countless small purchases in the other. Faint impressions lingered in the carpet where furniture had been removed.

Rounding the bed, she opened the gilt and ivory doors of a built-in wardrobe. Bare hangers rattled on the rail in one half; a dozen suits, jackets and an overcoat crowded the other. Several pairs of shoes, probably size twelve, were lined up beneath the hanging clothes. Shirts, knitwear, ties; bundled into carrier bags and piled on top of the shoes; awaited James Conway's return.

Samantha went over to an inner door, pushed it open and peered into a shadowy en suite bathroom. When she tugged at the light-cord, she saw it had the same abandoned look as the bedroom. There was a grittiness beneath her feet as she crossed the tiled floor to check a mirrored cabinet. A film of dust covered its glass shelves. They were bare except for a bottle of aftershave, a packet of sticking plasters, a cheap plastic razor and a can of deodorant.

There were three more bedrooms and another bathroom on the first floor. One had obviously been used by Helen Conway, the other by Jennifer, the third had served as an office. A dressing-table and a chest of drawers that matched the headboard in the master bedroom had been taken into what had been Helen's room. The chest of drawers was empty. The shallow central drawer in the dressing-table held underwear, the others scarves and belts, handkerchiefs and gloves, a scattering of buttons and cheap paste jewellery. Hidden away at the back of one drawer, Samantha found a baptismal candle, first-birthday cards, baby-clothes and a brown-paper bag containing locks of blond hair. In another, cuttings from newspapers that had covered James's trial were gathered together in an envelope. She checked a built-in wardrobe, then moved on to what had been Jennifer's room. She found nothing to indicate where they might have gone. In the makeshift office a cheap desk had dark patches where a computer and keyboard had stood. Its drawers were empty.

Returning to the ground floor, Samantha checked kitchen drawers and cupboards, a magazine rack in the sitting room, a sideboard and bookcase in the dining room. She found photograph albums, Jennifer's school reports, a dozen paperback novels, folders stuffed with old utilities bills and domestic correspondence, but no letters or estate agent's literature giving a clue to Helen's new address.

She wandered through the rooms again. Decorations were muted: shades of beige and cream with a beige carpet in the sitting room and plain rugs on polished boards in the dining room and hall. The kitchen was large and lavish, with granite work tops, hand-made cream-painted units, a shiny red Aga and a red quarry-tile floor. A huge refrigerator with double doors sported an ice-cube dispenser.

Standing at the kitchen window, Samantha gazed across a rear garden enclosed by high fences that were almost hidden behind shrubs and small trees. She'd drawn a blank. Just the dustbin to check, then she'd head for the town centre and make the rounds of estate agents on the off-chance one of them had been involved in the move; there wouldn't be many in this small country place.

Doors slammed at the front of the house. Samantha ran from the kitchen and glanced down the hall. She could hear men's voices, a woman saying, 'It shouldn't take long. Just one or two things from the bedrooms first; there's not much to go from downstairs.' A blurred shape moved past the rippled glass window beside the door, a key rattled in the lock.

Turning, Samantha darted into a short passageway off the rear of the hall. The back door of the house was at the end. It was bolted and locked and she didn't have a key. A door on her left opened into a utility room, a door on her right into a small swimming-pool covered over by a conservatory-like structure. Feet were treading down the boarded floor of the hall. Voices were louder and coming closer. Pushing through the door on her right, Samantha stepped out of her shoes, slipped them into her raincoat pockets, then ran, silent in her stockings, over blue tiles that bordered a rectangle of still water.

She entered a tiny windowless room where heating and filtering equipment sprouted pipes and ducts and cables. Standing behind the door, surrounded by buckets and mops, she waited in the darkness and listened. Feet climbed the stairs, then a woman's voice, its strived-for refinement still bearing a trace of Essex-girl, said, 'The dressing-table and drawers from this room; the bed and chest of drawers from the blue room across the passage, and the little desk from the lumber room at the end.'

Having issued her instructions, Helen Conway returned to the ground floor. Footsteps grew louder as she approached down the passageway, then echoed when she began to walk around the pool. They stopped. After a silence, Samantha heard a sigh, then heels clattered away across the tiles and there were faint sounds of cupboard doors opening and closing in the kitchen.

Men's voices could be heard again, feet shuffled on the stairs and there was a lot of grunting and puffing. They were bringing down something large and heavy.

The furniture removers were quick and adept. After a short

time Samantha heard Helen Conway saying, 'Just these now, the ironing-board and the boxes; this one's got china and glasses in it.' Her voice grew fainter. She was following the men into the hall. 'Have you got room for the sideboard? It's in the dining room. I've not emptied it, but ...' Her voice became inaudible.

'No problem, Mrs Conway. We could squeeze the dining table in as well at a pinch.'

Helen's feet sounded in the hallway again. 'I'm leaving the table. I don't have room for it. But perhaps one of the armchairs from the sitting room?'

After more grunting and feet shuffling, van doors slammed and a voice called out, 'That everything, Mrs Conway?'

'I think so. Everything I can find room for.'

'We'll set off then. Leave you to lock up.'

'Wait a minute.' Feet ran across boards. 'Have you got the address? I gave it to your wife when I phoned.'

'Better make sure she got it down right. It's on the docket. Where's the ... Ah, here we are: thirty-seven Marlborough Road, Cheltenham.'

'You've got it. When you get to Cheltenham, head for the town centre and drive up the Promenade. Go past the park, then straight across the little roundabout at the top of Montpellier. The house is about half a mile further on, off the Gloucester road. How long will it take you?'

'About an hour if the traffic's not too bad.'

'I'll try and get there before you arrive.'

Cab doors slammed and a starter whined. When the sound of the van's engine had faded, footsteps approached again, began to echo and mingle with sniffs and muffled sobs, as Helen Conway walked around the pool. Samantha listened to heels tip-tapping on tiles, then feet thudded up the stairs. Helen was taking a last emotional look around the rather fine house that had been her home.

There were some faint sounds of movement, then Helen

thudded down to the hall and the front door slammed. Samantha ran through to the front-facing sitting room. Standing well back, she noted the registration number of the red Volvo estate as it moved off down the drive. She recorded it in a small brown-leather diary, together with the address she'd overheard. She smiled. Just a little luck could make things so much easier.

Leaning back against the wall, she took her shoes from her rain-coat pockets and slid them on. Helen Conway still had to be asked whether or not she wanted to be contacted by her father-in-law. She'd follow the convoy to Cheltenham, pay her a visit, then have lunch at The Daffodil.

Samantha had expected a stuccoed Regency villa, small but elegantly proportioned, its roof hidden behind a parapet. Instead she discovered Helen's new home was a tired-looking bay-windowed semi-detached.

She'd parked on the opposite side of the road, far enough away not to be noticed, near enough to see what was happening. Helen Conway arrived first, drove down the side of the house and left her car in front of a garage that enclosed the rear garden. Minutes later, the white van turned into the road and squealed to a stop across the driveway. The men dropped down from the cab. One of them opened the rear doors while the other went to the house and rang the bell.

Samantha got her first clear look at Helen Conway when she appeared in the porch. Her natural blond hair was shoulder-length, and she'd lost weight since she'd worn the black ball-gown. If anything it had made her figure even more head-turning. Long legs were sheathed in faded jeans, and her red jumper had a polo neck. It was tricked out with a necklace of large and iridescent red beads. She went back into the house and the men began to unload the furniture.

Feeling a vibration against her thigh, Samantha groped in her raincoat pocket, found her mobile phone and keyed it on.

'That you, Sam?'

'Who else would it be?'

'How are you?'

'Fine.'

Laughter rustled out of the earpiece. 'It's good to hear that sexy voice again.'

'You're just a smarmy old charmer, Marcus. What do you want?'

'I'd like to talk to you.'

'You are talking to me.'

'Not over an open phone; in private. Can we meet?'

'I'm busy, Marcus. And there's nothing I want to hear that can't be said down an open phone.'

'What I've got to say is going to interest you.'

'What you say usually ends up scaring the shit out of me. What's different this time?'

'Meet me and I'll tell you.'

'You're being infantile, Marcus. I'm not interested. I'm going to ring off.'

'Have dinner with me,' he offered hastily. 'Old-time's sake. Where are you? I'll come to you.'

She listened to his breathing.

'Sam ... You there, Sam?'

'I'm here, Marcus. If I have dinner and listen and still say no, will you leave me alone?'

'Of course.' He was laughing again. 'Where are you?'

Samantha watched the men struggling with a bed. She was still booked into the hotel in Tanford; she might have to return there to report Helen's whereabouts to Lord Conway. She'd nothing to wear, but an hour searching the boutiques in Montpellier before she left Cheltenham should solve that problem. 'Tanford,' she said. 'Small market town south of the City.'

'I know it well. There's a village close by, with a quiet little pub that serves good food. Where shall I pick you up, and what time?'

Samantha hesitated, decided he probably knew where she was

staying, and said, 'Braemar Hotel. It's just outside the town. Seven o'clock. I'll be waiting in the lounge.' She switched off the phone without offering a goodbye and returned her attention to the removal men.

After carrying in the cardboard boxes and the ironing-board they climbed into their van and drove off. Samantha stepped out of the Ferrari, crossed over to the house and rapped on the door. When it opened, Helen Conway's pale and slightly puffy face was looking out at her.

'Mrs Conway?'

'That's right.'

'I have a message for you, from your father-in-law.'

Fear widened Helen Conway's eyes, and anger roughened her voice as she snapped, 'Go away. I don't want any messages. Go away and leave me …' She tried to close the door.

Samantha leaned against it, holding it open. 'I'm here now, Mrs Conway. I've found you. You may as well listen to what I have to say.'

'Say it then, and go.'

'On the doorstep?'

The tension ebbed from Helen Conway's body. Closing her eyes, she sighed out her resignation and stepped back. 'Come in. You have no idea what you've done to me, but come on in.'

She led Samantha through to a small dining room at the rear of the house. Sunlight, pouring through French windows, was bright on faded primrose-yellow wallpaper and a blue floral-pattern carpet. 'Sit down.' She gestured towards a dining chair, then dragged another from beneath a gate-legged table and sat down herself.

'Lord Conway engaged me to find you,' Samantha said. 'He instructed me to tell you he misses you and Jennifer. He'd like you to come back to the house in Tanford.'

'And did he tell you about his son, James, my husband? Did he tell you what he did?'

Samantha nodded.

'You know James is being released from jail on Thursday?'

'Your father-in-law told me. He said he was sure you'd nothing to fear.'

'Nothing to fear? He should be in my shoes. Do you want a cup of tea or coffee?'

'No, thanks.'

'A drink then? I've got gin, whisky?'

'I'm driving, but you have one. I think you need one.'

'Too bloody right I do.' Helen rose, reached into one of the cardboard boxes stacked against the wall and lifted out a half-full bottle of Scotch. 'Sure you won't have one?'

'I'm sure.'

'Won't be a sec.' She went into the kitchen. There was the sound of a tap running, then she came back holding a glass and a jug of water. She poured herself a drink, then sat down again, her elbow on the table, the glass in her hand. She gulped at it desperately.

'You're afraid your husband might harm you?' Samantha prompted.

'I watched him kill a man; beat him to death with his bare fists. I kept on screaming at him to stop, but he just ignored me. I knew it was all over when Roy's face went lopsided and blood started to dribble from his ears. James threw him down on the bed, then went into the en suite and cleaned himself up. When he came out he pushed his face into mine and said, "Be afraid, bitch. Be very afraid. You'll never stop paying for this. I'm going to make you wish you were dead." Then he went to the police and told them what he'd done. I never saw him again until the trial. I've never spoken to him since.'

'He's had four years to get over it, Mrs Conway. And being on probation is a restraint.'

'He's been locked up for four years. He's had plenty of time to brood about it. He really meant it when he threatened me. And he's clever. If he wants to hurt me, he'll hurt me.'

'If he was going to harm you, surely he'd have done it that afternoon, in the bedroom?'

'He's a very controlled man. He never displays emotion. Silent, doesn't say much, just watches and thinks and keeps his thoughts to himself. Beating the man that afternoon drained him emotionally. He was sated, like he would be after sex. He'd no energy left for me. And he probably wanted to leave me terrified, wondering what he was going to do to me. He was saving me for later. When he threatened me after he'd cleaned himself up he was so calm it was chilling. He really meant what he said.' Helen Conway drained her glass, then switched the conversation on to fresh tracks. 'How did you find out where I'm living?'

'Followed the removal van. I got lucky.'

'I'm glad someone got lucky.' Helen poured herself another drink. 'What are you going to do?'

'That depends on you.'

'On me?'

'I agreed with Lord Conway that I wouldn't give him your address without your permission. He seems to have very firm views on how a gentleman should behave.'

'Fergus is OK. Bit fussy and over-attentive, gets on my nerves sometimes, but he's a very decent man.' She laughed. 'I think he fancies me. But then, he fancies anything in a frock.' She laughed again, then sipped at her drink. 'He's been very kind to us. Jennifer really misses him. I think she still misses her father.' Helen put her hand over her eyes and began to weep.

Samantha remained silent. After a while, she said softly, 'Why?'

'What do you mean, why?'

'Why did you get involved with this other man?'

'What's it got to do with you?'

'Nothing at all. I'm just curious.'

'You married?'

'Widowed.'

Helen sniffed and wiped the back of her hand across her eyes. 'I can't give you a reason. I suppose it was boredom. James was a good man, decent, a real catch; big, athletic, clever, moneyed background. His mother thought I was a brazen little gold-digger, but it wasn't like that. Met him at a party. I was engaged to a bloke called Woodward at the time. He'd had to go on a course, so his brother took me. When James came over and started chatting me up, I went dizzy and breathless. That sort of thing had never happened to me before: going all dizzy and breathless I mean, not being chatted up. Men try to chat me up all the time. It was lust at first sight. James felt the same. We couldn't keep our hands off one another. A month later I broke off my engagement to Alan Woodward and married James six months after that. His mother went ballistic. She never forgave me.'

'And you became bored?'

Helen was gazing through the French windows, down a long back garden that had become overgrown while the house waited for its new owners. 'We never talked much,' she said softly. 'All he was interested in was the business and sport; worked long hours, got home late, then played in some football team at the weekends. But he pulled the firm round. We paid cash for the house; no mortgage. After we were married he never seemed to notice me any more. I was the thing that made him comfortable and attended to his needs: childcare, hostess, housekeeper, sexual services; someone to have on his arm at dinners and functions. He never said anything nice to me; never told me he loved me. Nothing ever changed. I got bored.' She waved her glass. 'There were three – no, I tell a lie, four. Roy Carver was the one he caught me with. He was just unlucky.'

Turning from the window, she looked at Samantha. 'Sometimes I think Jennifer must hate me. She was twelve when it happened. Just becoming aware of adult things, but not really understanding, if you know what I mean. Now she's older she's less difficult.' Helen laughed. 'Strange that. When I got older, I became more difficult. She didn't argue when I told her we had to move to get her into a good sixth-form college – her school at Tanford didn't have one. But she doesn't understand why I'm so scared. She was daddy's little girl, you see.'

'You're sending her to Cheltenham Ladies' College?'

'Couldn't afford that. Got her into a small Church of England place: Hatherley Hall School for Girls.' She slid her glass on to the table. 'How's Fergus, then?'

'Like I said, missing you both. He was in tears.'

Helen smiled. 'He's a sentimental old thing. Bet Elizabeth's glad to see the back of us, though.' She suddenly frowned and looked worried again. 'You've not told me what you're going to do?'

'I take it you don't want me to give him your address?'

'Jesus, no. He'd tell James and James would come looking for me.'

'He could find you within hours. You'd have to change your name, your identity, and Jennifer's too, if you really want to lose yourself.'

Her face crumpled. 'I can't move again; can't buy a house one week and sell it the next. And I can't mess Jennifer about any more. I'll go and see the police, tell them I'm scared, tell them I'm sure he'll try to find me.'

'The police warned you he was getting out of jail?'

'They came to see me before we left Tanford.'

'But you haven't told them your new address?'

Helen shook her head.

'Might be best not to,' Samantha warned as she studied the pale, frightened face. Helen didn't seem to have heard her.

'Are you going to tell Fergus you've found me?'

'I'll wait a few days, then tell him I can't trace you. I'll tell him I think you might have left the country.'

Helen wiped her eyes with her hand. Her chin was trembling. 'Honest? You really mean that?'

Samantha smiled at her. 'Honest.' She clicked open her bag, took out a small square of white card, and wrote her mobile number on it. 'If you decide you want me to contact Lord Conway and act as a go-between, or if you're frightened and think I might be able to help, call this number.'

When Helen reached out to take the card she noticed Samantha's black-and-white Moschino dress, her Burberry raincoat, the designer bag and shoes. 'I suppose you're expensive?'

'Very. But don't worry about that. Lord Conway's paying.' Samantha rose to her feet. 'I'll leave you.' She nodded towards the boxes piled up in the corner. 'You have things to do.'

FOUR

'**B**eautiful frock, Sam. You always look ravishing in red. I suppose it's the latest thing?'

'Teeny bit last year, Marcus.' She smiled at him across the dinner table. He seemed quite taken by the dress she'd bought before she left Cheltenham.

There was more grey in his hair than she remembered, and the lines around his mouth were deeper, the flesh on his cheeks and chin a little less firm. But his blue eyes were still wickedly bright, and he still had that commanding presence. Bit like Lord Conway – ex Guards officers all seemed to be chips off the same block. And he certainly knew the best places to dine. The meal in the small private room had been more than pleasant. It had mellowed her. That was dangerous. Taking a deep breath, she warned herself to be careful. 'You were telling me about banks, Marcus.' She dropped a sugar cube into her coffee.

'Situation's worrying. Security systems are being breached, money's being taken.'

'Surely they have experts who deal with that sort of thing?'

'They have, and we've given them access to our people, but they haven't been able to resolve the problem.'

'Are all banks being penetrated?'

'We understand most British banks are being hacked into at will. British and Asian are the only people who've admitted to an actual loss, but there could be others. It's the sort of thing they'd want to keep to themselves. Depositors go elsewhere if there's the slightest hint their funds might not be secure. Been discussed at Cabinet level. They're desperate to avoid another banking scandal. Gave the chief a very hard time. She had to give the PM assurances.'

'Assurances?'

'That we'd take immediate and positive action.'

Samantha smiled. 'Sounds like the usual rhetoric.'

'She had to promise something to get out of the meeting unscathed.'

'And have you and Loretta decided what this urgent and positive action is going to be?'

He sipped his dessert wine and fixed her in a steady gaze. 'We were hoping you'd go in.'

'Me! What do I know about banks? What do I know about electronic security?'

'Bankers don't need anyone to tell them about banking, and they've got their own experts working round the clock on security. What's needed is a different mind, a different kind of intelligence, to take a look at the problem.'

'Has Fallon approved this?'

'Given it her full support. If she's able to tell the PM she's sending you in, he'll accept she's taken exceptional measures.'

'Cosgrave got his second term,' Samantha murmured. She picked up her coffee cup. 'I wonder how his secret love-child, little Benjamin, is getting on.'

'Fine, as far as I know.'

'I wonder if Cosgrave kept the turd in the jar as a memento?'

Marcus chuckled. 'He ought to have. If the Bassingers had got to the boy first we'd be serving under a different government.'

The smile faded from Samantha's lips. 'I'm not coming back, Marcus.'

'This is banking crime, Sam.'

'I'm trying to unravel myself, Marcus. I've finished with stalking and killing.'

'Bankers and computer hackers? This one's completely different, Sam.'

'It's something I know nothing about. I'd be no use to you.'

'Could be an internal thing. Surely you could investigate that. Anyway, if Loretta could tell the PM she'd put you in it would reassure the politicians, keep them quiet until the banks get round to dealing with it themselves.'

'Who's representing the banks?'

'Sir Nigel Lattimer. He's chairman of British and Asian, and he chairs the Banking Association.'

'Does he know what you're proposing?'

'I've discussed it with Nigel. He thinks it's a jolly good idea.'

Discussed it with Nigel. Probably over drinks at the club. Sounded like a stitch-up. 'I'm not coming back, Marcus. You'll have to find someone else to go in.'

'What if British and Asian were to engage you directly?'

Samantha began to feel interested. She was going to tell Lord Conway she was abandoning the search for his daughter-in-law; she couldn't, in all conscience, charge him. And her sessions with Dr Uberman were going to be expensive, frequent and in London. Working for City bankers would be lucrative and convenient. But there was a flaw. 'If the bank hires me, Loretta won't be able to tell the PM she's sent me in. And I might not be able to do the job without access to information you're holding.'

'We can get round that, Sam. We'd put you on a short-term contract, three months renewable. We'd pay consultants' rates; you'd negotiate a separate fee with the bank.'

'Can a servant of the Crown have two masters?'

'You'd be a consultant. Consultants are free to have more than one client.'

'You're being Machiavellian, Marcus.'

He smiled. 'It'll suit our purpose. We'd supply you with ID cards, an encrypted phone. You'd be able to access the information systems, the central data bases. And British and Asian wouldn't quibble over a decent fee.'

'I'd be tricking them, Marcus. I don't know a thing about banking security.'

'They're awash with banking experts and security experts. Just go in and get the feel of it, then report back.'

'To you or Sir Nigel?'

'Both. But I'd expect all the details. You could tell old Nigel whatever you thought appropriate.'

She fixed him with a reproachful stare. 'Machiavellian was too polite, Marcus. Cunning, devious and utterly without ethics would have been more accurate. Loretta wants the politicians off her back; you want to know what's going on. You're putting them under surveillance and they're going to pay for it. Solving the problem's not on your agenda. The fact that I know bugger all about banking and cyber crime really doesn't matter.'

He laughed. 'That's a bit harsh, Sam. We're keen for you to address the problem, it's just that we have other priorities.' He met her gaze for a while, then said, 'Consultants' rates are generous, Sam, and old Nigel wouldn't quibble over the fee.' He gave her his slow smile. 'Well?'

'Well what?'

'Are you in?'

'I must be brain-dead to even sit here listening to you, Marcus, but I'll go along with it.'

She could sense his feeling of satisfaction, triumph even, as he withdrew a narrow envelope from an inside pocket, took out a document, then shook a collection of ID cards on to the table. He unfolded the papers and slid them over to her. 'The standard consultancy agreement. The bank's not mentioned, and there are no restrictions on the clients you can work for, either during or after the agreement's expired. It's for three months, renewable. Monthly rate's indicated here,' he pointed to a figure entered by hand in black ink, 'and you sign here.'

Samantha noticed a signature in the same black ink. 'Loretta's already signed.' She glanced up. 'She must have been pretty confident your charm would win the day.'

'Loretta knows charm's wasted on you, Sam. I got her to sign on the off-chance you'd accept; save time. I want someone in there, and Loretta wants to stop the politicians banging on about it.'

Samantha clicked open her bag, found her pen and added her signature above Loretta Fallon's. Marcus tugged the forms away and handed her the copy. She picked up the ID cards. 'Don't care for the photographs.'

'You've not changed. It's still a good likeness. The name on the cards is Georgina Grey. I presumed you'd want that. I'll have the encrypted phone brought to you by courier. Where are you going to be staying?'

'In and around London. Tell whoever brings it to call me on my mobile before he sets off. I presume we'll have to exchange identification before he hands the thing over?'

'He'll say he's Marlon from Metro-City Courier Services. What's your name going to be?'

'Shirley Temple.'

'You don't look the least like Shirley Temple.'

'She was cute; all those ringlets.'

'You're glamorous, Sam, breathtakingly glamorous, but I wouldn't call you cute.' Huge green eyes, dismissive and icily remote, stared into his. Ruthless, he mused. Ruthless and deadly. That was the perfect description for Samantha Quest.

She slid the ID cards into a pocket in her bag.

'The appointment with Sir Nigel Lattimer is on Monday at eleven thirty. He'll be entertaining you to lunch.'

'You were sure I'd accept, weren't you, Marcus?'

He smiled. 'It was a provisional arrangement, Sam. If you'd refused, I'd have cancelled. And I know banking's a bit dull, a bit of a closed shop, but it's vital we find out what's going on. Bankers are so secretive.'

Samantha studied his big confident features. His mouth, with its heavy bottom lip, had curved in a reassuring smile. He'd deliberately made the job sound tedious and boring. If Loretta Fallon had rushed back to headquarters, wetting herself after a dressing-down from a Cabinet committee, it was too serious to be boring. If she hadn't been toying with the idea of a new Ferrari, she'd have turned the job down.

Helen saw a line of light under Jennifer's door as she rounded the top of the stairs. She tapped gently, pushed it open and peered around the edge. Her daughter was sitting at the desk the men had brought over that morning, her long blond hair gleaming in the light of the reading-lamp. Helen smiled. 'Still working?'

Jennifer smiled back. 'We've started calculus. I'm trying to get to grips with it.'

'Calculus? What's calculus? Don't bother trying to tell me.' Helen entered the room and sat on the edge of the neatly made single bed. 'New school still OK?'

'I like it. A lot of the girls in my year have just enrolled. They're going for the sixth-form college, like me.' She laid her book on the desk and took a closer look at her mother. Her face had that shiny, slightly puffy look it always had when she was really upset. Jennifer made her voice reassuring. 'I'm OK, Mum. Really. Everything's fine.'

Helen's face crumpled. 'You must hate me.'

Shocked, Jennifer left the desk, sat beside her mother on the bed and put her arm around her. 'Why on earth would I hate you, Mum? I love you.' Jennifer's voice was bewildered. Her mother's body was hot, feverish almost, and she smelled faintly of sweat, like she had after the police had called in Tanford and told her Daddy was being released.

'Because of your father going away, and now we've had to come here.'

Jennifer shrugged. 'Bad stuff happens, Mum. I got over Daddy going ages ago. It's the same for most of the girls at school. They've all got something they don't want to talk about, or if it's just happened they usually can't stop talking about it.' Her mother was weeping silently. Jennifer gave her a hug and pressed her cheek against hers. 'We're fine, Mum. Everything's OK.'

And things really were OK. Before she'd left Tanford, her form mistress had taken her aside and said, 'A new school, Jennifer. Two years and then university. You've got wings, take flight. You're young and free and life's a wonderful adventure; a cornucopia of opportunities. *Carpe diem*, my dear. Seize the day. Work hard and don't allow stupid boys to distract you.'

'But the new house is so ordinary,' Helen went on. 'And the decorations are awful and knocked about, and—'

The house is fine, Mum. I like the house. It's got a nice atmosphere. You can tell a happy family lived here. I never really liked Elm Trees after what happened. And Cheltenham's nice. And I've made new friends.'

It *was* nice. She liked the old Regency spa town. It wasn't sleepy like Tanford. It had more fizz. And men seemed politer. They'd smile and let you pass; open doors for you – some of the older ones did, anyway. The younger ones leaned out of van windows and whistled and yelled things. Gretchen, one of her new friends, said some men got excited when they saw older girls in their school uniforms: blazers, blouses, pleated skirts and opaque stockings. Old perves and young perves, Gretchen called them. And there were what they'd started calling presentable young perves. When they strolled, sometimes arm in arm, along the Promenade and around Montpellier, they compared notes on all the presentable young perves.

Her mother was still sniffing and tugging at her handkerchief.

Jennifer hugged her. 'What's wrong, Mum? Something's happened. What's—'

'A private detective called today; hired by your grandfather to find us and tell us he's missing us and that he wants us to go back to Tanford.'

'Private detective! Gosh, I've only ever read about private detectives. Was he small and sleazy or big and intimidating?'

'She: it was a woman. Slim, expensively dressed, jet-black hair, big green eyes.' Scary eyes, Helen reflected. Eyes that seemed to take you prisoner, make you say things you'd normally keep to yourself. 'She promised me she'd tell Grandpa she couldn't find us; that she thought we might have gone abroad.'

'Did she have a name?'

'Gave me a card.' Helen reached into the pocket of her jeans and tugged it out, glanced at the scribbled phone number then turned it over. The other side was blank. She passed it to Jennifer. 'Strange, she never told me her name.' Jennifer glanced at it, then dropped it on her bedside table. 'Her finding us has scared you, hasn't it, Mum?'

Helen nodded. 'I phoned the police in Cheltenham when she'd gone, spoke to a woman who deals with domestic violence. She was sympathetic, but she said there was nothing they could do unless your father made trouble. She said they'd contact the police in Tanford, get information from their files, and make a note that I'd called.'

'Do you think he'll try to find us?'

Helen shrugged. She was certain he would, but she didn't care to voice her fears. She gazed at her daughter. 'Do you miss him?'

'It's been four years, Mum. I know it sounds awful, but apart from remembering he was big and incredibly strong, I'm beginning to forget what he looked like. If I met him again, I'd feel embarrassed.'

'He adored you.'

'He was always working. The holidays abroad were nice, but I don't remember him ever being in the house much.'

'Grandpa: don't you miss Grandpa?'

''Course I miss Grandpa. He was kind. He made me laugh. Nicer than Grandma. I don't think she ever really liked me.'

'Elizabeth never liked either of us. We were intruders. She

begrudged us our share of your father's affection.' Helen rose to her feet. 'I'm going to have a bath. Can I make you a hot drink before I do?'

Jennifer shook her head. 'I'll struggle with the calculus for a while, then I'll turn in.'

Helen paused on the landing and looked back. 'I was talking to the woman next door this afternoon. Her son's good with computers. Perhaps I should ask her if he'd mind taking a look at yours. They're called Goodwin; Edith and Charles Goodwin.'

Jennifer smiled. 'The son's called Edward.'

'You've spoken to him?'

'Heard him talking to an Indian man who'd driven a van down the rear access. They were carrying things into that big shed he has at the bottom of the garden. The man kept laughing and saying, "Good old Eddie. You are my cleverest and most industrious worker. I would be bankrupt without you." He's cute.'

'The Indian man's cute?'

'No, the boy.'

'The next time I see his mother, I'll mention it. He might be able to fix it for you.' Helen closed the door and headed for the bathroom.

Beauty could be a dangerous thing. It could be a curse. Jennifer had matured too early and too quickly, just as she had. James coming back wasn't the only thing that frightened her. She dreaded Jennifer becoming too interested in boys. It was one of the reasons why she'd kept her at an all-girls school. She'd been putting off the evil day. She didn't want Jennifer to end up like her. You're man mad, her mother used to say. And look where it had got her.

FIVE

ady Conway was sitting on the back seat of the Bentley, shoulders turned so she could gaze through the rear window towards the gatehouse of Doncaster Jail. The small visitor's car park was full and Dobson had reversed on to a paved area near the access.

Reaching forward, she touched a button in the armrest. A sidelight slid down and chilly morning air began to mingle with her perfume and the fainter odours of leather and cigars; she wished Fergus wouldn't smoke his wretched cigars in the car.

The approach to the jail was deserted, quiet enough for her to hear the rush of river water as it tumbled over a cascade beneath a nearby bridge and the birds singing in a hawthorn hedge that separated the car park from a storage compound. Strong sunlight was making the high concrete walls of the jail seem a little less forbidding. It was glaring off the gatehouse windows, obscuring the guards within.

Her heart lurched. James was coming. It could only be James. Few men were as tall and broad as her big handsome son. She turned, reached forward, tapped on the glass partition, but Dobson had seen him through the wing mirror. The grey-liveried chauffeur was already climbing out of the car.

She'd never have to visit this awful place again. No more fingerprinting, no more humiliating mouth and body searches, no more sniffing dogs.

James was striding past the gatehouse. He was wearing a suit and tie again, swinging a plastic carrier bag that held toiletries and a few personal things. He looked leaner, fitter, even more handsome.

Dobson opened the rear door of the limousine and held out a hand. 'Welcome home, sir. It's good to have you back.'

'Good to be back, Dobson.' James grasped the extended hand and shook it vigorously.

Tears were flooding down Lady Conway's cheeks; her heart was in her throat. James lowered his head and joined her on the back seat. She wrapped her arms around him.

'I'm back, Mother. It's over.' His deep voice was quiet and matter-of-fact, devoid of emotion.

This was her son, her great big handsome son. She held him tightly, heard the car door close, the faint whine of the starter. Then the black limousine rolled off the pavement and whispered its way over the river bridge into Marshgate, heading south, out of Doncaster. She was taking James home.

Dr Uberman's voice betrayed his irritation. 'If you're to derive any benefit from our sessions, Miss Quest, if I'm to have the opportunity to carry out an analysis, you must be prepared to allocate the necessary time to it. If I'd known you were going to cut this second session short, I wouldn't have spent quite so long on word association.'

'Sorry, Doctor. Someone made the appointment for me. I'll make sure it doesn't happen again.'

'We'd better move on to your dream. Is it still progressing, still unfolding?'

'A little.' Her husky voice rustled out of the shadows.

'Are you comfortable? Are you relaxed?'

The waistband of her skirt was rather tight. Samantha unhooked it, eased the zip down a little, then let out her breath. 'Quite comfortable.' She was wearing an Ungaro suit, black with a bold red pinstripe. Her Zac Posen blouse was a rather fetching white silk creation. She'd chosen the clothes with bankers, not Doctor Uberman, in mind.

'Then you should begin. Recount the dream slowly. Try to recall small details, every impression. What seem to be trivial things can often be the most revealing.'

Samantha closed her eyes and collected her thoughts. 'I'm walking down a narrow valley,' she began, 'along the bank of a river. I'm wearing a white dress. My legs and feet are bare. I can—'

'The dress: can you describe it?'

'It's very plain. I would call it chaste. It has a high neck, long sleeves and a long skirt. Where was ... Oh, yes, I can feel the grass cool and wet under my feet. Suddenly the sky becomes dark and overcast and I feel rain falling on me. Warm rain. When I look down, I see my dress is streaked with red. It's raining blood. The river is quite shallow and I take off the dress and wade into it. Completely naked now, I splash water on to my legs and body, trying to wash myself, but the rain is clouding the water with blood, turning it red, and it smears over my skin.

'The river narrows and flows into a culvert. I have to find clean water, so I wade inside, into the darkness. The roof is low and I have to bend my head.' Samantha paused. Her breathing had quickened, just as it did in the dream.

Dr Uberman underlined *white dress and blood*. Then, in his small, neat handwriting, added: *First Holy Communion? Wedding? Menstrual blood or loss of virginity?*

'As I progress down the culvert the water becomes deeper. I can hear it lapping and swirling against the stones. It reaches the top of my thighs, and the current is stronger, drawing me along. The sandy bottom of the stream has gone. I'm walking on large pebbles that are smooth and round and slimy and strangely soft. A man is following me. He is calling to me in Arabic. His voice is loud and angry.'

'He is angry with you?'

'Yes. He is pursuing me.'

'One man?'

'Yes, one man.'

'And why is he angry with you?'

'I sense his anger, I can hear it in his voice, but I do not understand the nature of it.'

'How do you know he's speaking in Arabic?'

'Because it is a language I speak.'

'But you do not understand the words?'

'He is pursuing me, splashing in the water, and the sound is echoing and distorted in the culvert. I cannot tell what he is saying.'

Sighing, Dr Uberman turned back to his notebook. 'Please continue.'

'And then the culvert becomes higher and wider and I realize I'm getting closer to the outlet, which is hidden around a bend. There's more light now. I can see the walls, and on the walls the names of men are written in blood.'

'The names of men?'

'Seven dead men.'

'How do you know that these are the names of dead men?'

Sensing a need for caution, irritated by the interruption, Samantha said, 'I know in the way that one knows things in dreams.'

Recovering her train of thought, she went on, 'The culvert is becoming lighter and wider and higher. I look down at my body. It's still smeared with blood, and great clots and ribbons of blood are drifting all around me in the water. I sense that, when I emerge, when I wade on around the bend, I will find clean water and be able to wash away the blood. I will also learn something I need to know, something my life depends upon. Then I wake.'

Samantha opened her eyes, gazed up in silence at the shadowy blue-grey ceiling while she listened to the rustle of paper and the movement of Dr Uberman's pen.

Presently he asked, 'Do you feel fear when you experience this dream?'

'Yes. When I enter the culvert and hear the angry voice of the man who is pursuing me, I feel very afraid.'

'Shame or embarrassment at your nakedness?'

'No.'

'What is your dominant feeling?'

'Revulsion at the blood on my body and in the water all around me.'

'It makes you feel unclean?'

'Yes.'

'You said that when you emerged from the tunnel you would learn something you needed to know; something your life depended upon. What is it that you need to know?'

'I … I've really no idea.'

'What would you like to know?'

Samantha's thoughts tumbled. The simplicity of the question had caught her unawares. 'I'd like to know how I can recover my peace of mind, Doctor. Isn't that why I'm lying here, on this couch?'

After a silence, she heard the creak of his chair, the rattle of a blind, and watched a bar of sunlight creeping across the high ceiling.

'We have to end there, Samantha. We really needed more time together. Do try to avoid your sessions being curtailed by other appointments.' He leafed through the pages of his notebook. The word-associations were strange; bizarre even. Could she be concealing things, or trying to mislead him? He watched her slide her feet into her red-and-black shoes, then fasten and smooth her skirt. The jacket of her suit was folded over the back of a chair. He held it while she slid her arms into the sleeves. The blouse she was wearing was quite an exotic affair: layers of translucent white silk with a square neckline, full sleeves and long pearl-buttoned cuffs. His wife would covet such a blouse. Enveloped in her fragrance, he followed her to the door.

As he opened it, he said, 'Beautiful clothes seem to be important to you, Samantha.' Was it simple vanity, he wondered? Or was she hiding behind them, concealing herself from the world?

'Fashion, Doctor Uberman.' She smiled, remembering her earlier lie. 'I work in the industry. I have to promote it.'

They stepped out into the reception area.

'Bernice, would you arrange another appointment for Miss Quest. Soon: before the end of this week or early next.'

Bernice Forster beamed at him over her blue-rimmed spectacles. 'Certainly, Doctor.' She turned to Samantha. 'When would be convenient, Miss Quest?'

The doors of the executive lift rumbled open. Samantha stepped out on to the ninety-second floor. A woman was waiting for her. Blond hair perfectly styled, elegant in a black dress that had a hem well above the knee, she smiled and displayed perfect teeth. 'Miss Grey?' The American accent was Washington, not Tennessee.

Samantha nodded.

'I'm Penny Jordan, Sir Nigel's PA.' She held out a hand. 'They're waiting for you in the boardroom. If you'll follow me, I'll take you through.'

Two pairs of stiletto heels tapped over cream marble, then stabbed into blue carpet when they left the lobby and strode on down a corridor. Large modern paintings, mostly abstract daubs, were displayed in groups of three between leather-covered doors. The air was warm and fragrant, the ceiling rather low, the lighting focused on the art collection. Samantha made a mental note to double her hourly rates.

She turned to the woman. 'Have you been with Sir Nigel long?'

Penny Jordan smiled. 'Longer than I'd care to admit. I came over from the New York office almost twenty years ago. I wanted to retire last year, but Sir Nigel persuaded me to stay on until he goes.'

They approached double doors with large and ornate bronze

handles. Without pausing, the woman pushed them open and they swept through. Standing aside, she announced, 'Miss Georgina Grey for you, Sir Nigel.'

Sunlight gleamed on the dark surface of a long boardroom table. Men seated at the far end had their backs to a wall of glass and a panoramic view across the City.

Samantha headed towards them, her step jaunty, her gun-heavy Alberta Ferretti bag swinging. The men rose to their feet.

Charming, Samantha mused, and flashed them all an appreciative smile.

A short, bald man, dressed in a grey three-piece suit, shook her hand. 'Nigel Lattimer. Delighted to meet you, Miss Grey. Let me introduce you to the team. This is Damien Bradley, our data base administrator; Angus Fiens is in charge of electronic security; Morris Powell is our encryption specialist; and this is Walter Donlan, he heads up the Asian arm of our enterprise.' He beamed at Samantha and gestured towards an empty chair next to his.

They all sat down.

Sir Nigel's complete lack of hair and small pink features gave him the appearance of an aged and oversized baby. His plump hands were restlessly folding and unfolding a pair of heavy horn-rimmed spectacles. The head of Asian affairs was tall, grey-haired and dignified. His expression was grave. The rest were younger, perhaps in their thirties; all dressed in expensive suits, they seemed alert and rather nervous in the chairman's presence.

Sir Nigel cleared his throat. 'Before we begin, Miss Grey, I must stress the utter confidentiality of the proceedings. We wouldn't expose ourselves in this way to our colleagues in the banking industry, let alone outsiders.' He cleared his throat again. 'Client confidence is paramount, Miss Grey. If we lose that ...' He gave her a baleful look, then turned towards the sandy-haired man in charge of electronic security. 'Could you start us off, Angus?'

'Please, not too technical, gentlemen,' Samantha interrupted. 'Just give me the broad outline of the problem and your take on it.'

'To put it simply,' Angus began, 'the bank's systems are being hacked into indiscriminately.' He glanced at the man called Powell. 'Morris has increased the level of encryption, but no matter how complex he makes it, or how often passwords are changed, the hacker or hackers continue to break in.'

'Funds are being stolen?'

The dignified man with the grave expression shuffled his papers. 'Two large sums due for transfer to an account held by the Mundai Bank in Pakistan. A day later, funds intended for the Bank Nagrani Punjab were diverted.'

'Significant sums?'

'A total of more than thirteen million pounds, so far.'

'Other banks – are they affected?' Samantha asked.

Sir Nigel unfolded the horn-rimmed spectacles, slid them on and frowned down at a typewritten sheet. 'Don't have any confirmation of that, but I would think it likely. As I said, Miss Grey, this isn't the sort of thing the industry cares to broadcast.' He read out the names of four high-street banks. 'We think they're being hacked into, but we're the only bank to have suffered actual loss so far.'

'The banks in Pakistan; have they been affected?'

'The losses arose before the interbank transfers, but Walter's engaged in a discreet dialogue with their people.' He glanced at Donlan. 'Have you discovered anything?'

The grey-haired man shook his head.

Samantha looked around the group. Five pairs of eyes were watching her intently. Flashing them all a dazzling smile, she said, 'The funds that were being transferred; presumably they were payments for something. Who were the account holders?'

Walter Donlan opened a file. 'All of the payments were being made by a UK-based organization called Grassman Holdings. The transfers to the Mundai Bank were heading for Texmet Tools of Badrah and Banpur Engineering in Hyderabad. The transfer to the Bank Nagrani Punjab was a payment to …' He frowned down at his papers, 'Venture Import and Export, based in Shikarpur.'

'You've spoken to Grassman Holdings?'

'Their chief accountant raised it with us immediately they discovered the loss. To say the least, he was rather agitated.'

'And have you any idea how the monies have been diverted?' Samantha asked.

'As far as we can establish, they were transferred to a bank that no longer exists.'

'No longer exists?'

'It was an internet entity that had all of the industry-agreed codes and electronic signatures needed for it to function as a bank. After the funds had been deposited and moved on, it ceased to exist. Essentially, Miss Grey, it was set up to make it impossible for us to trace the final destination of the money.'

'So, the people who did this would have an understanding of the industry; an insider's knowledge?'

Sir Nigel nodded.

'And considerable technical resources,' Damien Bradley added. 'Setting up the fugitive bank was no small matter.'

'Surely you have safeguards to prevent sums as large as this being withdrawn without some sort of scrutiny?'

'Intricate safeguards,' Angus Fiens said. 'Unfortunately, they were overridden in some way.'

'And you've no hope of tracing these funds?'

'The bank was registered, briefly, in the Cayman Islands. We're in dialogue with the authorities there, and with the internet service providers, and we may be able to trace the source of the instructions to deposit and withdraw. But even if we managed to do that we'd still be some way from recovering the cash. Fact is, Miss Grey, we've accepted that British and Asian will probably have to stand the loss.'

Sir Nigel sighed and glanced at Angus Fiens. 'How's the tracking going, Angus? Are you any nearer to sourcing the instructions?'

'Working on it with Morris and Damien. They were routed in a complex way and we're not having much success.' He grimaced and gave Sir Nigel a shamefaced look. 'Fact is, we've not had any success.'

'If you can't trace the cash, can you locate the hackers?' Samantha asked.

'If enough resources are put into it, we usually can,' Angus said. 'It takes time but, with a little co-operation from foreign governments, banks have been able to do it. This one's going to be difficult. Hackers use all sorts of tricks to preserve anonymity, and these people have been particularly clever. And the program they're using to actually hack in is completely unknown to us. Whoever's devised it has been doing some very original thinking.'

'You're working on this?'

'With Morris. Eighteen-hour days. We monitor the system round the clock, lock on to the hacker when he breaks in, then record what he's doing until he leaves. When we try to block him, or do a trace, he mocks us.'

'Mocks you?'

Angus glanced at Sir Nigel. When Sir Nigel nodded, he tapped keys on his open laptop and turned it so that Samantha could view the screen.

The head and torso of what looked like a ventriloquist's dummy appeared: apple-red cheeks, startled eyes, gaping mouth, a sailor's hat tilted at a rakish angle. The head began to turn from side to side, the eyes rolled, the torso swayed, then manic laughter screeched out of the laptop's speakers.

Samantha tried hard not to smile.

'Apparently the thing's called a Laughing Sailor. They used to put them in glass cases in amusement arcades. Penny in the slot and he starts to laugh.'

They were all looking at her, waiting for a comment. Samantha peered at the screen again. 'Jolly Jack Tar's been embroidered on his hatband; uniform's a bit moth-eaten, his face is chipped. Have you any idea where…?'

The men shook their heads, then the one called Powell, the

encryption specialist, said, 'There're a few in museums in seaside towns. They usually have the name of the town on the hatband. This chap isn't one of them. A Miss Ryman at the Victoria and Albert Museum wrote a monograph on the things, and they've actually got a doll and mechanism catalogued. We've shown her the image but she can't place it. Seems they were fairly popular in amusement arcades in the forties and fifties.'

'And what's happening when Jolly Jack Tar's on the rampage?' Samantha was struggling to keep a straight face.

'Funds are transferred, to and fro, between accounts, in what seems to be a haphazard way,' Angus said.

'Other banks are affected?'

Angus nodded. 'The system continuously retotals balances, then, as far as we've been able to make out, the funds are restored to the proper accounts.' He turned the laptop, made a few key strokes, then presented it to Samantha again. There were ripples of movement up and down endless columns of figures. They stopped, then, after a few seconds, the movement began again.

Samantha glanced around the group. 'And funds don't go missing when this happens?'

'As far as we're aware, no.'

'Could it be a disgruntled employee?'

'Always possible, but I don't think a disgruntled employee would go to these lengths.'

'And why is nothing taken?' Morris Powell asked. 'Are they practice runs, persuading us we're dealing with a joker, while all the time they're getting ready to skim the accounts.'

'Before they removed any funds they'd have to set up multiple accounts under false names; different addresses, different banks; prepare to receive the money when they spirited it away. That would take time,' Angus suggested.

Sir Nigel seemed to want the meeting to end. Clearing his throat, he said, 'If there's nothing else you'd like to ask, Miss Grey, I think you and I may as well continue our conversation over lunch.' His plump fingers were still fidgeting with his spectacles. He turned to his colleagues. 'Thanks, all of you. I'm sure Miss Grey will want more meetings with you when she begins her investigation.'

They rose, gathered up papers and laptops, and began the long trek to the door.

Sir Nigel seemed to relax when the men had left. Perhaps the problem was weighing on him and he was looking forward to a pleasant diversion. 'Lunch, Miss Grey. It's being served for us in the executive dining room. Shall we go through?'

Samantha rose, moved closer to the wall-to-wall window and looked out across the city. When she turned, Sir Nigel was smiling at her, waiting for her to lead the way to the door. 'You survey the world from a very high place, Sir Nigel.'

'So I do, Miss Grey, but I find that mist often obscures the view.'

Lunch was a delicate meal of contrasting flavours, perfectly prepared and served by two Asian waiters who wore white gloves and white jackets with Mao collars.

'What do you make of it all, Georgina?' Sir Nigel had dispensed with surnames while they were tackling their Sole Veronique.

'We've got off to a bad start.'

He frowned across the table at her.

'We should have met secretly; just the two of us. You could have briefed me, then given me some sort of job that would have made it possible for me to mingle with the staff.'

'You think the culprit might be an employee?'

'Culprits. I think your systems are being penetrated by two parties.'

'Walter wondered that, but Angus thinks it's unlikely.'

'I've been seen,' Samantha went on. 'I can be recognized by security men, receptionists, the staff you invited to the meeting, the waiters who've served us. At least four of your people know why I'm here. I can't carry out a covert investigation now.'

'When Marcus said he'd try to persuade you to come, he agreed a preliminary meeting with key staff would be a good idea.' Sir Nigel toyed with his coffee spoon. His small pink features were arranged in an appealing expression. 'But you will take the job, Georgina? Marcus was so confident you'd be able to help us.'

'You employ very clever people, Sir Nigel. They devised the systems that enable the bank to function. If they can't understand how this is happening, what chance do I have?'

'Marcus said you'd approach the problem differently, and if you discovered an external cause you'd deal with it discreetly; there'd be no need for us to have recourse to law and the courts. This is how we usually resolve problems of this kind. What would it do for our credibility as a bank if litigation exposed the fact that we're vulnerable in this way? I accept your position's been compromised, but surely you can still help us?'

'I can try.'

He was smiling again. 'Then we must discuss your fee.'

'The outcome's uncertain, Sir Nigel. I'd feel I'd cheated you if I charged hourly rates for an investigation that dragged on and on and then floundered. How about a bounty payment?'

He looked intrigued.

'Like I said, I suspect you're troubled by two hackers. Jolly Jack Tar – so far he's just been a humiliating intrusion – and some people who are actually robbing you. How about a million-pound bounty if I resolve both problems, half if I only solve one.'

'A million pounds, Georgina?'

He was still smiling, but she could tell she'd shocked him. There was no possibility of a successful outcome. She wouldn't waste much time on it, just enough to keep Marcus quiet and stop him complaining about the consultant's fee he was paying. And the men she'd just met, men who were experts in the field, were working night and day on the problem. They might not recover the lost funds, but they'd soon find a way to block intruders from the system. She returned his smile. 'A fraction of your annual bonus, Sir Nigel.'

'Those days are over, Georgina.' He took a deep breath. 'I'm planning to retire next year. I don't want to leave this behind and I want it dealing with in a discreet way. How would I know you'd solved the problem?'

'It would end.'

'It could end without your intervention. If I have to explain to the board why I sanctioned payment of a million pounds, I'd need tangible proof that you were the sole cause of it ending.'

'I'd give you proof: details of how the hacking was done, how they unscrambled your encryption. Your experts could look it over and verify it. Knowing how would be important to them. And there's a very remote chance I'd recover the funds.'

His baby-face wrinkled in a conspiratorial smile. 'I think we can do business, Georgina. Shall we seal it with a brandy?'

'I shouldn't. I'm driving.'

'It's rather special. Perhaps just a small one?'

Samantha laughed.

Sir Nigel unstoppered the decanter the waiters had left behind and poured. They clinked glasses. 'A million pounds it is, then, Georgina. Before you leave, I'll ask Penny to type a formal agreement for us both to sign.'

Samantha swung the Ferrari on to the exit ramp and accelerated out of the basement car park. She nosed between cars lining the side street, then cruised towards a junction with a broader artery that served the commercial quarter. The afternoon sun, low and dazzling, began to flicker through gaps between glass and concrete office buildings as she drifted with the stream of commuters. Horns blared when she made a cheeky left across a line of traffic, hoping to find a less congested route. She heard them blare again, behind her, and glanced in the mirrors. A black cab had copied her manoeuvre. It swayed as it followed her down the connecting road.

Suspicious, she picked up speed, began to twist and turn aimlessly through the network of streets. She made a left on to a major road, merged with eastbound traffic, then checked the mirrors. The black cab was winding out of the junction. It was three cars behind.

She was being followed. She'd been right to have doubts about it all. Marcus would have known the boardroom meeting was a bad opening move, exposing her before she'd begun. It had been calculated. Her entry on to the scene had provoked a response; brought things out into the open. She was never meant to solve the banker's problems. She was a pawn in some bigger game. She glanced in the mirrors. The black cab was only a car away.

Flicking her indicators, she gave plenty of warning before turning into a labyrinth of narrow lanes that linked old wharves. She drove on, down gloomy canyons formed by towering warehouses, occasionally catching a glimpse of the river. She was moving sedately now, making sure the black cab didn't lose her.

An enclosed timber walkway, its paint peeling, its windows blackened by grime, spanned the roadway, connecting warehouse to warehouse. Samantha passed under it, then turned on to a wide swath of concrete. On one side the river, dark and oily, its choppy surface glittering in the sunlight; on the other a ramshackle collection of metal and timber buildings, all derelict and deserted. In the distance, some massive Victorian warehouses were being demolished. Gigantic yellow machines were crawling over a mountain of rubble, scooping it up and crashing it down into high-sided lorries.

Samantha checked the mirrors. The black cab hadn't appeared on the waterfront. Up ahead, the doors of a big corrugated-iron shed were rolled open. She braked hard and swung the Modena over. The place had been a workshop or garage. She bounced over the threshold, parked between oil drums and a heap of scrap metal, then climbed out and ran back to the door. When she tried to slide it along its tracks, it moved enough to screen the car, then jammed.

Standing just inside the opening, she narrowed her eyes against the sun and glanced back down the strip of uneven concrete. The black cab was approaching. It slowed to a crawl as it rattled past, the driver looking this way and that, fearing he'd lost his quarry.

Hand in her bag, Samantha stepped out. The cab rolled to a stop and the driver wound his window down. She walked towards him.

'You're following me.'

'Following you?' Wet lips almost hidden behind a frizzy grey beard parted in a smile. Jaundiced eyes crawled over her. 'I am looking for an address, answering a call.'

Samantha slid the gun from her bag and brought the muzzle close to his face. 'Get out of the car.'

'Are you mad? I'm searching—'

'Get out of the car.'

She stepped back. The cab door opened. He was wearing a brown tweed sports jacket, baggy and old, over his nightshirt-like kameez. His cotton trousers were loose, his boots had thick rubber soles, and he wore a round woollen hat, the sort of thing Afghans call a *pakol*. His haj belt, his money bag, nestled on top of his paunch.

'Drop the knife you're hiding in your sleeve.'

'I have no—'

She levelled the gun. 'Drop the knife from your sleeve.' It clattered on to the road. 'Put your hands behind your head and walk into that building over there.'

He scowled at her, bristling with outraged dignity. 'You filthy little whore. Who are you to tell me where to walk?'

'Just walk.' She motioned towards the shed with the gun.

He dragged up mucus, spat it out at her feet, then combed fingers into wiry curls and strolled, with a leisurely insolence, through the parting in the doors.

Samantha picked up the knife and followed him in. 'Over there: stand by that guard rail next to the inspection pit.'

He ambled over to a rusty rail, then turned and leaned back, feigning nonchalance.

'Your name?' Samantha demanded. 'Tell me your name.'

'Fazel Nasari.'

'Not the name on your forged papers: the name Allah the Compassionate, the Merciful, will whisper when he calls you home.' She spoke the words in Arabic.

He was eyeing her warily now. 'Abdulgader Walgadi.'

'Take off your clothes, Abdul. Start with the boots.'

Consumed with rage, he snarled, 'I am a man. How dare you show such disrespect. Who do you think you are?'

'I'm your worst nightmare, Abdul.'

One of the massive lorries, big as a house and laden with rubble, was approaching, its engine roaring, its tyres rumbling. The metal walls of the garage began to reverberate. The sound rose to a crescendo, drowning out the words he was screaming at her. She fired three shots around his head. The bark of the gun, the crash of bullets tearing through metal, were loud, even above the din of the lorry.

When the sound had faded, she snarled, 'Strip or die, you hairy bastard.'

He began to undress.

SIX

D r Jeffreys snapped a surgical glove over an elasticated cuff, adjusted his rubber apron, and scowled at the plain-clothes policeman. 'Was this absolutely necessary? Six in the morning! Surely it could have waited a few hours?'

'The commissioner's very grateful, sir.' The inspector made his tone deferential. 'He's under considerable pressure with this one. He needs an early confirmation of the cause of death and your observations on the abrasions to the wrists.'

'Cause of death's bloody obvious,' Dr Jeffreys muttered scathingly. He turned to a tall gaunt young man with close-cropped fair hair. 'And you'll be my pathology technician, I suppose?'

'That's right, sir. Shaw, sir. Stephen Shaw.'

The doctor turned to the policeman. 'And your name is?'

'Detective Chief Inspector Saunders.' He challenged the doctor's haughty stare. Arrogant bastard. He wasn't the only one who didn't want to be in this cold damp hole where even the smell of their vile disinfectant couldn't mask fouler odours. His face was sore after a hasty shave. A greasy canteen breakfast was heavy and undigested in his stomach.

Lips pursed, the doctor's gaze wandered over the policeman's crumpled brown suit, then settled on his face. 'And do we know the name of the deceased?'

DCI Saunders flicked through a notebook. 'Fazel Nasari. Lived with six other drivers above a taxi firm's offices in Newham.'

'Do you want me to estimate the likely time of death?'

'We know that, sir, to within an hour. He called the office, told them he was turning out of Dock Lane and heading east through an old industrial area by the river. They called him on the radio half an hour later. When they got no reply they sent another cab to see if he was OK – a couple of drivers have been mugged recently. Found his taxi, then found him in an inspection pit in a derelict garage. Fuller's Wharf area, it's being cleared and redeveloped, riverside luxury apartments.'

Dr Jeffreys stepped over to the stainless-steel dissection table and drew back the green sheet. 'You've laid him face down.'

'That's right, sir.' The technician's voice was defensive. 'Had to clean him up for you: lower back and legs. He'd been lying in old sump oil. I used swabs, a mild detergent and a low-pressure spray. Shall I turn him?'

'Leave him for now. I'll check the posterior first. And I'm not going to open him up today. I'll do that tomorrow.' He began to move his gloved hands over the body, squeezing, touching, all the while staring intently at the plump brown flesh. He glanced across the table at the technician. 'Get me a pair of scissors and a small sample wallet, will you? And a razor.'

When he had the scissors, he snipped away some of the thick grey curls at the nape of the man's neck. The technician opened the plastic wallet and held it out. Dr Jeffreys dropped the hair inside, handed back the scissors, then took the cheap plastic razor and began to shave away the stubble.

'Mmm ... Large-bore weapon: at least nine millimetres. Fired at fairly close range.' He kneaded the flesh around the the wound. 'Shattered the base of the skull and the vertebrae at the top of the spine.'

DCI Saunders approached the raised rim of the table and took a look at the hole in the circle of shaved skin. The reek of the peculiar disinfectant was overpowering, the fluorescent lighting harsh and shadowless, the air cold and damp. Twenty-five years in the force and he still loathed autopsies. At least he wasn't going to suffer the dissection, the removal and weighing of the organs. Some other poor sod could attend that.

Having completed his examination of the back of the corpse, Dr Jeffreys parted buttock cheeks and peered into the cleft; ran his fingertips over arms, checked the hands and the soles of the feet. He glanced at his technician. 'Shall we turn him?'

Stephen Shaw stepped up to the table, took a firm grip on an arm, and dragged the body over to the raised rim. Straining, he heaved it on to its side. Dr Jeffrey grabbed a hip and thigh and pulled. Fazel Nasari rolled on to his back.

'Jesus Christ!' DCI Saunders made a dash for a sluice and began to vomit up his still recognizable breakfast.

Dr Jeffreys chucked softly, gratified by the policeman's distress. Serve him right for calling him out at this god-forsaken hour. He grinned across at the technician. 'We're not going to need the cranium chisel or the brain knife when we do the autopsy, are we, Stephen?'

The sound of retching became violent. The gaunt young man smiled back, enjoying the fraternal moment with a fellow professional.

'Plug a lamp in, there's a good chap.'

Stephen groped under the outlet end of the table, uncoiled an extension lead and placed a torchlike lamp in the doctor's outstretched hand.

'Bullet emerged beneath the left eye socket and we've lost … Mmm,' he peered inside the gaping hole, 'lost most of the brain, the left eye and the left upper jaw. Right eye's still in place. Very powerful weapon loaded with expanding ammunition: passage of the bullet's evacuated the cranium.' He glanced up. 'Got a long spatula?'

The technician crossed over to a steel table, returned with a strip of hard white plastic and handed it to the doctor.

'Hold the lamp for me. Direct the beam into the cavity; top and back of the skull.'

Dr Jeffreys inserted the plastic strip. 'Mmm … Part of the right hemisphere's still there, but …' He probed. 'There's very little of it.' He tossed the spatula into a bin, then ran searching fingers over the body, beginning with the neck beneath the beard, before moving to the chest with its frosting of grey hair, then on to the abdomen and down to the thighs and calves.

He examined the abrasions on the wrists. 'Handcuffs,' he pronounced. 'The ratchet type that can be squeezed tight. Not rope or cord. Metal edges have cut through the flesh in places.' He glanced up. 'You can sheet him over now, Stephen. We'll open him up tomorrow, but it's going to be little more than a formality.'

'There's a cut, Doctor. A stab mark. Inner left thigh. Noticed it when I was cleaning the oil away.'

'A cut?' Dr Jeffreys's manner became brisk again. 'Part the legs; let the calves hang over the edge of the table.' He examined the soft flesh, saw a tiny incision. 'Plug the lamp in again and bring it over.' He reached for a scalpel, inserted the blade into the cut and opened it gently. 'Mmm … I'd say six millimetres deep and about five long. Probably made by the point of a knife. And what's this?' He cupped a gloved hand under Fazel's genitals and lifted them clear of the groin. 'Bring the lamp closer … No, get it right down, on the table; shine the beam up into the crotch.' He lowered his head until his cheek was touching a thigh. 'Interesting. There's a transverse cut across the back of the scrotum. Not deep: it's not severed the scrotal sac.' He chuckled. 'But jolly painful. Wouldn't like that done to me. How about you, Stephen?'

'Definitely not, sir.'

'Right, cover him up.'

The technician stowed the light, gathered up the scalpel and rolled the green cotton sheet back over the corpse.

'You can look now, Inspector. It's all over.'

An ashen-faced DCI Saunders turned from the sluice. He was dabbing his mouth with a square of paper towel. He fumbled in a pocket, pulled out his notebook and clicked his pen. 'So, Doctor.'

He coughed, cleared his throat, then began to write. 'The man was killed with a powerful gun loaded with expanding ammunition. The bullet entered at the base of the scull and emerged through the left cheek. Death would have been instantaneous?'

'Absolutely,' Dr Jeffreys said drily. 'The poor bugger had no brains left.'

'And the abrasions to the wrists were probably caused by metal handcuffs?'

'I'm pretty sure of that.'

'And there was a stab wound at the top of the left inner thigh, and the scrotum had been sliced across with a knife.'

'A sharp knife.'

'Why do you think someone would—'

'Motives are your domain, Inspector. Perhaps pain was inflicted, castration threatened, in retribution for some wrong, the breaking of some sexual taboo. Or perhaps someone was trying to elicit information. You're well versed in the wickedness of men; you decide.'

'And you're going to carry out a full autopsy tomorrow, I think you said.'

'You'll definitely have my report before the end of the week, but I'd be very surprised if the autopsy adds anything to what we've learned today.'

Quiet street, James reflected. Pleasant town. Helen had chosen well. House looked tired, though. The front hedge was overgrown, a rainwater pipe was broken, garage doors were falling apart, and the whole place needed painting.

Someone was emerging through the gap between the garage and the house, walking down the short drive. It was Helen. She still carried herself well. Long blond hair gathered back and tied with a blue ribbon; the splendid breasts that pimply-arsed bastard had been fondling. Who else in Tanford had given them a suck and a squeeze?

She stepped out of the gate and began to walk towards him. She was wearing a grey coat and sensible black shoes; carrying a brown-leather document case. She must have found herself a job. Probably had to. She was walking briskly, approaching fast. He slid down in his seat. She was still some distance away, on the other side of the road, but if she looked across ...

She'd lost weight. It suited her, made her look younger, much ... It wasn't Helen. It was Jennifer! Four years. How much could happen in four years? God, she was the image of her mother. Hair was the same, face was prettier, features more refined, the same sensational figure. She hadn't seen him, hadn't spared him a glance. He watched her through the rear-view mirror until she disappeared around a corner, heading towards the main road. All the things that mattered had been stolen from him. He suddenly felt disorientated, as if he'd lost his bearings in space and time.

A sergeant at the police station in Tanford had told him Helen's new address for the price of a home-cinema system: when you wanted something, you became vulnerable. He'd wanted Helen the moment he'd set eyes on her at that football club dance. The blond hair, the pretty face, the body in the little black dress; most of all, the body in the little black dress. By the end of the evening his desire had become unbearable. And the more you wanted something, the more vulnerable you became.

He had to know. He had to get into the house and find Helen's keepsakes, her little collection of mementoes. Closing his eyes, he took a few deep breaths. He must control himself. Whatever happened, he couldn't go back to jail. He climbed out of the black BMW and walked the short distance to the house, kept his head down behind the overgrown hedge, then strode quickly up the path and stepped into the shallow porch.

His heart was pounding. He hadn't expected it to affect him like this. He rang the bell. A radio was playing inside the house. Beyond the hedge a delivery van rumbled down the street and mothers chattered while they walked children to school. As he was reaching up to press the bell again, the door opened.

He watched Helen's eyes widen, her features slacken with shock. She lifted a hand to her throat, then tried to slam the door, but he'd planted his big shoe inside the step and it stayed open. Her hair was shorter now, a little unkempt; and the skin around her eyes, those cornflower-blue eyes, was pale and waxy. She'd aged, but it was still the same sexy voluptuous Helen.

'Go away,' she gasped. Then her voice rose to a wail. 'Go away. I don't want you here.'

She was terrified. He relished that. Her wide eyes were fastened on his, and some musky perfume on her red sweater was mingling with an unpleasant undertone of fear-induced female sweat.

'We need to talk.' He managed to keep his voice low and calm.

'About what?'

'Things; the marriage. Can I come in?' He felt a sudden rush of anger, an eruption of rage that had been long suppressed. The feeling was so intense it made him giddy. Closing his eyes, he held on to the doorframe to steady himself. Why should he have to stand here, begging the faithless bitch? His hands trembled with an urge to take her by the throat and choke the life out of her. He breathed deeply. He had to calm himself. No way was he going back to jail. 'Please,' he said softly. 'I just want to talk. Give me ten minutes, that's all I'm asking.'

'You scare me. Don't you realize that? You scare the hell out of me. How do I know you won't—'

'Please. Just let me talk to you. I won't harm you. I won't even touch you. And if we start corresponding through lawyers it'll cost money you might not want to spend.'

Helen kept a tight hold on the door. He looked anguished, distraught, on the verge of tears. This was the thing she'd dreaded, the thing that had given her bad dreams: being confronted by him, being overwhelmed by guilt for what she'd done, fearing his violence. She was unable to close the door. She couldn't get rid of him. It would be embarrassing if her new neighbours saw and heard....

James opened his eyes and looked at her. 'Please,' he begged. 'I mean you no harm. It's been four years. There's been time for things to heal.'

Standing back, Helen kept well clear of him as he entered the shabby hall. 'Go through there.' She nodded towards a door. 'Sit down. I'll bring you a cup of coffee. You're as white as a sheet.'

She followed him at a distance, watched him enter the dining room, then dashed into the kitchen and rummaged in her bag for her mobile phone. She keyed in 999. A female voice was asking her which service when she heard feet moving across the hall. She switched off the phone, slid it behind the bread bin and opened the cutlery drawer. Standing with her back to it, she put her hand inside.

James pushed through the kitchen door. 'Feel a bit unwell. I think it's the shock, the emotion, seeing you again after ... Can I use the bathroom?'

She wrapped her hand around the handle of a knife. 'Sure. Upstairs. Door at the end of the landing. It's a bit scruffy. I've not had time to ...'

He'd gone. She could hear his huge feet thudding on the stairs. She snatched up the phone and dialled again. When she'd been put through to the police, she began to babble out her fears.

James glanced around the tiny bathroom. The walls had been painted pink above crazed white tiles that were decorated with plastic stick-on fish. He lifted the seat on the WC, made sure it clattered against the cistern, then pressed the flush and turned on a tap.

He crept out and entered the bay-windowed front bedroom. It was Helen's room. The bed she'd slept in was unmade, the sheets and pillows rumpled, just as they had been when he'd found her with her lover that afternoon. Stay calm, stay calm, stay calm. He whispered the words to himself, like a mantra, as he breathed in the musky fragrance that seemed to pervade everything she'd touched.

Her ivory-and-gilt dressing-table was in the bay. He tugged open drawers, found tights, scarves, tatty jewellery, knickers. He searched with his hand amongst it all, but he couldn't find Helen's hoard of treasured things, the cards, the candle, the locks of Jennifer's baby-hair.

He tidied it all up as best he could, tried to leave everything looking as he'd found it, then crossed the landing and entered a room that overlooked the back garden. His gaze took in pink rose-buds that dotted faded blue wallpaper, some new pink curtains, a flimsy desk, a neatly made single bed; then came to rest on a silver-backed hairbrush on a silver tray on a chest of drawers. He darted over. There was a comb on the tray. He ran it through the bristles of the brush, then ran it through again, collected a ball of fine blond hairs and, without touching them, slid them into the plastic wallet the firm had sent. *Avoid any contamination*, the instruction leaflet had stressed. On his way back to the bathroom, he peeled tape from an adhesive strip and sealed the flap. He let the WC seat clatter down, turned off the tap, pressed the flush again, then headed for the stairs.

Helen was standing beside some French windows. He noticed she'd opened them a crack. Her line of escape. She was visibly shaking. Her legs in the faded blue jeans were tightly pressed together. Such long shapely legs. How many men, he wondered, had she spread them for?

'Your coffee.' She nodded towards a mug on a ring-marked dining-table.

James pulled out a chair and sat down.

'You said you wanted to talk.'

'Access,' he said, trying to keep his voice calm and reasonable. 'I want to see Jennifer.'

'I don't think I'd like that.'

'She's my daughter. I want to see her, get to know her again.

And she's sixteen; at Christmas she'll be seventeen. Doesn't she have a say?'

'You didn't bother much before. When you weren't working you were playing football and when you weren't playing football you were at your club.'

He gripped the mug of scalding coffee. He wanted to throw it over the sharp-tongued bitch. He wanted to pound the fucking shit out of her, just like he'd pounded her scabby lover. Stay calm, stay calm. He dragged in deep breaths, mentally chanting the mantra. 'All I want is to see Jennifer. If I go to court, they'll grant me access. Can't we be reasonable about it? And she's not a kid any more. Why not let her decide. If she says she doesn't want to see me, I'll stay away.'

'You've been jailed for murder. Do you think she'd want—'

'Manslaughter, not murder. And let's not forget who provoked it.' He'd allowed irritation to sound in his voice. That wasn't good.

'I want a divorce.' She blurted out the words, deliberately changing the subject. Arguing with him like this was making him angry. She felt even more afraid.

'Fine, have a divorce. I'm surprised you didn't go for one while I was in jail. Can we talk about my seeing Jennifer?'

There was a hammering on the front door.

'I'll just see who that is.' Helen edged past him, her nervous eyes challenging the ice-cold anger in his.

James heard her run down the hall, the door open, then a man's voice saying, 'Mrs Conway? You called us ...'

'Come in. He's in the back room. Make him go. Please make him go.'

James smiled wryly. The crafty bitch. She'd phoned the police while he was upstairs. Turning on his chair, he faced the door and kept up the smile.

A policeman, peak-capped, bulky in his protective jacket, pouches and handcuffs fastened to his belt, stepped into the room. He was followed by a rosy-cheeked policewoman, cute in her little hat. Helen squeezed past them and resumed her position by the French windows.

'You'll be the lady's husband, sir?' The policeman looked down at James. James's smile became genial. 'Your wife would like you to leave, Mr Conway.'

James shrugged. 'She invited me in; made me a cup of coffee.'

'I understand you've recently been released from prison, sir. You'll be on parole.'

'I wanted to see my wife. There were things, family things, we had to discuss.'

'Your wife's told us she's very frightened of you, sir. I've got to ask you to leave.'

'She invited me in. We've been having a quiet conversation.'

'I know that, sir. A frightened woman – she probably felt she had to.'

James rose to his feet. 'If my wife wants me to leave, officer, then of course I'll leave. I don't want to upset her. I don't want to upset anyone.' He glanced at Helen. The fear had gone. Arms folded beneath her breasts, she looked defiant now. 'I'll telephone you, Helen. About Jennifer and the divorce.' He smiled, kept his voice calm and gentle. 'You don't mind if I phone you, do you?'

Back in the car, he looked down the street towards the house. A white police car was parked across the drive. He'd got what he came for, and the waitress at the Station Hotel had saved him the coffee cup Alan Woodward had used at the Rotary dinner. He smiled. He'd frightened Helen. He'd scared her out of her wits. And it was only the beginning. He didn't care for the talk of a divorce, though. The cheating bitch would be awarded maintenance, she'd get half the value of the house he'd worked his nuts off for. Things might have to be speeded up a bit.

The policeman and policewoman appeared on the step. Helen was standing behind them in the doorway. When the policeman touched his cap and turned to leave, James started the car and pulled out, heading back to the motorway and Tanford.

Marcus reached for the internal phone.

'What did you find out, Marcus?'

'I'm pretty sure it's Quest, ma'am. I've just had a call from the commissioner of the Met. He got the pathologist out at first light to look the corpse over. Killed with a large-bore weapon after being stripped naked and handcuffed. He'd probably been fastened to a metal guard rail – there were scrape marks on it. Shallow stab wound on his inner thigh, scrotum almost cut through.'

'Almost?' Loretta Fallon chuckled softly. 'Samantha's slipping.'

'The clothes and an intact money belt were by the body. Lining had been torn from a jacket and the left boot was missing. No documents or papers. The taxi had been cleaned out. She must have searched him and tried to extract information.'

'Is the man known to us?'

'We've had him under surveillance, on and off. Goes by the name of Fazel Nasari here, Abdulgader Walgadi when he's travelling in the Middle East. Attends a London mosque that hosts radical preachers, and he's attached to Islamic Jihad Union in the UK. Been involved with Al Umar Mujahideen in India and al-Qaeda in the Arabian Peninsula. Asylum seeker; he's been refused, but he's appealing.'

'Quest's certainly set the hares running. Presumably she'll give you a report and hand over any papers?'

'I'll phone her, ma'am.'

Loretta chuckled. 'I don't envy you. She'll know now that you've set her up. Keep me informed. Oh, Marcus ...' She held him on the phone.

'Ma'am?'

'That business about Quest undergoing analysis: have you found out what she's been saying?'

'Should have a copy of Uberman's notes before the end of the week. If there's anything untoward, I'll deal with it.

*

Samantha scowled at the ankle-length rubber-soled boot. The moulded heel had been sliced away and replaced with another, secured by screws. After deciding it was a hiding place, not a bomb, she'd bent a fork and two of the hotel's knives trying to prise it off. Abdulgada's secrets were safe until she could get her hands on a screwdriver.

She'd found nothing of interest amongst the papers she'd taken from his jacket. When the knife had begun to slice into his flesh he'd screamed, 'I know nothing. I drive taxi; that's all I do, drive taxi. Rashid Naveed, a worker at the bank, summoned me; he instructed me to follow you.'

If she'd had longer, if she hadn't been afraid of being discovered, she might have learned more.

She still had to look through the message slips and fuel receipts she'd removed from the taxi. She began to leaf through pages torn from a pad; mostly pick-up and drop-off addresses, some with times, most in and around the City. One message had been penned in Arabic. She read:

Abundant black hair, straight, just concealing her ears, and with a deep fringe. Eyes of a jinnee, body of a houri, mouth the colour of freshly spilt blood. A painted Kafir whore in a black pinstripe jacket, silk blouse and black pinstripe skirt. Car a silver Ferrari Modena with Polish plates, ZT59609, parked in a visitor's bay to the left of the exit ramp.

After folding the note into her ID wallet, she gathered up the rest of the papers and dropped them into a Gucci carrier bag. She glanced at her watch. It was almost noon. She'd have lunch at the hotel, then head back north to Barfield, spend a few days at home and consider her position. She might decide not to return.

SEVEN

Jennifer stared at the meaningless riot of colours on her laptop screen. Tapping it didn't make it work any more. She had to get the thing fixed; she needed it for her essays. Grandpa would have bought her a new one, but she wasn't in touch with him any more. And she didn't want to trouble her mother again. Her mother had looked pale and ill when she'd arrived home from school; said she was tired, couldn't face the mess the new house was in. Jennifer knew it was more than that. She was probably scared out of her wits at the thought of Daddy calling.

Something changed at the edge of her vision. She glanced out of the window. A light had flicked on in the shed at the bottom of the garden next door. She remembered her mother saying the boy called Edward fixed computers, that he might be able to repair hers. Jennifer shut the machine down and closed the lid. When she stepped out on to the landing she could hear laughter and voices on the television in the sitting room. Her mother would probably tell her not to be so forward, to leave it to her to ask the boy's mother, but she needed the thing fixing. She descended the stairs quietly, crept out of the back door, then ran down the long back garden.

Leaning the laptop against the high fence, she stood on a tree stump and looked over at the green-painted shed. 'Edward?' She called his name, surprised at her own bravado. 'Are you in there, Edward?' A light was shining from a window and through chinks around the door, but she could hear nothing. She stepped down, searched for pebbles in the flower bed, then climbed back on to the stump and threw a couple at the door. As she was drawing her arm back to throw a third, it rattled open. The escaping light illuminated her blond hair and the pale oval of her face. A tall, bespectacled boy was gazing up at her.

'Edward!' The smile and helplessly beseeching look were boy-control things she'd been practising in the mirror. 'Hullo, Edward. My name's Jennifer. We're neighbours.'

Edward blushed. He felt bewildered; amazed that this stunningly attractive girl should be talking to him in such a friendly way over the top of the fence.

'Can you help me, Edward? My laptop's broken and your mother told my mother you know all about these things.'

'I know a little,' he said evasively.

She coaxed him with her eyes and smile, lowered her voice, made it more intimate. 'Your mother said you know absolutely *everything* about them, Edward. Could you possibly look at mine?'

He glanced up at her again, then jerked his gaze down to the fence. His blush had deepened. 'I … er … suppose I could take a look. When would—'

'I've got it here with me,' Jennifer said. 'You're so kind, Edward. Shall I bring it round?'

'Why not pass it over the fence? I'll look at it when—'

'It's right here,' she pressed on, ignoring him. 'Unfasten your back gate and I'll bring it through.' She climbed down from the tree stump and struggled with rusty bolts on her own gate. When she emerged into the rear access, Edward was waiting for her. She trotted past him and stepped up into his brightly lit workshop. He followed. After staring at her disbelievingly for a few moments, he closed the door and unrolled a square of grey cloth on a wooden bench.

'Put it on here.'

Jennifer laid her laptop down. He clicked it open and lifted the screen. 'What's the problem?'

She thought he sounded tense; a little irritable even. Perhaps she'd been too overwhelming. She was standing quite close to him and when he turned he couldn't avoid her gaze. Shaping her mouth in an unhappy pout, she said, 'There's just colours on the screen, all jumbled up, no words, no pictures.' She gave him her helpless look.

He stared down at the laptop.

'Is it serious?' she asked.

'Could be, or it might just be the connections to the screen. You want me to take a look?'

'Please. I need it desperately, for essays. Can I stay and watch?'

'I'll get you a chair.'

'I don't mind. I'll just stand here.' She beamed at him, congratulating herself on the way she'd persuaded him; amused at his embarrassment and confusion. A lot of boys were like this, she'd found. Shy when you had them on their own and with very little to say. It made them easy to manage.

Edward prised a strip of plastic from the top of the keyboard and inserted a screwdriver. He had huge hands with long, bony fingers. In fact, everything about him seemed long and lean and bony. With his long face and arms and legs, and those broad shoulders, he looked half-formed; a youth in the process of becoming a man. But the brown eyes and tightly curled brown hair made him quite good-looking, she thought, especially when he wore his little trilby hat and leather bomber jacket. Gretchen would probably say he was very presentable.

He dropped screws into a white china dish, then lifted out the keyboard. 'Did you bring the power supply?'

'No, sorry, shall I—'

'It's OK.' He glanced at the back, inserted an adaptor, then plugged in a cable and pressed the 'on' button. After a few seconds, colours scintillated on the screen.

'There,' Jennifer said. 'That's what it looks like.'

Long fingers reached for a ribbon of fine wires that had been hidden beneath the keyboard and pressed it deeper into a connecting strip. Words and a logo appeared on the screen, sharp-edged and bright.'

'Gosh, you're clever,' Jennifer said, with feeling. 'It must be wonderful to be able to fix things like that.' She beamed at him. He risked a glance and returned her smile before blushing and looking away. That was another thing she'd discovered about boys: like pet dogs, they were incredibly susceptible to praise and flattery. The right look, the right smile, a few well-chosen words, and they'd sit up and beg, particularly the shy ones.

'We'll leave it running for a few minutes,' he said. 'If you've been switching it on and off while the screen's been faulty it'll need to restore itself.' He laid the keyboard back in place, used tweezers to pick one of the tiny screws from the dish, and dropped it in its hole. He applied the screwdriver.

'You repair them for the Indian man, don't you?'

He nodded and picked up another screw. 'Mr Sharman. Been working for him for a couple of years. He's OK. Pays me well.'

'Is it your job?'

'Going to Oxford. Got a place, but I'm taking a year out to get some cash together. I'm going to read maths.'

Impressed, Jennifer glanced around the workshop, at the tools arranged neatly in racks on the walls, the components in tiny plastic drawers, the test equipment lined up along a bench, the computers waiting for repair, each labelled with the owner's name and address. 'Bit like the Tardis,' she said.

'Tardis?' He glanced up and smiled. His face wasn't quite so red now.

'Your shed. It looks small on the outside, but it's quite big when you're inside.' She pointed to a row of desktop computers ranged along the back wall. 'Are those waiting to be repaired?'

'They're mine; linked to combine the memory so they can process data quickly.'

Her skirt swirled as she turned to face him. 'What do you want them to process data quickly for?' She gave him her wide-eyed, innocent look.

Shrugging, he said, 'Fast calculations, number crunching, that sort of thing.' He tightened the last screw then pressed the plastic cover strip back in place. He felt overwhelmed by the attractiveness of this girl; by the mysterious power of her femininity. And she was so fragrant: the apple-scented stuff she'd used to wash her hair, the perfume in her soap, rode over the smell of insulating resin and plastic and dust that permeated the workshop. He watched a progress bar creep across the laptop screen. 'It's done a disk scan,' he said. 'Everything seems OK. If you've any problems, bring it back.'

'Is there any charge?' She watched him blush crimson again.

'On the house. Anyway, there wasn't much wrong; just the connections to the screen. It happens sometimes.'

He found the neat way she dressed rather captivating, too: her grey pleated skirt, her grey stockings and shiny black shoes, her white shirt and blue striped tie. She was completely different from the girls at Crossgate Comprehensive. They used to smile behind their hands as he approached, then collapse into helpless giggles when he'd passed. She wasn't the least bit like those stupid idiots.

'I think you're very kind, Edward,' Jennifer said. 'And incredibly clever.'

'It's Eddie,' he mumbled. He could feel his cheeks burning. He hated himself for blushing.

'I don't care for Eddie,' Jennifer announced, a little imperiously. 'And Edward's such a manly name. If you don't mind, I shall call you Edward.' She let out an exaggerated sigh. 'Essays to type, and you've got computers to repair. I'd better let you get on.' She swirled over to the door, then paused. He remained glued to his workbench. He didn't dash over and open it for her, so she pressed the latch and opened it for herself. As she stepped outside she held up the laptop and smiled back at him. 'You're incredibly sweet, Edward. And I'm very grateful.' She began to close the door.

'Perhaps ...' His voice tailed away.

'Yes?'

'Perhaps we could have a coffee or something together sometime? That is, if you don't ...'

She gave him an encouraging smile. 'That would be nice, Edward. I'd like that.'

'I, er, well—'

'Tomorrow evening, after I leave school. I have to go to the bookshop opposite that strange hare and minotaur sculpture. What if I meet you there about five?'

'Cool,' he said. 'I'll see you then.'

Closing the door on his crimson face, she skipped back to the house.

The dark-green four-by-four cruised down the crowded urban street. 'What's the place we're looking for?' Lawrence Grassman peered through tinted windows at brightly lit shops.

'The Pond Street Centre for Islamic Studies.' Stuart Grassman slowed and stopped at some lights. Women dressed in hijabs and abayas; men, mostly wearing white skull caps and top coats, surged across. Morris Grassman muttered, 'Could have sworn this was down-town Calcutta.'

'Not Calcutta,' Stuart corrected. 'Saris in Calcutta. It's hijabs and abayas here: more like Karachi.'

'Where's Karachi?'

'Pakistan. We were invited there when we clinched the deal with Virendra, but we didn't go.'

Morris tapped Stewart's shoulder. 'Up ahead, Pond Street, make a left.'

They turned into a street where small terraced houses crowded the backs of pavements and the road was lined with parked cars.

Beyond its dark and diminishing perspective, the floodlit dome of a mosque rose above the rooftops.

'Over there,' Morris said. 'Just past that red van; three or four houses knocked together.'

Stuart Grassman turned into an even narrower street. 'Virendra said park in the rear yard and go in the back way.' He swung the four-by-four through an opening in a high brick wall and docked it next to a white Mercedes. The three Grassman brothers and their associate climbed out and strode over to an unpainted door sandwiched between boarded-up windows. Lawrence gave the plywood a pounding, then led the group into a dimly lit passageway.

A short, slightly built man, wearing a crocheted skull cap and a kameez, appeared through a doorway. He smiled. 'Lawrence, Stuart, Morris; good to see you all again. You are well, I trust?' He shook hands with the stocky grey-haired Grassman brothers. The family resemblance was strong. Dressed in dark bespoke suits, they all had watchful eyes and hard mouths, and exuded a brutish confidence that bordered on the menacing.

Virendra, their host, led them into what had once been a large back kitchen. A photocopier stood against a wall where books and pamphlets were displayed. A long table, circled by an assortment of chairs, filled the remaining space. Plywood covered the window. It had been crudely nailed in place. The cold harsh light of a single fluorescent tube heightened the drabness of the room.

'And this is?' Virendra took the hand of the fourth man. He was tall and obese, and his fair hair was combed back from plump, pasty features.

'That's Chris: Christopher Blessed. He understands computers,' Morris said. 'We thought he might be handy so we brought him along. He knows all about the business.'

Lawrence, his Crombie overcoat draped over his shoulders like a cloak, pulled out a chair and sat down. His brothers and the fair-haired man ranged themselves on either side of him. Virendra Khan joined the two kameez-clad Asians facing them across the table and made introductions. 'Arza Mahmood,' he said. A bearded man smiled. 'And Habib Alani. They also are fully conversant with our business.' He beamed around the table. 'So, we can speak openly. Can I offer you tea, coffee?'

Lawrence shook his head. 'Best get down to it. Did you uncover anything; anything at all?'

'A little,' Virendra said. 'One of the waiters in the executive dining room is a member of our group. He's told us they had a special meeting to discuss the losses, attended by a woman he thinks was sent by the Government. We had her followed when she left. The man who followed her was found an hour later. He'd been stripped naked and shot through the head.'

Morris Grassman sniffed. 'She must have had an accomplice.'

'She left alone.'

'Must have met up with him later, maybe called him on her mobile and led the tail to him.'

The three Asians glanced at one another, then Virendra went on, 'Our man has heard important people at the bank discussing the problem; just snatches of conversation, no more. They seem perplexed by it. He has heard the bank's computers are infested by an image of a laughing man.'

Lawrence drew his overcoat around him. The room was damp and cold. 'Laughing man?'

Virendra nodded towards the Asian called Habib. Habib lifted a crease-marked paper from an attaché-case and slid it across the table. 'The waiter's brother's wife is a cleaner at the bank. She found this in the office of one of the men who manages the computer system.'

The Grassman brothers studied the laughing face.

'The problem is most worrying,' Virendra said, 'but so far it has had no effect on us. You have had your shipments; the banks in Pakistan have assured us that British and Asian are going to stand the loss and our people there will be paid, but one can't help being concerned about the situation.'

'It's more than worrying,' Morris said. 'Why us? Why are funds being siphoned from our account? Is anyone else affected?'

Virendra shrugged. 'We were hoping you would have the resources to investigate that.'

The Grassman brothers turned and looked at the corpulent fair-haired man. Blessed gestured with his fingers and they slid the picture towards him.

'Presumably this was downloaded from the bank's computers?'

The Asian called Habib said, 'We do not know. They have been talking about a laughing face in meetings; this was retrieved from a waste-bin. It seems likely.'

Stuart leaned forward and rested his elbows on the table. 'We thought the Government might have had a hand in it, but this gives the lie to that. They wouldn't put silly faces on the screen.'

'And this is England.' Virendra smiled. 'The Government would observe the rule of law; obtain court orders before seques-tering funds.'

'Bastards would do anything,' Lawrence muttered. 'Look what they did to the Bassingers: took cash, property, paintings, the yacht, every fucking thing.'

'Government wouldn't mock the bank, though,' Morris said. 'They might snatch the cash but they wouldn't leave a laughing face.'

'Hardly likely,' Lawrence conceded. He gave the three Asians a grim smile. 'Still, as you said, no real damage done yet, but we've got to watch it. Something's stirring if one of your blokes has been shot for doing a tail job. Perhaps we should look for other ways to transfer the cash.'

'Gold?' Virendra raised an eyebrow.

'As a last resort. Lot of bother handling gold.'

'The material is reaching you OK?' Arza Mahmood asked.

'No probs,' Morris said. 'Eveything's fine on that score.

Sealing it in with that stinking wax seems to be fooling the sniffer dogs.'

Arza displayed uneven teeth in a smile. 'And you have many fine tools and machines, all made in India and Pakistan.'

'Many?' Lawrence laughed. 'England must be full of blokes in garden sheds turning table lamps on lathes. Don't make a fortune selling the tools, but it's a good front, something to keep the taxman quiet, launder a bit of cash.' He spread heavily ringed fingers on the table and grinned across at the Asians. 'Not much more we can say, is there? We'll stay in touch as per usual; no phones, no internet; just send a messenger with a request for a meeting.'

'Can I keep this?' Christopher Blessed held up the print-out of the laughing man.

Habib reached into his attaché-case. 'I can give you a black-and-white copy. Would that be acceptable?'

Christopher nodded. They exchanged papers.

'If that waiter and his brother's wife uncover anything useful, call another meeting. If Chris gets anywhere, we'll do likewise.'

The Grassman brothers and Christopher Blessed rose to their feet. Virendra was the only Asian who rose and shook hands before following them to the rear yard. He waited until they'd driven off, then returned to the room.

'Filthy kuffar,' the bearded Arza muttered.

'We need them,' Virendra said softly. 'We need their organization to distribute the heroin, we need their money to fund the jihad.'

Habib Alani closed his attaché-case. 'They pay us to enslave their brothers to an addiction; their money funds our struggle against them. They are like pigs, defecating where they eat and sleep, defiling the very place where they live.'

'Take heart, Habib,' Virendra said. 'A new age will dawn. We will not see it, our children may not see it, but we will have been instrumental in ushering it in.' He rose to his feet. 'Come, let us offer the last prayers of the day.'

*

Stuart Grassman turned the four-by-four on to the main road and headed back towards the city centre. 'Didn't spend much time in there.'

'Nothing more we could say,' Lawrence muttered. 'And we've got to meet to talk. Daren't use letters or phones or the internet, especially since the cash went missing. Some bastards have got their eye on us, and I still think it could be the government, laughing face or no laughing face.'

'Fancy spending an hour in a club?'

'Don't know anywhere decent in Leicester,' Morris said. 'How about driving over to Birmingham?'

Lawrence yawned. 'We could drive back to London.'

'Booked into the hotel now. No point wasting it.'

'Birmingham it is, then.'

'Count me out,' Christopher Blessed said. 'I'm bushed after the drive up. Drop me off at the hotel.'

Stuart negotiated roundabouts, then turned past the railway station. Halfway up the rise he turned off London Road and pulled up outside a hotel. Blessed clambered out. 'See you all at break-fast.' He slammed the door. Stuart drove off, heading for the motorway.

'We've got to give Chris the account passwords and security codes if he's going to do this job,' Morris said. 'Are we all OK about that? I mean, can we trust him?'

'With our mother's life,' Lawrence said. 'We've put him and his computers in that store room at the Coventry depot, and I've told the office manager to keep an eye open and report back if anything worries him. More important, we've got the dirty little pervert by the balls. He's already on the Sex Offender's Register. One word from us about his paedophile ring and they'll lock him up for life.'

'Why do they do it?' Stuart muttered. He turned on to Narborough Road.

'Because they fancy little boys and girls.'

'We should maim the bastard,' Morris said. 'Save the police a job.'

'We need him,' Lawrence insisted. 'He's a genius with computers; people who organize paedophile networks have to be to stay ahead of the cops. If he can't suss it out, no one can.' He looked over his shoulder at Morris on the back seat. 'Do you know where he learned his trade, got his experience?'

Morris shook his head.

'National Child Welfare Agency. He was one of the team who set up the computers and developed the systems. Would you Adam and Eve it?'

Samantha used the remote control to raise the garage door, then eased the Ferrari inside. Opening her laptop on the passenger seat, she began to interrogate the security system. The rooms were surprisingly neat and tidy; the bathroom and kitchen gleamed. Crispin had been. When she flicked to the camera in the sitting room, she saw he was still here, relaxing on the sofa, watching television. Stubble darkened his cheeks and jaw. His blue-striped butcher's apron was spotlessly clean.

She climbed the stairs to the house above the garage and stepped into the sitting room. Crispin glanced up. Pleasure showed in his smile, but his eyes were sad.

Samantha dropped her keys on a coffee table and laid her bag on the arm of the sofa. 'Thought you'd be out on the town with Timothy.'

'Said he had to visit his mother, but I'm pretty sure he was lying. He's gone to that new club near the bus station. He'll be chatting up the talent.'

She sat down beside him. 'I'm so sorry, Crispin.'

'It happens, love. Trouble is, he works for me at the salon, so things could get a bit fraught. I might have to ask him to leave. And I vowed I'd never get involved with an employee after all that trouble with Daniel. I never learn.' He switched off the television. 'Glad you're back, Sam.' His voice softened, lost its bitter edge. 'There's a beef casserole in the fridge and I brought a bottle of decent red over.' He pushed himself out of the sofa. 'I'll go through and switch the oven on.'

She followed him into the gleaming black-and-white kitchen. 'You've been busy.'

'Came over, tidied the place up and gave it a good clean. How do you do it, Sam? There's only you, you don't do any cooking and you're out most of the time, but the place is always like a tip after a couple of days.'

Laughing, Samantha stood on tiptoe and kissed him on the cheek. Crispin berated her like this on a regular basis. 'Leave the casserole for a while. I'm going to get out of these clothes and soak in the bath. Come through and talk to me.'

He followed her into the bedroom. 'How was the banker?'

'Old, completely bald, baby-faced and a perfect gentleman.'

'What you need, love, is young, handsome, rough and raunchy.' He laughed. 'Come to think of it, that's what we both need.'

'Unzip my skirt.'

He moved behind her, unfastened the waistband and pulled down the zip. 'Bet he liked the suit and the Zac Posen blouse?'

'Don't think he was too interested in the suit, but he seemed captivated by the blouse.'

'It's your perky tits, dear, trying to push their way through the silk. Bet he was gasping for it.'

Samantha wiggled her hips until the skirt fell around her ankles, then stepped out of it. Crispin picked it up and clipped it on to a hanger. The expensive clothes, her absences, the lack of a routine, had convinced him she was a high-class whore. It suited her to let him go on thinking that. The idea that she sold herself for sex didn't cause him any problems, but if he knew she dealt in death he'd be appalled.

'Your mobile's bleeping, love. Shall I get it?'

Bleeping, not ringing. That meant it was the encrypted phone. She closed her eyes. She needed to be angry when she spoke to Marcus, and right now she was too tired to be angry, but if she didn't answer he'd keep on calling. 'Please, Crispin,' she said, then took off her jacket and began to unbutton the blouse.

He returned with the bleeping phone, gathered up the jacket and closed the door as he left the room. Flopping down on the edge of the bed, she pressed the receive key.

'That you, Sam?'

'You treacherous bastard, Marcus.'

He ignored the invective. 'Where are you?'

'Barfield. At home. Crispin's just running my bath.'

'I presume you dispatched the taxi driver?'

'You set me up, Marcus. You sent me into the bank to provoke a response. You never intended me to investigate their problems.'

'Sam, I can—'

'I'm going to ring off, Marcus. Tell Loretta she can shove her short-term contract.'

'Sir Nigel was very impressed.'

'With what? I didn't do anything. I hardly said a word at the meeting you agreed to. And why didn't you announce my visit in the *London Gazette*? It wouldn't have exposed me any more than that meeting did.'

'He was impressed with the robust way you approached the problem; the way you suggested a bounty instead of a fee.'

'We both know I'm not going to solve his problems. It wouldn't have been ethical to charge an hourly rate when there's no chance of a successful outcome.'

'He was impressed, Sam. He took to you. You inspired confidence. You've got to see it through.'

'Don't keep flannelling me, Marcus. What you mean is, because I was stupid enough to let you talk to me into this, I've exposed myself, put myself in danger, and now I've got stay with it until I eliminate the risk.'

She crossed over to the bathroom, no longer listening to the agitated voice in the earpiece. Taps were running. Crispin was stirring the water, shaking in perfumed oil. She put her hand over the mouthpiece. 'Let's have a whisky, Crispin. Fetch two big ones and sit with me. Neither of us should be alone tonight.'

'Sam? You there, Sam? Is someone with you?'

'I'm just about to step into the bath. Crispin was in here. He's gone for a couple of whiskies.'

'Did you get anything from the cab-driver?'

'Only his forged documents. He told me he'd been called in to do the tail by someone called Rashid Naveed who works at British and Asian.'

'I'd better sign off if your valet's hovering around,' Marcus muttered, then, suddenly curious, 'One of the taxi-driver's boots was missing. You didn't take it away, by any chance?'

'What would I want with a taxi-driver's boot? Tell the police to search harder.'

'I'll have a disk couriered to you tomorrow: everything we have on the people we think might be involved. Where shall—'

'Barfield railway station. Under the display board outside the ticket office, 10 a.m. I'll be Shirley Temple. What's your man going to call himself?'

Crispin swept in with whiskies in cut-glass tumblers, put them on the rim of the bath, mouthed, 'Sorry!' then darted out.

'It's a she,' Marcus continued. 'I'll tell her to say Judy Garland. And Sam ... You still there, Sam?'

'I'm here, Marcus.'

'Thanks for staying with it. Keep in touch.'

'I didn't know I had.'

'Had what?'

'Stayed with it.' Samantha clicked off the phone and called out. 'It's OK, Crispin. He's gone.' She finished undressing.

He was smiling when he returned through the door. 'Didn't know you did role-play, Sam?'

'Role-play?'

'Sex with Shirley Temple: ankle socks and ringlets. Kinky!'

Samantha slid into the hot scented water and picked up her glass. 'You're learning all my secrets, Crispin.'

He sighed. 'Don't want to learn yours, love. I've got enough of my own.'

EIGHT

Swaying to and fro in his swivel-chair, James gazed through the window at the brick gatehouse on the far side of the factory yard. He watched the barrier rise, his mother's Bentley whisper in, then cruise sedately towards the office block. She was coming to collect him; making sure he went to High Gables for what she called a decent meal.

He spun the chair and brought his knees under a desk as big as some of the prison cells he'd languished in. Files and catalogues and sales charts were beginning to hide its shiny surface. It was good to be back, holding the reins, running the family firm again. And there'd been no embarrassment, no one had asked questions, they'd just welcomed him. He sensed the women were sympathetic and the men respected him for what he'd done. The pace had slackened while he'd been away, but his father and the managers hadn't done a bad job. The order books were pretty full and next month they'd be launching the new range of industrial circuit breakers. He lifted the phone.

'Yes, Mr Conway?'

'I'm having lunch with my mother, Ella. Her car's just pulled into the yard. I'll probably be a little late back, say about three.'

'Very good, Mr Conway … Mr Conway, reception brought a letter up for you. Recorded delivery. They had to sign for it. It's marked personal. Shall I bring it in?'

'Please, Ella.'

The door opened and a white-haired matronly woman, her bright-blue dress tight across her hips, approached the desk. When she handed him the envelope, she gave him a quick smile and said, 'It's good to have you back, Mr Conway.'

'Good to be back, Ella. Do you know what I missed most?'

'I've really no idea.'

'Your coffee, Ella. I used to dream about it.'

She laughed. 'I'm sure you're being fanciful, Mr Conway. Shall I show your mother in when she comes up?'

'Bring her straight through.'

When the door had closed he picked up a paperknife and slit the envelope open. The letter was headed, *Broxholme Laboratories, Rochdale*. Flicking through the first two sheets, he went straight to the final paragraphs and read:

We are able to advise you that the DNA profiling results, based on the cheek swabs and hair sample, exclude the possibility of paternity. The man who supplied the swabs cannot be the father of the child who supplied the hair.

The test results based on the saliva sample (recovered from the cup) and the hair sample, are, however, consistent with paternity. Whilst tests involving extracted saliva samples and hair lack the certainty of tests using blood, sufficient matches were observed for us to be able to say that the result has a certainty of the order of 85%.

We trust that this report meets your requirements. If you have any queries, please do not hesitate to contact us.

The door swung open, he heard his mother gushing, 'Lovely to see you again, Ella. You really are looking well,' and then she was sweeping into the room, her face a little heavily made up, her sleeveless fur jacket looking rather elegant over her black suit.

'You're deathly pale, James. Are you feeling unwell?'

He managed to say, 'I'm fine, Mother,' then he folded the letter and slid it into an inside pocket. 'Perhaps I'm ready for lunch.' He rolled his chair back, rounded the desk and kissed his mother on the cheek.

'You need some decent food. I do wish you'd come home and let me look after you.'

'I am home, Mother. In my own home.'

'I don't know how you could bear to go back to the place,' Lady Conway muttered. 'I certainly couldn't.'

'Is Father lunching with us?'

'He said he might, but I'll believe it when I see it. Magda's preparing something special for you. I think you're going to enjoy it.' She turned and began to chatter to Ella through the open connecting door.

James suddenly felt dizzy and icily cold. He'd considered the possibility while he was in jail, but having his vague suspicions confirmed had been a cruel blow. He laid a hand on the desk to steady himself, ran trembling fingers over his brow. He had to pull himself together. He drew in a breath and said, 'We'd better go, Mother. Don't want the meal to spoil.'

Lady Conway took her son's arm as they descended the stairs. 'You know your father hired someone to find Helen and Jennifer? A private investigator, a woman, quite charming, very attractive.'

James held open the door to the lobby, then followed his mother through. 'He didn't mention it to me.'

'She phoned him this morning, said she couldn't trace her. She thinks Helen's taken Jennifer abroad. Does that upset you, dear?'

Don't reveal what you know, he warned himself. 'Of course it upsets me. I'm her father. I've got rights. Helen can't just take her away like that.'

They paused by the entrance doors. His mother was giving him a long, steady look.

She knows, James realized. She's always known; a woman's instincts. That's why she never warmed to the child. He pushed at the heavy glass door and followed his mother down the steps.

Dobson was holding the rear door of the Bentley open. James helped his mother inside, then slid on to the seat beside her.

A sick rage was burning deep inside him. The report from the laboratory changed things; in some ways it made them simpler. Casting his mind back to Jennifer's birth, he realized Helen must have been having it off with Woodward right up to the wedding. While the dirty little slut had been sleeping with him, she'd still been having sex with her ex-fiancé.

Perhaps that was why Woodward hadn't made a fuss, hadn't said a word, when Helen ended their engagement. Ending it had been no more than a formality. And by that time Woodward would have realized Helen was a promiscuous slut. He'd have been more than relieved that the town idiot was going to take her off his hands.

James sank back into the leather. The beating of the blood in his ears was so loud he could hardly hear his mother chattering on about the house and the servants. He had to play this very carefully. Above all, he had to conceal the fact that he knew Jennifer wasn't his child.

Bernice Forster gazed at the bouquet of roses. She couldn't stop looking at them. The florist had cut the stems rather short and bound them with silvery ribbon to make the dusky-pink blooms form a tightly packed cluster. They were quite beautiful.

Such a charming man; no longer young, but sensitive and gentle, and with such kind eyes. Certainly not the type of man to make one constantly afraid he was going to pounce. He'd held the lift door open for her while she ran down the corridor, insisted she share his taxi rather than struggle on the tube. Then he'd asked her to have dinner with him, right out of the blue, just like that! And when she'd said she wasn't dressed for it, he'd said she looked perfect, utterly perfect. Bernice sighed and read his note again:

Meeting you quite by chance like that, dining with you, spending those few delightful hours with you, gave me so much pleasure. You

*were enchanting. Perhaps when I visit London again I might call
on you at your office and we could renew our acquaintance?
Warmest regards, Vincent.*

She was so glad she'd followed her instincts, thrown caution to
the winds and said yes to his invitation. People were so cynical.
Romance wasn't dead.

She ought to put the roses in water. She didn't have a vase, but
she could put the stems in a mug and prop the bouquet against the
wall to keep it upright. Bernice heard the door open and close and
glanced up. The client with the compelling green eyes, the one
who always left Dr Uberman so irritable and exhausted, had just
stepped into reception. Crimson suit, crimson gloves and bag,
crimson shoes: she looked eye-catchingly smart.

Bernice smiled. 'Good morning, Miss Quest.' Still preoccupied
with thoughts of Vincent and his bouquet, she could hardly stop
smiling. She picked up the phone. 'I'll just see if Dr Uberman …
Miss Quest is here for her appointment, Doctor. Shall I … Yes, of
course.' She smiled at Samantha. 'Please go through, Miss Quest.
Dr Uberman is waiting for you.'

The blinds were drawn, even though the day was overcast. Dr
Uberman was sitting in his chair, a vague shadowy form, his notebook and hands the only illuminated things in the near-darkness of
the blue-grey room. 'I hope we have time for a full session today,
Samantha. I hope you're not going to dash off to a business
meeting?'

Samantha sat on the couch. 'All the time you need, Doctor. 'She
kicked off her shoes, swung her legs up and settled her head on the
paper that protected the pillow.

'And the dream? Has it progressed?'

'A little.'

'Then perhaps we should begin by your recounting the dream.'
He flicked through his notebook. 'During our last session you
described wading, naked, along a dark culvert. Your feet were

treading on soft, slimy pebbles; your body was streaked with blood and the water was red with it. You could hear the voice of an angry man, calling to you in Arabic. He was pursuing you. You were moving towards the light and you could see the names of dead men written in blood on the walls. Have I got that right?'

'Perfectly, Doctor.'

'Then please continue.'

'I emerge from the culvert into strong sunlight. Grass covering the steep river banks is lush and green and sprinkled with flowers; the sky is blue and cloudless. In the river, great clots of blood drift past me. Between the clots are patches of clear water and I can see the bottom. I am walking on eyes that have been torn from their sockets, the veins and membranes that once attached them writhe and swirl like strands of scarlet weed in the current. They are men's eyes. They are watching me. As I wade past, they swivel and follow me.

'The left bank of the river is lined with women wearing black burqas made from some fine material that shimmers in the light. Even their eyes are concealed behind threads of silk that criss-cross the narrow apertures. They are chanting. It is a gentle, ethereal sound: the murmuring of angels. They are reciting the twenty-ninth sura of the Koran.'

'The twenty-ninth sura?'

'The twenty-ninth chapter. It is known as *Al-Ankabut: The Spider*.'

'And why is it called *The Spider*?'

'Because there are lines that compare those who serve other masters than God to spiders who spin webs to make the frailest of dwelling places.'

'They are chanting in English?'

'In Arabic.'

'It is a language you speak?'

'Fluently. I think I have already told you that.'

'And you have knowledge of the Koran?'

'I can recite much of it.'

'These women, dressed in black; you say they are angels. How do you know they are angels?'

'Because their eyes are concealed. In my dream I am aware that mankind could not bear the gaze of angels.'

Dr Uberman recorded the exchange in his notebook, then added: *Death has caused the patient much trauma. Do the women dressed in black symbolize death? Religion and religious imagery deeply ingrained in the psyche of the patient.* Glancing up, he said, 'The angels can observe your nakedness. Are you shamed or embarrassed by this?'

'No. I feel only an urge to wade on, with the current, because I know that when I round the bend in the river I will discover something of great importance to me.'

'How important?'

'My life will depend on it.'

'And then?'

'And then I hear the voice of the man who has been pursuing me down the dark culvert. His words are angry and violent.'

'Is he angry because other men have died; men whose names are written in blood on the culvert walls?'

'No!'

Dr Uberman smiled. Her response had been too quick, too emphatic. Perhaps he was, at last, beginning to make a little progress. He leafed through his notes, fingers and pages fluttering in the tiny circle of light. 'Does the angry voice of the man make you afraid?'

'Yes.'

'Is fear your only emotion?'

'No. I also have an overwhelming urge to continue my journey down the river.'

'To receive this important information?'

'And to find clear water so I can wash the blood from my body.'

'But your fear of the man is your dominant emotion?'

'It is the thing that wakes me from sleep.'

In his small neat handwriting, Dr Uberman wrote: *Blood, naked-ness, angels; guilt, vulnerability, death.* Then he said, 'That gives me much to think about, Samantha. But now I would like to return to word-association. Are you happy with that?'

'Fine.'

'I think you are not fine. In the past when we have attempted the exercise, you have not participated as you should. You must let go, allow your mind to drift freely, and when you respond to a word, you must tell me the first word, the first thought, that enters your mind.'

Samantha sighed.

'River,' he began.

'Blood.'

'Husband,' he whispered.

'Doctor.'

Dr Uberman ticked his notes. 'Kibbutz.'

'Killer.'

He made another tick. 'Sister.'

'Child.'

'Sister's child.'

'Sick murdering bastards!' A low roar of grief and anguish escaped his patient's throat.

Dr Uberman glanced up, saw the black-haired woman swing her legs to the floor, heard her laboured breathing erupt into harrowing sobs. She sagged forward, her head in her hands, her elbows on her knees, her body racked by the violence of her emotions.

Marcus flicked through the photocopied sheets. Bit sparse, he reflected, but the handwriting was legible. He sipped his coffee and his eye came to rest on a marginal note. *Relationship with male homosexual friend is one of some intimacy: e.g., he sits with her in her bathroom and they talk while she bathes.* Marcus sighed. What an awful waste! He leafed on. *Wading through culvert … blood … angry voice … pebbles.* What's this? He peered at the tiny handwriting. *Manipulative and misleading responses in w.a. test.* He smiled. Nothing here to frighten the horses. Hardly worth the bother and expense, but he'd had to be sure.

There was a loud rap on the door. He turned. Loretta Fallon was frowning down the room at him.'

'How did Quest respond, Marcus?'

'She's staying with it.'

Loretta smiled. 'She has to now she's been exposed.'

'I've had a disk couriered to her. Grassman brothers, and the cell in Leicester.'

'Did she get anything from the cab-driver?'

'Only the name of his contact at the bank.' Marcus glanced down at the papers on his desk. 'Just reading through her analyst's notes.'

'Is she telling secrets?'

'Only her own. Seems her valet sits and talks to her while she takes a bath.'

Loretta's lips parted in a smile. 'The one called Crispin?'

Marcus nodded.

'I've seen his photographs in the Sunday supplements. He could sit and talk to me while I bathe. How did you get hold of Uberman's notes?'

'Sent Vincent Perry in to befriend the receptionist. He managed to get impressions of all the keys.'

'Perry could charm the knickers off a nun.'

'Do you want to read Uberman's notes?' Marcus held up the papers. 'First two sessions.'

Loretta shook her head. 'If there's nothing there to worry us, shred them, Marcus.'

'I'm minded to give it another couple of weeks, then send Perry in again, just to make sure Quest's not being indiscreet.'

'I think that would be wise, Marcus. I'm heading for Downing

Street. Our political masters want a progress report on the bank business. Hang on until I get back. You might care to drive me home.'

Jennifer clicked the word-processor icon, then gazed out of her bedroom window while the programme loaded. Light was shining from Edward's workshop. He was in there, repairing computers for Mr Sharman. Mr Sharman supplied the parts and paid him a flat rate of thirty pounds for every repair.

Edward had told her that while they were in the rather nice coffee bar at the top of Montpellier. He'd been incredibly shy, and his tall angular body had seemed so awkward and graceless, just like his manner. But he had bought her coffee and some rather nice cakes. The trouble was, he had no conversation. He only came close to relaxing when she tried to talk to him about computers or mathematics. He'd explained the rudiments of calculus to her, helped her to understand it in a way that Miss Rossiter never could. He didn't seem all that interested in music, he'd probably curl up and die at the thought of dancing, but he was incredibly clever. It was useful to have a boyfriend who could help you with difficult subjects, someone who could fix things.

How would she describe him to Gretchen and Monica? She'd tell them he was extremely intelligent, going to Oxford to read maths, that he'd offered to fix her laptop and then insisted on taking her for coffee. She'd thrown them off the scent; told them she was meeting him in the museum. If she'd revealed she was meeting him in the bookshop opposite the sculpture, they'd have gone there to take a look at him and embarrassed them by giggling behind the bookshelves.

She brought her mind back to her essay: *The Human Nervous System*. The word-processor programme had loaded. It was a great relief to have her laptop working again. Edward really was very sweet, and he might lose his shyness when they knew one another better. The problem was, the embarrassed silences encouraged her to chatter and she was tempted to tell him things she'd normally keep to herself. Telling him her parents were separated was no big deal. Anyway, he must have guessed that. She hadn't mentioned her grandfather having hired a private detective to find her and her mother. That was weird. She'd certainly not told him her father had killed a man. That would have scared him to death.

And she'd found out why her mother was so irritable and depressed. During their evening meal, her mother had told her that Daddy had called at the house. She was sure he'd got the address from the police in Tanford, not the private detective; she seemed to trust her. Daddy had asked for access, asked to see his daughter on a regular basis. She simply couldn't understand why her mother was so upset at the prospect of Daddy seeing her again. After all, he *was* her father. Meeting him would be awkward at first, but they'd get over that. And for her, if not for her mother, it would be a way back to Grandpa and the family.

She hadn't done anything to upset her father. It was her mother who'd been with that man. Her father had absolutely no reason to be anything but his former loving self towards her. *She*'d no reason to be scared of him.

NINE

Hands behind his back, James strolled around the clear, still water in the pool. He paused by the glass doors and looked out over the back garden. Drifts of leaves made curving shapes across the neglected lawn, and the shrubs he'd planted were almost hiding the fences now. Little girls weren't the only things that got bigger every day.

When he was in jail he used to lie in his bunk, walking the house in his imagination, moving through the rooms, taking in the views from the windows. He'd missed the place then. The sense of loss had hurt so much it had made him weep. Now he was back he realized that the house meant very little to him. It was a symbol of his wealth, his status, but nothing more. It wasn't the loss of his house, it was the loss of his marriage, the companionship, the intimacy, that hurt so much.

What a dreadful sham his marriage had been. Helen had made an utter fool of him. He was the saddest cuckold in the whole of Tanford. He'd provided and cared for a child, loved a child who wasn't his, while all the time Helen had been enjoying the attentions of other men. What had she been like with those other men; with Woodward, her fiancé? Had she been as abandoned, as insatiable, as she had with him those first nights in the back of his car? He should have listened to his mother when she'd sat him down on the long sofa in her dressing room and told him he was proposing to marry a whore. Of course, she hadn't been quite so

115

blunt; she'd hedged the message round with ladylike euphemisms, but he'd understood what she was saying. He hadn't listened. Helen had won. So fair of face, so perfect of form, how could she lose?

He felt a throbbing in his temples, a dull ache creeping across his chest. Suddenly breathless, he went through to the sitting room and lowered himself into the one remaining armchair. He reached down the side and lifted up the whisky bottle; a couple of doubles left. He groped for the glass he'd used the night before, poured a generous measure, then sank back and sipped it, hoping it would calm him and take away the pain.

He closed his eyes. Suddenly he could feel his hands around that smooth scented throat, squeezing, crushing; hear the soft sexy mouth gasping for air, see the blue eyes bulging with terror. Slut! The dirty fucking …

The glass shattered in his hand. Slivers stabbed into his thumb and palm and the spirit made the cuts sting. He glanced down. Blood was dripping on to the cream linen cover that protected the arm of the chair.

He went through to the kitchen, picked out the splinters of glass, then wrapped a tea towel around his hand before taking a bucket and cloth back to the sitting room to clean up the mess. Stay calm, stay calm, stay calm. Whispering the words to himself, he rubbed at the red blotches until they were reduced to a faint pink stain.

He was supposed to be having lunch with his sales director, going over the marketing strategy for the new range of circuit breakers, but he was too distracted by personal things. Not wanting to appear badly briefed and indecisive, he decided to call Ella, tell her he'd been detained, ask her to cancel and reschedule. But first, he'd call Helen, keep up the pressure, keep the fear simmering. He picked up the phone from a table beside his chair and keyed in her number. Stay calm, stay calm; appear gentle and reasonable; she could be recording her calls.

The line clicked. A familiar voice said, 'Hullo?'

He listened to the faint rustling.

'Hullo … Who's there? Hullo?'

'It's me, Helen,' he whispered softly.

'You! I don't want to—'

'Don't put the phone down, Helen. If you won't speak to me over the phone I'll have to visit the house, and I think you'd like that even less.'

'You scare me, James. Just the sound of your voice scares me. I want you to leave me alone. Please—'

'You've no need to be afraid. I don't want to harm you. I don't even want to touch you. I just want to talk.'

'I did a bad thing to you, James,' he could hear her crying now, 'and I'm sorry. I'm so sorry. But I watched you kill a man for it; watched you beat him to death. And then you threatened me. I've got every reason to be scared.'

A man's angry words, said in haste, usually forgotten by him in a minute but remembered by the woman for a lifetime. But he'd never forget those particular words, snarled into Helen's terrified, tear-streaked face. The memory of it was embedded in his mind: her naked body crouching on the pillows, huddling against the headboard, one hand pressed between her thighs, an arm hiding her breasts, her lips swollen, the stink of sweat and love-making clinging to her creamy flesh. He was glad she remembered his angry words.

Stay calm, stay calm. James drew in a breath and made his voice gentle. 'That was four years ago, Helen. Four years is a long time.' He listened to her snuffling for a moment, then went on, 'I just want to talk to you, about seeing Jennifer. She's my child. I've a father's right to—'

'I want a divorce.' She blurted out the words.

Whenever he talked about access, she demanded a divorce. 'That's OK,' he said evenly. 'Get a solicitor. Start the process. But can we talk about my seeing Jennifer?'

'I don't want you to see Jennifer. I want you to stay away and stop bothering us.'

He felt a rush of satisfaction. This was hurting her. She didn't want to share Jennifer's affections; didn't want to risk him taking her child from her. 'She's my daughter, Helen,' he said softly. 'You're not being reasonable.'

'What do you mean when you say you want to see her?'

'Just that. Meet her. Take her for a meal somewhere, get to know her again, buy her things.' He paused, then plunged in the knife. 'Have her stay over for the weekend if she wanted.'

'Stay over?'

'At Elm Trees.' He lowered his voice. 'It's her home, Helen. Elm Trees is her home.'

'I've got to think about this.'

'What is there to think about?'

'I watched you kill a man, James. You're a murderer. That's what I've got to think about. I don't want Jennifer to have anything to do with you.'

Blood was beating in his ears. He felt a sudden urge to scream: *Do you think a father would want his daughter living with a fucking whore?* He swallowed hard, took a breath, reminded himself that Jennifer wasn't his child, that her moral welfare was no concern of his. 'I'm not going to hurt her, Helen,' he said softly. 'And I've no intention of hurting you. In fact, if you want helping in any way, all you've got to do is ask.' He smiled, pleased with himself. The offer of help was a clever touch. He hoped the conversation was being recorded. He went on, 'Have you told Jennifer I called at the house?'

'Yes.'

'Have you told her I'd like to see her?'

'No,' she lied.

'Then tell her. See what she says. I'll call again in a few days, give you chance to talk it over with her, OK?'

James listened to the rustling, then the line clicked and went dead. After replacing the phone, he unwrapped the tea towel. The bleeding had almost stopped. Suddenly remembering that there used to be bandages in the cabinet in the en suite, he rose and headed for the stairs. Helen was still going on about a divorce. Had she seen a solicitor? The possibility lent an urgency to things. He didn't want to have two motives for killing the bitch.

He rounded the half-landing and began to climb the second flight. His mother would be horrified if she knew he was using the master bedroom. He'd made that decision months before he was released. To have chosen another room would have been an admission of defeat, made him an even bigger loser. The old mattress had gone. Bloodstained, it had probably been carted away and burned. He'd slept on the couch the first night, had a new mattress delivered the following day. He ought to hire a cleaner. Perhaps his mother could find someone, or maybe ask one of the women who cleaned at High Gables if she'd come over a couple of times a week.

He elbowed the bedroom door open, went into the en suite and tugged at the light-cord. He held his hand under the basin tap. When the blood had washed away, he dabbed the skin dry, then opened the mirror-fronted cabinet. No bandages, but there was an old packet of plasters. He peeled the backing from a couple of large ones and applied them over the cuts.

Someone had to be found who could deal with Helen. He daren't deal with her himself. How were such people hired? He'd read reports in the papers of people who'd paid for a killing and been discovered, but he hadn't read many, so a lot of successful attempts must remain hidden. Distancing himself from the killer would be crucial. He had to be certain Helen's death couldn't be traced back to him. An accident would be the thing, if one could be contrived. He'd have a word with Bob Andrews at the club, tell him he was being threatened and wanted to find someone who could sort the problem quickly and without fuss. Bob knew people in the city who had dealings with the criminal fraternity; people who could arrange things for the respectable. Bob would put him in touch with someone who'd be discreet.

And he'd take a drive over to Cheltenham. When he'd seen Jennifer the other morning she'd been dressed in grey and been wearing a blue-and-grey striped tie. Her school uniform. It should be enough to enable him to discover where she spent her days.

Helen lowered the phone. James's calm, reasonable voice had made her flesh crawl. He'd changed. He was no longer the easy-going, work-obsessed football fanatic she'd married. Everything about him had been so predictable: what he wanted for his meals, what he wore, the day he played football, the evenings he went to his club, the time he'd leave for the office, the time he'd return home. He'd broken the habit of years when he'd climbed the stairs and crept into the bedroom that afternoon. He'd probably heard her when he wandered into the hall, recognized the sounds she was making, come up to investigate. How long had he stood there, in the doorway, watching?

A person's eyes told you so much about them. Her mother used to say eyes were the windows of the soul. James's eyes weren't kind any more. They were cold and watchful, the eyes of a man with a purpose, a predator choosing its moment to strike. She shivered. She almost wished he'd make his move, declare his hand, so she'd have something to complain to the police about.

Had he found out about Jennifer? Did he suspect? The way he kept going on about being her father had made her wonder. But how could he possibly know? She'd not been sure herself at first. It wasn't until Jennifer was eight or nine that she'd accepted she was probably Alan Woodward's child; only when she'd become a teenager and begun to mature that she'd been absolutely certain. When Jennifer's features were lit in a certain way, when she gazed at you with those serious eyes, smiled at you with that rather prim mouth, it was as if Alan Woodward were looking out of her daughter's face.

Her mother-in-law would have noticed. Men were invariably blind, but women were quick to recognize these things. And Elizabeth was as shrewd as they come. She'd have suspected from the very beginning. Had she told James? It would suit her to turn him against Jennifer, to persuade him to sever all ties so she could claim back the son she thought she'd lost.

Helen recalled the satisfied look on James's face when he'd sat in the dining room and told her he wanted access to his daughter; the gloating sound in his voice when he'd talked about her staying over at Elm Trees. The last thing he'd want was access to another man's child. Unless … A sudden fear gripped her. She shivered. Surely he wouldn't do anything to harm a child? But Jennifer wasn't a child any more. She'd grown into a beautiful young woman. Was he thinking of using Jennifer to take his revenge on her?

Legs trembling, Helen sat at the foot of the stairs and put her head in her hands. She felt so alone, so vulnerable. Should she tell Jennifer? She'd already blighted her life enough. If she revealed that her entire childhood had been a lie, her daughter really would hate her. But it might stop her wanting to see James.

Rain had begun to fall during the drive south. It was raining now as Samantha watched and waited in the East London street. She'd decided to return and confront the situation Marcus had embroiled her in. She'd no alternative. She'd been seen, identified; her security, her safety, had been compromised.

She switched on the wipers for a couple of swings to clear the rain from the windscreen. From where she was parked, she had a clear view of the small terraced house. The cream paint on its stuccoed walls was flaking, slates were missing from a ground-floor bay; behind low railings weeds were growing through pavings that covered a small front garden. There was darkness beyond the windows. The man who worked as a waiter in the executive dining room at British & Asian hadn't returned home yet.

The narrow street connected with a main road that was lined with small shops, eating places, takeaways. A red neon sign, *Turkish Kebabs*, glared out from a window and made a streaky reflection across the wet pavement. Above it, a smaller sign flashed *Halal Meat*. Cars, vans and buses appeared fleetingly as they rumbled past the junction, tyres hissing in the rain.

Abdulgader the cab-driver had been included on the disk Marcus had sent her, and there was a decent image of him leaving a taxi call centre. He'd been under surveillance. Rashid Naveed, the waiter, was mentioned, too. In the Yemen he was called Saeed al-Wahishi, one of the names on the list she'd eventually managed to remove from the heel of the cab-driver's boot. There had been more than thirty names passwords and e-mail addresses, written in a neat Arabic script, on the tightly folded, polythene-wrapped square of paper.

Samantha angled her watch to catch the light. It was after 7.30. She'd been waiting for little Rashid Naveed, aka Saeed al-Wahishi, since before five.

Another half an hour elapsed before the slight figure, wearing a white cap and buttoned-up raincoat, turned the corner. Head down, shoulders hunched against the rain, he approached along the opposite side of the street. He pushed through the gate, fumbled with keys, and let himself into the house. A glow appeared behind a fanlight above the front door.

Samantha glanced into her bag. Her gun was lying on top of the clutter, silencer attached, butt uppermost. She took out her wallet of identity cards, then stepped from the car, trotted over to the house and rapped on the door. It opened almost immediately and the small dark-haired man was staring out at her. Recognition gleamed in his quick, birdlike eyes. She allowed him a glimpse of the cards inside the wallet. Recognition escalated into fear.

'What do you want with me?'

'Just a talk.'

'What do you wish to talk about?'

'Can I come inside, Mr Wahishi. It's raining.'

He didn't move, just stood in the narrow opening, frowning at her, water dripping from his unbuttoned raincoat.

Samantha pushed at the door. It caught his shoulder and he staggered back. Stepping up into the narrow hallway, she slammed the door behind her.

'I did not give you permission to enter. Do you have the authority to force your way into my home? And my name is Naveed. Who is this Wahishi?'

Samantha slid the ID wallet into her bag and drew out the gun. 'Don't go all coy on me, Wahishi. That's what they call you in Sana'a, where you were born.' She peered into the gloom at the top of the stairs and at the end of the hall. 'Who else lives here?'

Nervous brown eyes flickered over her face. He was deciding what to tell her. Presently he said, 'I share the house with two others.'

'Are they here?'

'I do not know.'

'What are their names?'

He shrugged. 'They are new here. They come, they go; I do not know their names.'

Samantha leaned back against the door, gripped the gun in both hands and levelled it at his face. 'Who are they, Wahishi?'

'I tell you, I am not Wahishi. Who is this Wahishi you keep talking about?'

She nodded towards the door to what had once been the front parlour of the house. 'That your flat?'

He nodded.

'Let's go inside.'

Glaring at her, he turned a key in the lock and pushed.

'Don't put the lights on. Just go inside and draw the curtains around the bay.' She prodded him with the gun.

He took off his dripping raincoat, hung it over the back of a chair, then closed the curtains. Samantha ran her hand down the wall, just inside the door, felt a switch and flicked it on. Light from an unshaded bulb revealed a sparsely furnished but neat room.

Samantha followed him in and closed the door. 'Why did you call Abdulgader the cab-driver and instruct him to follow me?'

'I don't know any Abdulgader. I don't—'

'Fazel Nasari, Abdulgader Walgaldi; pick a name. He knew you. He told me you'd called him.'

'I tell you, I don't know any Abdulgader, or Fazel, or Wahishi.'

Samantha pulled the breech of the gun against its spring and let it clatter back. 'You want me to make you a martyr? Tell me who you're working for.'

'Who I am working for? British and Asian. The executive dining room. Mr Jarvis, the catering manager, engaged me.'

Footsteps scraped on the path beyond the window and there was the sound of male voices and laughter. The front door opened. A ratchet click-clicked as a bicycle was wheeled inside, then came a rattling as it was leaned against the wall. The outer door slammed; voices continued to chatter in Arabic.

'You home, Saeed?' There was a tapping on the door.

The little waiter relaxed and a faint smile of relief moved over his fleshy lips.

Samantha stepped back, gripped the gun in both hands and held it with arms outstretched. The door swung open. A young Asian man in a dark business suit, the strap of a laptop case over his shoulder, entered. He was closely followed by a bearded man wearing a grey overcoat. They froze when they saw Samantha. Two men could be covered for a while, but three were dangerously unpredictable. Samantha squeezed the trigger, felt the recoil, winced at the muffled thud in the confined space. The bearded man swayed back and collapsed in the bay window.

Waving the gun at the other two, she snapped, 'Put your hands behind your head.'

Saeed, eyes bright with fear, jerked his hands up. The other man's movements were slow, his expression scornful. Outrage at being dominated by a woman was blunting even his fear of death. 'Anyone else live here?' Samantha asked.

Saeed shook his head.

'And what's your name?' Samantha looked at the dark-suited man.

'Tahir Bukhari.'

She glanced at the body on the floor. 'And him?'

'Shazad Hussain.'

'Are you all AQAP members?'

'AQAP?' Saeed gave her a blank look.

'Al-Qaeda in the Arabian Peninsula.'

'I work at the bank. What do I know about al-Qaeda and the Arabian Peninsula?'

'Your seriously pissing me off, Saeed. You were born in Sana'a. You lived in Aden for thirty years. You're a member of al-Qaeda. Who do you liaise with here?'

'Liaise? I work for Mr Jarvis at the bank. I—'

'I'm going to count to three, Saeed. If you don't—'

The man in the suit allowed the laptop to slide from his shoulder, caught the straps and used them like a sling to hurl the machine at Samantha. She stepped aside, heard it crash into a cabinet behind her as she squeezed the trigger. Blood and brains spurted up the wall and Tahir Bukhari toppled back on to a shelf of books.

Raised voices erupted in the adjoining house, a fist pounded the wall; the neighbours were upset about the noise.

'No more time-wasting, Saeed. Who do you liaise with? I'm going to count to three.'

'Virendra Khan. The Centre for Islamic Studies.' He blurted out the words, terrified now his friends were dead.

'There must be hundreds of study centres. Which one?'

'Pond Street in Leicester.'

'And why did you have me followed?'

'There are problems with the bank's computers that I do not

understand. Virendra instructed me to keep my eyes and ears open. I tell him about the laughing face. The big men at the bank are all worried. Mr Fiens is scared he's going to lose his job. Then I hear them talking about a woman, to be sent by the Government, someone sure-fire guaranteed to fix the problem. I report to Virendra. He tells me to find out all I can. Saddique warns me when you arrive, so I—'

'Saddique?'

'The security man who watches over the executive lift. When I see you in the dining room, I call Abdulgada the cab-driver, ask him to follow you when you leave. Just follow, see where you go, not do you any harm. While you were eating, Saddique played back the basement security videos so he could locate your car and let me have the details.'

'Abdulgada would report back to you?'

He shook his head. 'To Virendra. We all report to Virendra.'

Samantha nodded towards the bodies. 'Did they report back to Virendra?'

'Tahir did. Shazad was waiting to serve. He had not yet been called.'

'Tahir is the guy with the computer?'

Saeed nodded.

'And what does he do?'

'He is employed by a bank that has also been troubled by the mocking face. He is freelance; a consultant.'

'He's trying to deal with the problem?'

'The problem is very secret. Others at the bank are struggling to overcome it. He merely watches and listens and reports to Virendra.'

'And why is Virendra so interested in the bank's problems?'

'Money which was to have been transferred to banks in Pakistan disappeared.'

'AQAP's money?'

He shook his head. 'Al-Qaeda in the Arabian Peninsula has no money. It merely trains and supplies operatives. Its work is funded by others.'

'Then whose money is it?'

'I do not know. I am merely a waiter who overhears things. Tahir might have known.'

Samantha eyed him down the barrel of the gun. His thin body was shaking, his face was taut, his eyes were jittery with fear. This insignificant little agent had probably told her all he knew. It was a tragedy he'd ever seen her; that he'd discovered she served the State. Marcus was an utter bastard. The blood was on his hands.

'What's at the end of the hall?' she asked.

'A kitchen we all share.'

She had to get away from party walls. More sudden noises might bring the neighbours round. She gestured with the gun. 'Go out into the hall.'

He stumbled over the sprawling legs of Tahir Mahmood, stepped gingerly around Shazad Hussain, then waited obediently beside the front door until Samantha joined him. Dim light from a single economy bulb revealed that the hallway had recently been decorated cream and white. A black mountain bike was leaning against the wall. There was a half-glazed door at the end of a passage that ran down the side of the stairs.

Samantha gestured with the gun. Saeed shuffled towards it. 'Go through, turn on the light and stand where I can see you.'

He did as she asked.

She followed him into a narrow kitchen that projected from the rear of the house. A cheap sink unit, cooker, fridge and washing-machine were lined up beneath the window. A yellow-Formica-topped table stood on old red-and-black tiles. A gas-boiler was mounted on the wall. Some greasy Venetian blinds had been closed.

'Put your hands back behind your head.'

His arms jerked up and his fingers laced together.

'What's through there?' Samantha nodded towards a door at the end of the room.

'A small chamber for storing food.'

'Go and open it.'

The tiny waiter moved forward, opened the door, then slid his hand back behind his head. He gazed at her with apprehensive eyes.

The closet was smaller than a telephone booth; a stone shelf took up most of the space. Cardboard boxes filled with cans and packets of food were stacked on and under it.

'Take those boxes from the shelf, then sit on it.'

When he was staring out at her, she said, 'I'm going to close the door. Count up to a thousand before you come out. Do you understand me?'

Relief flooded his features. He nodded vigorously.

Samantha swung the door shut with her toe and slid one of the boxes across it. Her heels clattered over kitchen tiles, then drummed on boards in the hall. She turned, tiptoed back, lifted the gun and fired two shots through the food-store door. There was a faint thud as his body slumped forward, then the door slipped off its latch and swung open until it hit the cardboard box.

Back in Saeed's flat, she peered around the edge of the curtains that covered the bay. The street outside was deserted. Faintly from the adjoining house came the sound of a television theme-tune. There were no angry voices. Everything was as it should be in the quiet residential street. She drew on a pair of surgical gloves and began her search of the house and the bodies of the men she'd killed.

TEN

With the fading of the light, the afternoon had become cold. Shivering, Helen Conway drew the lapels of her coat together before stepping out of the perfumed warmth of the hairdresser's. She'd had her hair cut and styled – a luxury she'd almost forgotten – and she'd bought a skirt and jumper in the autumn sales. She was feeling calmer. Almost a week had passed since James had phoned and she'd seen and heard nothing of him since. Perhaps she'd been silly to be so afraid. When he'd visited, when he'd phoned her, he'd been composed. He'd not been angry or aggressive. There had been nothing in his behaviour that she could complain about. And when the police had asked him to leave her home he'd gone without making a—

Helen caught her breath. James was no more than ten paces away, standing beside one of the Grecian statues that decorated the shop fronts. She dodged into a doorway. Busy studying something on a slip of paper, he hadn't seen her. He screwed the paper into a ball, tossed it down, then strode off between parked cars. He glanced up and down Montpellier Walk, waiting for a break in the traffic. When it came, he crossed the road and tugged open the door of a black BMW. His belted overcoat had a bold herringbone pattern. It was unfastened and she glimpsed a perfectly tailored light-grey suit. His shoes were shiny, his tie colourful and extravagant; he'd always been very particular about his ties.

The chill in the air suddenly sliced through to her bones and she began to shiver. She watched him slide behind the wheel, draw the coat over his knees, then slam the door. God, he was so smart, so handsome. But she felt no desire or affection for him now. The sight of him aroused only fear.

'You all right, love?'

Helen turned. An elderly woman, plump, carrying a shopping-bag, was staring at her in a concerned way. 'I'm fine, thanks. Absolutely fine.'

'It's just that you look as if you're having a bit of a turn. I have little turns, little dizzy spells. They can frighten you. I know what it's like.'

'I'm fine,' Helen repeated. 'Really I am. But it was very kind of you to ask.'

Helen heard a starter whine. Glancing back across the road, she watched the black coupé pull out and head towards the round-about at the top of Montpellier. Smiling her thanks at the woman, she stepped from the doorway and went to the spot where James had been standing. She picked up the ball of paper and unfolded it, saw a rough plan: Lansdown Road, the A40 to Gloucester, Hatherley Road, Warden Hill Road; it was the network of streets around Jennifer's school. Was that why he was in Cheltenham? It was almost four. Was he going to the school to meet Jennifer?'

Panicking, she ran towards her car, threw her bags on the back seat, slid behind the wheel and reversed out. Fear made her impa-tient as she waited for a break in the traffic. Her chance came, she moved off, accelerated towards the roundabout and turned into Lansdown Road. After a few hundred yards, she caught sight of the new-looking black BMW, moving slowly, as if the driver were searching for a particular street. Lights turned red and the line of cars slowed and stopped. When they changed back to green, James turned left. Helen followed, began to drive past big old houses, set well back from the road and almost hidden behind high walls and hedges.

Brake lights flared, the black BMW slowed, then pulled over to the kerb and parked at the end of a line of cars. They'd been left there by mothers who were waiting to collect their daughters from Hatherley Hall School. Helen swept past and bounced the Volvo on to a grass verge opposite the entrance. Girls in grey coats and skirts and blazers were emerging. Jennifer came into view down the long drive. She was with Gretchen and Monica. Helen climbed out of the car and crossed over the road. Jennifer saw her, left her friends and ran towards the gates.

'You OK, Mum?' There was a concerned expression on her face.

'I was in town. I thought I'd drive past on my way home and pick you up.'

'I thought something had happened.' Suddenly brightening, Jennifer said, 'You've had you hair done. It looks nice – different – it suits you.'

Freckle-faced red-haired Gretchen and dark-haired Monica joined them. Smiling, Helen said, 'I was passing so I thought I'd pick Jennifer up. Would you two like a lift?'

'Please,' Gretchen said.

'I've only got to walk to the end of the road,' Monica said. 'But thanks for the offer, Mrs Conway.'

Helen glanced down the line of parked cars, saw a vague shape behind the windscreen of the black BMW, then opened the rear door for her passengers. The girls scrambled inside; she slid behind the wheel. Hands still trembling, she keyed the ignition, checked the mirrors, then lurched off the grass verge. Should she tell Jennifer that James had been waiting for her? She'd no idea what to do. Half an hour ago she'd been feeling better. Now her nerves were shot to pieces again.

The two girls were chattering in the back of the car, discussing their studies, sounding so mature, so earnest. Jennifer had inherited her looks, thank God, but she had Alan Woodward's bookish intelligence, his rather dull conformity, his determination to do well academically and be a success.

After playing the field all those years ago, she'd decided she wanted to marry a man who could provide, who'd give her a comfortable life, someone steady and reliable. Alan had fitted the bill. It hadn't been difficult to enchant him, to make him eager to marry her. And staid-and-boring was a price she'd been prepared to pay for status and security. Then she'd met James: old money, his position in the town already established; genial, confident, tall and handsome. And an exciting and rather overwhelming lover.

She'd been wild when she was Jennifer's age. From thirteen on, books and school hadn't interested her in the slightest. Boys, then men, had been her only preoccupation; dancing and parties and sex her only pastimes. Thank God Jennifer was different. It was all in the genes. Some people took to books and studying; others were obsessed with pleasure and sex. It was the way you were made. You couldn't help yourself. But the all-girls schools, keeping Jennifer away from boys, had probably helped. Now she wanted to be a doctor. Fancy, her little girl, a doctor!

If she told Jennifer that James had been watching and waiting outside the school, she'd probably look out for him. On balance, it would be best not to tell her. Instead, she'd warn her she must never go anywhere with him without first getting her permission. Going with James could be dangerous. Jennifer was physically mature and very attractive. There was no blood tie; no consanguinity. James had murdered a man. He'd broken one powerful taboo, he could break another. And if he had discovered he wasn't Jennifer's father, his feelings towards her might change.

Lawrence Grassman settled his overcoat on his shoulders and studied the faces ranged along the opposite side of the table. Habib Alani and the bearded Arza Mahmood were seated beside Virendra Khan. A stranger was with them tonight. He was tall and powerfully built, his mouth ringed by a narrow moustache that curved down to a short beard. Dressed in Western clothes, his blue suit looked handmade, his cream shirt crisp and new, the wine-red silk tie and matching pocket handkerchief carefully chosen.

Diamonds studded his gold cuff-links; Lawrence guessed the gems would be a carat apiece, at least.

Virendra smiled. 'May I introduce you to Dr Martin Manson. He understands the nature of our business. You can speak openly in front of him.'

Lawrence tugged out a handkerchief; the room was so damp and cold his nose was running. What did these people wear under their nightshirts and baggy pants that kept them so warm? Still challenging the newcomer's gaze, he muttered, 'My brothers, Stuart and Morris.' He nodded towards the big man with slicked-back fair hair. 'And this is Christopher Blessed. He's our IT expert.' He turned his gaze on Virendra. 'You said you had news for us; things we should discuss.'

Virendra pressed his fingertips together. 'Three more of our people have been killed. Rashid Naveed, he was the man we had in the British and Asian Bank, and two others.'

'Where?'

'At a house in East London.'

'Police been informed?'

Virendra nodded. 'They're investigating it, but they don't seem to have much sense of urgency. We carried out our own investigation amongst the Asian community there. A neighbour reported seeing a black-haired Western woman push her way into the house after showing our brother some sort of wallet.'

'You're suggesting the woman who killed the cab-driver killed these three?'

'That is so. We have a picture of her. A guard at the bank rewound the security tapes and photographed the image on the monitor screen. It's rather blurred, I'm afraid.'

Arza Mahmood reached into a folder, drew out a large photograph and slid it across the table. Lawrence studied it. 'Blurred's the word, but I suppose someone who knew her could tell who it was.' He handed it to Stuart and Morris. They glanced at it, then passed it to Christopher Blessed.

'She's worked in the Coventry warehouse.' Christopher Blessed tapped the photograph. 'Last week. Only stayed three days. Polish piece. Justyna Lukaszewski.'

'You're sure about that?' Lawrence Grassman scowled down the table.'

'Certain. Remember her very well.' He laughed. 'Frank Field won't forget her in a hurry. My office looks down on the packing bay. I heard this commotion and went out on the decking. Frank was hopping around and screaming. He'd crept up behind her and given her arse a feel. She'd jumped on his foot with her stiletto heel, stabbed it into the flesh, broke bones. They had to take him to Accident and Emergency in a car. The packing women were ecstatic. Frank the Feeler, they call him. He's the floor manager. He likes to stroke arse. The black-haired piece went up to the office, told them she was going to make a complaint about sexual harassment, collected her cards and walked out.'

'Was she Polish or was she faking?'

'Talked to the other women in Polish; sounded Polish when she was giving them grief in the office.' He studied the image again. 'It's her all right. The fringe, the black hair, the big eyes. Wasn't dressed like this, though. Wore a tatty old skirt and a baggy sweater on the packing-line.'

'The car parked in the basement at the bank had a Polish registration,' Virendra reminded them.

'She come to the warehouse in a car?' Lawrence asked.

'Firm's bus. Transport's laid on from a pick-up point in Coventry.'

The men eyed one another across the table. Lawrence Grassman was scowling. Things were getting serious.

From a room on an upper floor came the sound of young Midlands voices struggling with unfamiliar Arabic as they began to recite the Koran.

Virendra raised his bushy eyebrows in a questioning way. 'I understand you have some news for us,' he prompted.

Lawrence turned his scowl on the overweight man. 'You tell 'em, Chris. But for Christ's sake, keep it simple. I've got a headache after hearing about the woman.'

'I've penetrated the bank's systems. Used the Keen-Bright Tools account as a doorway. I stayed logged on until the hackers appeared and started playing tricks with the figures. When they put the face on the screen, I tried to locate the source. I couldn't – they're being clever with the routing and using high-level encryption – but I managed to put a trace on the packets and get IP codes for most of the servers they went through.'

'Packets ... IP codes?' Lawrence Grassman scowled down the table at Christopher Blessed.

'Packets are chunks of data sent between computers via the internet. Every device it's routed through has an identifying letter-and-number sequence; what's called an internet protocol, an IP code.' Christopher Blessed paused. The faces of the men around the table were still blank and uncomprehending. He tried again. 'All computers and servers have a number; bit like a car registration number. Internet service providers can use it to identify the owner and the location of the equipment. But, like I said, I may not have the numbers for all of the devices in the chain, and some that I do have could be false.'

Arza Mahmood stopped combing his fingers through his beard. 'We only have numbers. The service providers have the addresses, and you say some of the identifying numbers you do have could be false. That's not a lot of use to us. These people could be anywhere.'

'I could probably send them a message for you,' Christopher Blessed suggested. 'At least, send a message back to the first server in the chain. They probably own the first server so they can control it, modify the logging software, stuff like that; and if they're using it for serious hacking, they'd keep checking it out.'

'Scare the shit out of the buggers,' Morris Grassman muttered.

The men eyed one another thoughtfully. Young voices in the upstairs room were chanting in unison now. Stuart Grassman asked, 'Has British and Asian honoured the payments?'

Virendra nodded. 'Monies were transferred to the Mundai Bank in Pakistan four days ago; to the Bank Nagrini Punjab yesterday. We have suffered no loss, and you have suffered no loss.'

'But we can't have crazy buggers plundering the account,' Lawrence said. 'And the bank might not stand the loss next time. They might decline our custom. They might find out things we don't want them to know when they're investigating. Maybe that's why the black-haired piece has been sniffing around the Coventry warehouse.'

'Would a British bank hire a Polish woman to search and kill?' Virendra asked.

'They've lost thirteen million quid. They've had their security breached. If that got out they'd be seriously compromised. They're so desperate, they'd do anything.'

'So,' Christopher Blessed interrupted, 'do I try to send a message to the people who hack in with the laughing face?'

'I think we should,' Lawrence growled. His brothers nodded.

'We're not yet able to reach them physically,' Virendra said. 'To send a message would put them on their guard. Surely it would be prudent to wait until we know more?'

Lawrence shivered. Jesus, it was cold in here. He scowled across the table. 'Three months from now and we'll be doing another deal. We want this cleared up before then. We're comfortably bedded-in with British and Asian. They're not asking awkward questions about cash deposits. If we look for another bank there could be difficulties. And there's a limit on how much money we can launder in three months. I think we should send a message. Try to scare the buggers off.'

Virendra glanced at the bearded man in Western dress. 'Do you have any reservations about that, Martin?'

'My task is to find and kill the woman. I don't think sending a

message to these people will make that any more or any less difficult, so I have no views on the proposal.'

'What's it to be then?' Lawrence glanced at his brothers.

'Send a message,' Stuart urged. 'Say, "We know who you are.
We know where you are. We're coming to get you, you thieving
bastards. Have the thirteen million waiting when we call."'

'I'm still concerned about revealing our hand,' Virendra
cautioned. 'We should wait until we know more, then act.'

Lawrence looked down the table at Christopher Blessed. 'Is there
a chance we could locate them? I mean, physically locate them.'

'They're clever. They've done everything they can to remain
anonymous: used encryption, used multiple servers, probably used
at least one server with the logging disabled. We might not be able
to discover their true IP number, let alone where they're actually
located.

Virendra said softly, 'We have brothers working for most of the
internet service providers. We have brothers working in the telephone companies. Why not let us take what information you have
and at least try to discover the location of these people?'

Blessed shrugged. 'Anything's worth a try.' He slid a printout
across the table. 'You can have that, for what it's worth. It's a
schedule of the IP numbers for most of the servers they're pushing
data through.'

Virendra looked at Lawrence. 'Christopher could liaise with us
on this. If you wish, I'll set up a meeting.'

Lawrence Grassman's eyes narrowed. 'I want Stuart to be in on
everything. It's all got to go through him. And we all attend any
meetings.'

'Fine,' Virendra said. 'I have no problem with that.'

'And in the meantime, we send the message,' Lawrence insisted.
'We could be messing about for months and something needs
doing now.'

Christopher Blessed gave Lawrence a nervous glance. 'Do you
want me to send what Stuart said?'

'Yeah, what Stuart said,' Lawrence growled. 'But ask for twenty million, not thirteen.' His gaze shifted to the man Virendra had introduced as Dr Martin Manson. 'It's our account that's been hacked into. The Laughing Sailor is ours. The black-haired woman is yours.'

Manson's smile was chilling. He didn't speak.

'That's reasonable,' Virendra said. 'Of course, any money recovered will represent new income, the bank's already made good the loss. If we locate the people, I think we're entitled to a share.'

'*If* we recover anything,' Lawrence said bitterly. '*If* we do, we'll split, fifty-fifty. How's that?'

Virendra nodded. 'That would seem fair. And the black-haired woman – you'll check the records at your Coventry warehouse and send us what information you have?'

'Tomorrow,' Manson urged. 'I'd like to receive it tomorrow.'

'Don't think there'll be much, but I'll get someone to drive over with what there is. Can't trust phones.' Lawrence frowned at Virendra. 'I hope this place is secure?'

'We have it checked, swept as you say, before every meeting.'

'If there's nothing more?' Lawrence Grassman looked at each face in turn, then pressed his hands on the table and pushed himself to his feet; the cold had stiffened his joints, made his body ache. There was a scraping of chairs as his brothers and Christopher Blessed rose, then they all filed out.

Virendra escorted them to the rear yard, waited until they'd driven off, then returned to the meeting room.

'Do you trust them?' Martin Manson asked.

'We need one another,' Virendra said. 'I have to trust them. And there is mutual respect.'

Arza sneered. 'Respect? Who is there amongst that godless bunch to respect? They make free with the women they employ; they own places where men drink alcohol and gamble and consort with whores, they blaspheme.'

'They are clever,' Virendra said softly. 'Wise in the ways of men.

Like us, they are ruthless and determined, and that has made them rich and powerful. Unlike us, they serve only their own selfish ends. True, they are coarse, depraved, unenlightened; but never underestimate them.' He turned to Martin Manson. 'If you find the woman we must question her before you kill her, discover who she is and what she knows.'

'*When* I find the woman,' Manson corrected. 'Do you have a place where she can be taken?'

'We have a house, on London Road. It's large, in its own grounds. We intend to convert it into a school for girls.'

Martin Manson smiled. 'Prepare a room. This Georgina Grey, or Justyna Lukaszowski, can be your first pupil.'

The four-by-four negotiated a roundabout, then turned on to the ring road and headed south. Morris was driving, Lawrence was in the front passenger seat, Stuart was in the back with Christopher Blessed. 'It's not late,' Morris said. 'Should we head back to London or should we do a club?'

Lawrence held his cigar in a lighter flame. 'Neither. We'll go to the warehouse in Coventry, talk to Frank Field, the bloke who manages the packers, see what he can tell us about the black-haired Polish piece.' He puffed at the cigar, got it burning evenly, then glanced over the seat at Stuart. 'Give Arthur Bateman a call on your mobile. Tell him to collect Frank and have him at the warehouse in twenty minutes.' He turned to Christopher Blessed. 'Could you send that message to the Laughing Sailor people while we're there?'

Christopher shook his head. 'Can't do it just like that. Got to devise some means of making an attachment so we can send it back. And I've got to make sure I've identified the first server in the chain.'

'How long will it take?'

'Two days and nights, maybe three.'

'But you can do it?'

'I'm pretty certain.'

Lawrence licked his little finger and dabbed the end of his cigar to even out the burning. 'I don't like this. It's got a bad feel to it.'

'Bet that's what Frank Field said when he grabbed the Polish woman's arse,' Maurice muttered.

Laughter rustled in Lawrence and Stuart's throats. Christopher Blessed stared out at the brightly lit Leicester streets.

Lawrence went on, 'A black-haired bitch is on the prowl and on the kill, thirteen million quid's gone missing, and some joker's putting laughing faces on computer screens. They're seriously taking the piss.'

'That bloke with Virendra; what did he say his name was?' Stuart asked.

'Manson; Martin Manson,' Lawrence muttered. 'Probably Abdul something or other. If his real name's Martin Manson, mine's Percy the Parrot.'

'Cold-eyed bastard. Wouldn't like the evil fucker chasing me. Reminded me of that bloke the Bassingers used to call in when one of their women got out of order. The things he'd do to 'em. Turn your stomach over.'

'Talking about keeping women in order, Terry mentioned something to me today.' Morris glanced over his shoulder, then filtered on to the motorway behind a lorry.

'Terry?'

'He manages the Swanley showroom for me; trucks and vans and four-by-fours. Said he'd been asked to arrange a killing. Some bloke's wife.'

'Do we know who she is?'

'He wouldn't say. Same old story: she's been screwing around and the husband wants to dump her, but he doesn't want to give her the house or pay maintenance.'

'How much is he paying Terry?'

'Twenty grand.'

Laughter erupted. 'Twenty grand! He could have got it done for five.'

'Told Terry he wanted to distance himself. Terry had to guarantee nothing would get back. And the bloke wants an accident.'

'Stupid bugger,' Lawrence growled. He flicked his lighter and held the flame to the cigar again. 'Best thing's a quick kill; strangle the bitch, then get rid of the body. It's sure and certain. You know where you are. Victim's gone missing, and with no body there's not a lot the cops can do. How's Terry going to handle it?'

'Bloke he knows, drug-dependent, fancies himself as a driver; paying him five grand to nick a car and do a hit and run.'

'So, Terry gets fifteen grand for fuck all!' Lawrence settled back in his seat and puffed on the cigar. 'Some of us are born lucky.'

Helen tapped on Jennifer's door, then stepped inside. Her daughter was still working, bent over textbooks and a notepad, all neatly laid out on an uncluttered desk.

'Brought you some cocoa.'

Jennifer glanced up and smiled. 'Thanks, Mum.'

'Isn't it time you finished? It's after ten.' Helen rested the mug on a coaster near the desk lamp. 'How are the calculations going?'

'The calculus?'

'That's it, the calculus.'

'Fine since Edward explained things.'

Helen smiled. 'You like Edward, don't you?'

Jennifer picked up her mug, began to take tiny sips while she gazed at her mother over the rim. 'He's nice, but he's unbelievably shy. Absolutely no self-confidence, yet he's so clever. He's going to Oxford next year, to do maths. I wouldn't mind doing medicine there if I could get the grades.'

They sat in silence, sipping cocoa; Helen on the bed, Jennifer at her desk. Helen was trying to think of a way of warning her about James, still wondering whether or not to tell her he wasn't her real father. No, she daren't do that. She couldn't predict the outcome.

Jennifer might begin to loathe her; she might demand to know who her real father was; she might take it into her head to confront Alan Woodward. What a nightmare that would be.

'You're upset, Mum. I can tell. It's Dad again, isn't it?'

Helen slid her mug on to the bedside table. 'He wants to see you, but I don't want him to.'

Jennifer shrugged. 'He's my father. Could be a bit uncomfortable until we got to know one another again, but I don't have any problems with it.'

'He might come to Cheltenham, look for you, try to make contact with you without my knowing.'

Jennifer gave her mother a puzzled look. She was really obsessed with this.

'Will you promise me something?' Helen asked. 'Promise me you won't go anywhere with him without talking to me first.'

'I promise.' She studied her mother's face, saw the worry and fear in her eyes. 'He really scares you, doesn't he?'

'I'm terrified of him,' Helen said.

'He wouldn't hurt me, Mum. He's no quarrel with me.'

'He might try to hurt me by hurting you.'

Jennifer let out an amazed laugh. 'That's crazy. You're being paranoid, Mum.'

'All the same, you promise me you won't go anywhere with him; not even get into his car to talk?'

'If it's so important to you, Mum, of course I won't.'

There was something she had to ask her mother. The days were passing and she couldn't wait much longer, and this seemed to be as good a time as any. She wrapped her hands around her mug and rested it on her knee. 'Edward asked me if I'd like to go to the coast with him on Saturday.'

Her mother smiled and raised her eyebrows.

Encouraged, Jennifer went on, 'He has to go and check a holiday bungalow they have before the bad weather sets in, turn off the water, collect mail, that sort of stuff. It's on the seafront at a tiny place called Lindon Sands, somewhere near Sidmouth. It was his grandparents'.'

'I've been told about it,' Helen said.

'About the bungalow?'

'About your being asked out. His mother invited me round for coffee this morning. She presumed I knew. I think she was wanting to tell me she was worried about Edward being distracted from his studies.'

'Distracted?'

'By you. She was hinting she didn't want him to become seriously involved with a girl.'

Jennifer laughed.

'Mothers and sons,' Helen said. 'It's something you'll learn about.'

'But it's so silly. I've no designs on Edward. And it's only a day trip to the coast, for heaven's sake. He's just a friend. I'd rather go with Gretchen or Monica.' Sighing, she muttered tetchily, 'I suppose it's off, then?'

'I told Mrs Goodwin I was just as concerned about your education being disrupted, but I was happy with the outing if she was.'

'And was she?'

'After our talk, yes. I asked her to tell Edward he had to call for you. I want to have a word with him about his driving before you go.'

Jennifer's pleasure was tarnished by the knowledge that her personal business had been discussed; that she was still being treated like a child.

Helen gathered up the mugs and headed for the landing. She paused in the doorway and looked back. Jennifer was wearing her offended look. 'Finish soon,' Helen said. 'You've worked long enough tonight.'

She closed the door and went down the stairs. She didn't want Jennifer distracted; didn't want her interest in boys to be awakened. But with James mooching around Cheltenham, it would be safer for Jennifer to be out of town on Saturday, and she couldn't imagine a more harmless boy. And it was understandable that Jennifer should want a male presence in her life. Gauche and awkward as he was, she'd feel much safer if it was Edward and not James.

ELEVEN

The car door jerked open. Long legs slid under the dashboard and Marcus settled himself in the passenger seat. He slammed the door.

'I see you've still got the Ferrari, Sam. How are you?'

'How do you think I am, Marcus? Shitty, and it's entirely your fault.'

'Sam!' His voice was mockingly reproachful. 'All I've done is put a job your way. We both thought it was an easy number.'

'Rubbish. You were using me. You sent me into the bank and exposed me. You set me up. Now I'm saddled with the mess until I sort it out.'

Irritated by her rebuke, his tone became brusque, almost dismissive. 'Did you find anything in the London house?'

'You're an utter bastard, Marcus.' Samantha reached over the seat and lifted a laptop in a canvas bag into the front of the car. 'You don't give a damn what you do to people.'

'You took the job, Sam. And things are dire; yesterday we upgraded the security threat to critical. We can't afford finer feelings.'

'What's new? Things are always dire.' She handed him the bag. 'This laptop was being carried by a man who called himself Shazad Hussain. He was an IT consultant working in a bank that's been troubled by the laughing face. He threw it at me and it hit the wall. It won't boot up, but your people should be able to extract the data from the disk. Documents and papers I found in the London house and on the bodies are in the laptop bag, and the stuff I found on the cab-driver is in there, too.'

Marcus slid the zip across and peered inside. 'Quite a collection. Anything useful?'

'Names and contact details. A lot are new. They're not on the disk you sent me.' She caught and held his gaze. His eyes slid away, lingered on the lapels of her tiny jacket, then swept down to a black skirt that hugged her hips and thighs. He glanced up. 'That's a beautiful suit, Sam.'

'Don't try to flatter your way out of this one, Marcus. I've begun to loathe you.'

He laughed. 'It's not flattery, Sam. Crispin's doing a great job, looking after your wardrobe. How is he, by the way?'

'Don't patronize me, Marcus. And don't sneer when you talk about Crispin. At least I can trust him.'

'Have you got anywhere with the banking business?'

'Nowhere. All I've done is eliminate men connected with the waiter who served in the executive dining room. They all answered to someone called Virendra Khan. He's based at an Islamic Studies Centre in Leicester.'

'Pond Street; we've had someone in there for the past two months. He didn't discover anything untoward. Last night he was found dead in his car – throat cut.'

'I presume the police are investigating the London house killings?' Samantha asked.

'Waiter's sister-in-law found the bodies the next day. She called the police. Bateman's not very pleased.'

'Bateman?'

'Police Commissioner. He thinks we're trying to muscle in on his counter-terrorism role. He's whinged to the chief, complained to the PM.' Marcus watched a woman in an imitation leopard-skin coat lift a hatch and begin to load groceries into her car. Still watching, he said, 'That message you sent; why did you go into Keen-Bright Tools?'

'It's a subsidiary of Grassman Holdings. Copies of statements issued by the Pakistani banks show the bulk of the funds that went missing were payments to tool exporters. The Grassman brothers import a lot of tools from India and Pakistan.'

'We've looked at Keen-Bright. We've looked at all the Grassman Brothers' businesses: gambling clubs, new and second-hand cars, pharmaceuticals. We've done bogus Health and Safety checks, asked the tax people to call in their accounts for scrutiny. We haven't found anything we can take action on.'

'Thirteen million for Indian tools, Marcus?'

'It wasn't thirteen million for tools. It was something like ten for tools, three for pharmaceuticals.'

'OK, ten for tools. That's still a lot of cheap Indian tools. And they make three, sometimes four, purchases every year, never less than ten million pounds. There's something more valuable hidden inside the tools, Marcus.'

'That possibility hasn't escaped us, but the packing warehouse at Coventry was clean when we checked it, and the Keen-Bright Tools accounts and balance sheets tally with their annual reports.'

Persisting, Samantha went on, 'The tools arrive at the Coventry packing warehouse from two places. Some straight from the docks in lorries laid on by the shippers; some from an agricultural machinery depot about ten miles from Loughborough, delivered in Keen-Bright's own vans. The sort of stuff that comes via Loughborough includes lathes, pillar-drills, band-saws; things with long hollow tubes and gearboxes. They're seriously heavy so the weight of any drugs packed inside wouldn't be noticed. And they're covered in the residue of some vile-smelling wax. You can see lumps of the stuff where it's not been melted away. The things that come straight from the docks don't smell like that. Tools are probably being taken to the depot near Loughborough to have the wax cleaned off and the drug packages removed.'

'You've checked this?'

'Not thoroughly. Just followed a Keen-Bright van from

Coventry to the agricultural machinery place near Loughborough. Keen-Bright van reversed into a bay at the rear. I didn't get inside, but the big doors were open and I did a couple of drive-pasts. As far as I could make out, the main enclosure is full of farm machines that they sell and hire out. The tools are probably dealt with in a separate place round the back.'

She glanced at Marcus. He was frowning thoughtfully through the windscreen. The woman in the imitation leopard-skin coat had slammed down the rear hatch and was wheeling her empty trolley over to a collection point.

'Thirty or forty million a year for cheap tools,' Samantha went on. 'It doesn't make sense. I think the monies that went astray were mainly payments for heroin from Afghanistan. Exporting agents probably collect the tools from the manufacturers and arrange the drug packaging before shipment. The strong-smelling wax is meant to put the sniffer dogs off if customs do a search.'

Still frowning, Marcus unbuckled a battered leather document-case resting on his knees and searched through the contents. He selected some photographs and handed them to her. 'Grassman brothers,' he said. 'Lawrence, Stuart and Morris. Did they visit the Coventry warehouse?'

Samantha flicked through the images. 'Not while I was there. I'd have seen them if they had. It's just a huge metal shed with offices on an upper gallery that overlooks the packing and storage areas. You can see the office staff moving around behind big windows. There's a general office and two small rooms.'

'How about the Studies Centre in Leicester? Checked that out yet?'

'I was thinking about driving up today. Presumably it's where people working for the suppliers in Pakistan oversee the UK end of the organization. The waiter and his friends reported to the place, and quite a few of the people included on your disk seem to be involved. I suppose I've got to look it over.'

'Most just visit or pass through, but three are permanently

based there.' He searched in the document-case and withdrew a typewritten sheet. 'According to the man we lost yesterday, Virendra Khan seems to be in charge, Habib Alani acts as accountant, and Arza Mahmood handles a lot of paperwork. And a couple of days ago, someone called Irfam Shehri moved in. Name on his passport's Martin Manson. He's an American national and a doctor of some sort.'

'Is that significant? His arriving at the centre in Leicester, I mean.'

'He's on a list of nationals the Americans are uneasy about. He travels a lot and he's known to be associated with the Islamic Jihad Union in the UK, Al-Aqsa in Europe, Asbat al-Ansar in the States. Never stays more than a few weeks in a place. Always returns to New York; he has an apartment there.'

'You think he's been brought in because of the banking problems?'

'Possibly. He's here for some reason.'

'You're telling me you want me to check him out?'

'I'm advising you to be vigilant.' Marcus flicked through his papers and produced another photograph. 'That's him.'

Samantha studied it. 'Cute little beard. Very smart suit and tie. He's almost as big and handsome as you, Marcus.'

'Family's Saudi Arabian. Very well connected.' Marcus dropped the flap on his document case. 'You keep telling me you've not got anywhere, but have you had any thoughts about the banking problem?'

'Just hunches. I think the banks have been penetrated by two parties. Someone's showing them how clever he is, hacking in at will and making a funny face pop up when they try to do a trace. And there are the people who actually removed funds. I'm beginning to wonder whether that might be the Grassman Brothers.'

Marcus smiled. 'Taking their own money?'

'No longer their money. It was filched at the point of transfer to the banks in Pakistan. Who else would know about the transaction?

And being account-holders might have made it easier for them to penetrate the system. They knew the bank would stand the loss; perhaps they've clawed the money back.'

'They'd be playing a dangerous game, Sam. They'd risk discovery by the banks, risk upsetting their suppliers in Pakistan.' Marcus slid straps through buckles.

'Don't forget these.' Samantha held out the photographs.

'Keep them. You may need them to identify the Grassmans and Manson. Decent images of Khan, Alani and Mahmood are on the disk I sent you. You've seen them, I suppose?'

She nodded, then said thoughtfully, 'A small room next to the general office in the Coventry packing place had computers and a display screen in it. Serious stuff, not business or domestic. A women on the packing line told me the room used to be a stationery store. They cleared it out about a week before I arrived and a big pasty-faced man came and installed the equipment.' She clicked open her bag and slid the photographs inside. 'He was there while I was on the packing line. Hardly ever came out; still working when the packers and office staff were leaving and the place was shutting down. I wondered whether he was involved in this banking business in some way.'

'Probably their legitimate business, Sam. Goods in, goods out, accounts, payroll.'

Samantha took a sideways look at him. Usually relaxed and good-humoured, he seemed edgy and preoccupied. Perhaps the threat to security really was as bad as he claimed.

Sensing her eyes on him, Marcus turned and smiled. 'You really are looking marvellous, Sam. I suppose the suit's by Dior or someone?'

'Balenciaga. Autumn collection.' She repaid his compliment with a scowl. 'You're still the same old charmer, Marcus, but it doesn't work any more. I can honestly say I've begun to loathe you, and I utterly despise Fallon.'

His smile widened, creased the corners of his blue eyes. Big shoulders began to shake with silent laughter. 'Did the charm ever work, Sam?'

'I'm not joking, Marcus.'

'I know that, Sam.' Trying to deflect her anger, he changed the subject. 'Dined with Sir Nigel yesterday evening. He was hoping for a progress report.'

'I haven't made any progress.'

'He'd like to give you lunch again. They're monitoring their systems round the clock. Face is still popping up and they've found signs of another penetration.'

'Signs?'

'He just said his people think someone else is hacking in.'

'Has any money gone?'

'Not as far as they're aware, but they're very agitated. Keeping it under wraps is as worrying as the problem itself. Why not call him, Sam? Have lunch, let his people explain what's happening.'

'Can't understand it when they do, Marcus.'

'But you could listen to what they say, check on developments and report back to me?'

Samantha laughed in spite of herself. 'OK, Marcus. I'll dine with Sir Nigel and report back to you. In the meantime, what are your priorities? The study centre in Leicester, or the machinery depot in Loughborough?'

'Study centre in Leicester. The cell reports to Virendra and he's based there, Martin Manson's moved in, and our man's had his throat cut. Something's happening. Take a look at it, Sam. The Grassmans and the trafficking can wait.'

He pushed open the door, swung his long legs out and struggled to rise from the low car. 'Give Crispin my regards. Tell him I think he's looking after you very well.'

She gave him a wicked smile. 'If he met you, Marcus, I might lose him.'

'You're making my flesh crawl now, Sam.' He slammed the

door, then grinned at her through the windscreen before striding off across the supermarket car park.

Samantha watched until he'd disappeared around the corner of the building, then keyed the ignition and headed for Harley Street.

'I must say, you're looking better, James.'

James spread a linen napkin over his knees and smiled across the table at his mother.

'You're losing that pale, haggard look.'

'It's called prison pallor.'

Lady Conway shuddered. 'Please don't use that word, James. I don't want the place mentioning, ever again.' She pushed her shoulders back and sat up even straighter in her chair. 'What have you been doing with yourself?'

'Running the firm. Got the decorators in at home. Had some furniture delivered.'

'You didn't tell me. I could have helped you choose things.'

'It's only the bedroom, Mother. Magnolia emulsion and a new carpet.'

Elizabeth let out an exasperated sigh. 'Elm Trees is a nice house, James, but Helen never turned it into a home; all those bland colours, no patterns, no pictures or ornaments. It's more sterile than a dentist's surgery.'

'She's an architect's daughter. It was her father's influence.'

'Architects? What do architects know about making homes? Look at that Le Corbusier man. "Less is more." What utter tosh. He was trying to hide the fact that he couldn't handle ornament and decoration. Same with Helen's father. Council dogsbody. Bus shelters and public conveniences, that's all he ever did.'

James laughed. 'It's good to be home, Mother.'

'Why don't you come and live here? I could look after you. You could talk to me. Your father never talks to me. I'm lonely, James.

He knew you were coming, but he wouldn't even lunch with me today. I think he's got a girlfriend.'

'He'll be dining at his club. All the magazines and newspapers are there, there's a bar, a billiard room, friends to talk business with.' James saw his mother's dubious look. He'd known for years that his father indulged in little dalliances.

He let his gaze wander over the white marble fireplace, the ornate gilt clock on its mantelpiece, the pale-blue-and-white chinoiserie wallpaper, the darker-blue-and-gold carpet and lacquered bamboo furniture. 'You're very good with decoration and ornament, Mother.'

Lady Conway began to smile.

'You've got flair, a sense of style.'

Her smile widened.

'You could have given old Corbusier lessons.'

She laughed happily. 'You're very sweet to me, James.' Her voice became girlishly coaxing. 'Won't you come and live here? Please.'

'I'm a forty-five-year-old man, Mother. Can't be under your feet. And that cleaner you organized's started.'

Wheels rattled in the passageway, there was a gentle tapping on the door, then Anna Tyminski came in, pushing a hostess trolley.

'Just plug it in and leave it beside me, Anna,' Elizabeth Conway said. 'I'll serve.'

Anna gave the mistress's handsome son a quick glance, then uncoiled a cable and pushed a plug into a socket by the fireplace.

'Thank you, Anna. And please thank your mother for me.'

The Polish maid smiled at James, then left the room, closing the door softly behind her. Elizabeth began to ladle soup into bowls, all the time keeping up a stream of chatter.

James nodded, offered the occasional word, but he wasn't really listening. He was thinking about the time he'd spent in Cheltenham, his sightings of Jennifer. He was still amazed at how much she'd changed in four years. She was no longer the child

153

he'd known. She was the woman Helen might have been if she'd not been such a promiscuous slut: young and fresh and unsullied. They looked like sisters now.

He'd hoped to catch Jennifer on her own, say hullo, begin to rebuild their relationship. But her friends were always with her, and the last time he'd seen her Helen had been hovering around, too. On reflection, it was just as well. It wouldn't be prudent for him to talk to Jennifer until her mother had been sorted. When that happened he'd be listed as Jennifer's next-of-kin and the authorities would expect him to take care of her.

Next-of-kin! His mother suspected, but she didn't really know. No one knew except him. He'd have to be very careful with the girl, make her feel secure with him, win over her affections again, make her dependent on him emotionally as well as financially. Then he could reveal he wasn't her father, tell her there was no blood tie, begin to reshape their relationship.

He wished Helen could be there to see it. It would destroy her. But she had to be dealt with. If she wasn't removed, she'd fight him, try to influence the girl and ruin his plans. And there was the threat of a divorce. He didn't want to pay maintenance, didn't want to lose Elm Trees. Above all, he had to erase the emasculating vision of those long lily-white legs spread wide over rumpled sheets. Only death, his or hers, could do that.

'James ... James?'

'Sorry, Mother.'

'You haven't listened to a word I've said.'

'Business, Mother. I was thinking about the business. We've just launched the new circuit-breaker range. I'm sorry. What were you saying?'

'How many lamb chops? Magda's cooked them beautifully. The whole meal smells heavenly.'

'Just one.'

'I'll give you four. You need building up again.'

James smiled. Men were always boys to their mothers. He half-listened to her chatter while she heaped his plate. His thoughts were confused. It wasn't easy to come to terms with the way his feelings, his intentions, towards Jennifer were changing. Could she be his new beginning, someone who represented all that might have been, and still could be? He had to be patient. Spend a year drawing her close, then, when she moved away to university, try to establish a different and deeper intimacy.

He felt a sudden urge to see her again, just one more time, before Helen was sorted. He daren't leave his office for another day. Ella was becoming curious about absences not covered by a diary entry. He'd drive over, early Saturday. Jennifer would probably leave the house to go shopping in the town. Young women did that. If he was lucky, he might be blessed with a few sightings.

Dr Uberman leafed through his notes. Across the silence of the dim room he could hear Samantha's breathing, slow and regular, like a person in sleep. He could smell her perfume, restrained and fragrant; just see, beyond the end of the couch, the abundance of gleaming black hair on the pillow. But he could make no sense of her responses to the word-association test; discern nothing in his notes that would inform his thoughts on the case.

She'd been very controlled. No matter how carefully he'd chosen words, he couldn't trigger the anger and grief she'd displayed at the end of their last session. Was she trying to conceal something from him? Some emotional wound, an anguish she was unable to confront, an unbearable guilt, perhaps? The randomness of her responses, her clever evasions, were beginning to convince him she had dark secrets she was unwilling to expose. He was making no progress. There should have been some break-through by now.

He cleared his throat. 'Miss Quest – Samantha – you told me,' he flicked back through his notes, 'during our first session, that you work in the fashion industry. What exactly do you do?'

'Travel, view collections, talk to designers, meet buyers for the big retail chains; that sort of thing.'

'Has that been your only career?'

'More or less.'

'You've never served in the armed forces or the police or anything of that nature?'

'Never.'

Dr Uberman sighed. He could feel the beginnings of a migraine. There was no pattern to this, only inconsistencies. Glancing at his watch, he saw there were twenty minutes left. He'd ask her about her dream. He might gain some insights from that.

'Your dream – have there been any developments?'

'Just one.'

He leafed through his notebook again. 'At the last account, you'd emerged from a culvert and you were wading, naked, along a shallow river. The water was clotted with blood. Human eyes, like slippery pebbles, covered the river bed. They were watching you. On the river bank, women wearing black burqas were chanting …' he peered at a scribbled note, 'the twenty-ninth sura of the Koran, verses known as *The Spider*. Colours are vivid, the sky is blue. You are approaching a bend in the river. You sense that beyond it lies some profound revelation. Have I got that right?'

'Pretty much so.'

'Would you care to recount the development?'

'As I progress around the bend in the river, the water becomes deeper, up to my waist, and the current stronger. It draws me along. The sound of chanting, the angry voice from the culvert, fade, and I see, up ahead, a huge tree growing out of the riverbank. It's a very old tree; ancient, primordial. Its colossal trunk is twisted and gnarled; its tapering roots writhe down and plunge into the water. They are red with ingested blood.

'The current becomes stronger. I begin to slip on the slimy eyes. I am having difficulty standing. As I approach the tree, I comprehend how huge it is. Its vast canopy of leaves fills the sky. Suddenly I am standing beneath it. The ceaseless movement of its leaves makes a rustling sound, like surf on a shore. It is as if I'm standing in a vast cathedral with branches forming vaulting and tracery that criss-cross high overhead. I feel the roots, like tendrils, begin to wrap around my legs and thighs, holding me steady against the current.'

'Do the clutching roots make you feel afraid?'

'No. They make me feel safe and protected.'

'Do the roots arouse you sexually? Is there vaginal or anal penetration?'

'No. They just hold me. I feel secure.'

'Please continue.'

'That's it. I sense that the tree is going to reveal a truth of great importance to me, and in the moment of anticipation, I wake.'

Dr Uberman glanced at his watch. Only ten minutes left. He could end the session now. 'I think that's a convenient point to finish on, Samantha. How do you feel? How do you feel at this moment?'

'Relaxed and a little sleepy.' Samantha swung her legs to the floor and groped for her shoes.

He watched her reach for her jacket and draw it over a crimson sweater. Like all the other clothes she'd worn, her black suit looked stylish and expensive. The long skirt was smooth over her hips and stomach and thighs; the tiny jacket, with its padded shoulders and tight sleeves, a perfect fit. He'd encountered other patients with impenetrable minds who were fastidious about their dress and appearance, but this was exceptional. She was so elegant. The whole effect was quite beguiling.

He removed thick spectacles and pinched the bridge of his nose. Samantha picked up her clutch bag and cradled its weight on her arm.

'Until next week, then, Dr Uberman.'

Replacing his spectacles, he rose to his feet, 'Until next week, Samantha.'

TWELVE

'Lindon Sands,' Edward announced.

Jennifer gazed out through the windscreen of Edward's yellow Toyota Yaris. They'd just rounded the top of a hill. Below them, a small town nudged a crescent of grey sea that merged, seamlessly, with grey autumn sky.

'It's tiny,' Jennifer said. 'Did your grandparents retire here?'

'Lived here most of their lives. Owned a shop and the amusement arcade.'

Bungalows and semi-detached houses lined the road at the bottom of the hill. They passed a church, a school, a row of shops; then streets of mostly terraced houses began to connect with the main road. Edward slowed, turned right into an avenue where the houses had been converted into small hotels and bed-and-breakfast places.

'There's nowhere to eat in the town, especially out of season, and there's nothing in the bungalow, but there's a decent chippy at the end of the road. You OK with that?'

Jennifer laughed. 'Sounds good.' She was enjoying the outing. She'd thought she might not, but Edward had been less shy, a little more relaxed. And if he wasn't the most talkative person in the world, at least he didn't boast all the time and pretend to know everything, the way most boys did. And they were becoming more comfortable in their silences.

He parked in front of a small hotel. Smiling, Jennifer watched him cross over to the fish fryers; long legs striding, hands in the pockets of his brown-leather bomber jacket, the brim of his small trilby hat – did they call them fedoras? – tipped over his brow. Sad that such a clever person should be so withdrawn, so lacking in self-confidence. From what he'd told her, that big comprehensive school must have been like a lunatic asylum. It had turned him into a loner. It certainly didn't seem the best place to go if you were academically inclined. He must have been brilliant, really focused, to get a place at Oxford. She was realizing how lucky she'd been to go to a private school in Tanford and now the college in Cheltenham. But his parents were still together. He was fortunate in that way.

When he'd asked her what she intended to do at university, she'd told him medicine. He'd shrugged and turned the corners of his mouth down, remarked that that was a people thing, and people could be incredibly hurtful and difficult. With maths it was just you and your ideas; a solitary striving to develop a mastery over the world of numbers.

Edward returned, opened the door of the car and slid behind the wheel. Jennifer took the warm parcel and settled it on her knees while he started the engine and drove off. Properties became sparse as they wound along a narrow coastal road. The sea was more distant here, separated from the shore by a wilderness of pools and mudbanks and waving reeds.

'Salt marshes,' Edward said. 'Supposed to be important for birds and wildlife. They're protected.'

The sea disappeared for a moment as they drove between high banks tufted with coarse grass, then the road curved steeply upwards and the bungalow suddenly came into view. It was set back, on the crest of a rise. White-painted walls, a roof of glazed green tiles, long windows and a sunrise front door: nineteen-twenties Art Deco.

Edward parked in front of a garage that was built beneath the far end of the bungalow, then they climbed steps that rose through a terraced garden to the entrance.

He led her inside, down a wide hall and through another sunrise door into a dining room. A green carpet with a swirling pattern of lighter green covered the floor; cream paper with pale-green stripes decorated the walls. The sideboard, table and chairs were modern and made from a dark wood with a pronounced grain. Some amateurish watercolours of local scenes were hanging in two neat rows above a grey-tiled fireplace.

While Edward found plates and knives and forks, Jennifer stood by a long window and gazed out over reed-choked pools and an expanse of muddy sand that ran down to the sea.

'Come for your fish and chips before they get cold.'

She joined Edward at the table. 'It's a nice place,' she said, while they were eating their meal. 'The bungalow's so light and the view from the window goes on for ever.'

'Lots of sea frets,' he said. 'Mist blankets the marshes and hides the sea. I used to spend the summer holidays here when I was a kid.'

'You miss your grandparents?'

'Heaps. I adored my gran. She was really kind to me.'

'I miss my grandfather. Since we moved from Tanford I don't see him any more.' She glanced up. Edward was gazing at her.

He finished chewing, then swallowed. 'After my gran, I think you're the nicest person I've ever known.'

Jennifer laughed, touched by the sentiment, amused at being compared to his grandmother. 'It was very sweet of you to say that, Edward.'

Edward smiled at her. He wasn't blushing. 'I'd better check the place over, drain the water off, make everything secure for the winter.'

Jennifer rose and began to gather up the plates. 'Let me wash these first. Is there any tea or coffee in the kitchen?'

'Try the wall cupboard next to the window.'

*

Helen changed gear, slowed, then turned into the roundabout. Had she got everything from the supermarket and the farm? Probably not. Jennifer usually went with her to do the Saturday morning shop and prompted her memory. She'd gone off with the boy next door today. Things were changing. Jennifer wouldn't be her companion for much longer. In a couple of years she'd be away at university.

Perhaps she should get a job. Could she get a job? It was seventeen years since she'd worked in the tiny insurance office in Tanford High Street. If she divorced James, she'd be free to marry again. She should have done it while he was in jail. Somehow she'd been afraid to; afraid to do anything that might antagonize him and make him more vengeful. Fergus, his father, had kept on dropping hints, begging her not to, and he'd been so supportive with money she hadn't wanted to upset him. Anyway, after the trauma in the bedroom, the trial, all the embarrassment and shame, men hadn't been on her agenda. And if they had, her notoriety would probably have attracted the wrong kind.

Leaving the roundabout, she accelerated down a slip road, then merged with the traffic on the bypass. A silver Jaguar, one of the big old ones, moved in behind her. She remembered seeing it in the supermarket car park and at the organic food place. Suddenly apprehensive, she peered in the mirrors. The silver car was quite close. There was a man behind the wheel. He was young and fair-haired. Her heart stopped fluttering. It wasn't James.

Darren Norby felt good about the car. It was a shame to waste it. He'd looked for something big and heavy, plenty of power and old enough not to have high-security locking. He'd snitched it from a used-car lot. Taking it had been easier than he'd expected; silly sods had hidden the keys behind the visor. And the run down had warmed it up, got the oil circulating. It was more responsive now. He took a couple of deep breaths. Everything was under control. He felt good. While she'd been in that health-food place he'd got his head down behind the dash and snorted a line. He was really up for it now.

Lingering on in Cheltenham with a stolen car wasn't a good idea. He didn't want to drive around in it much longer. And it was no use waiting for a deserted stretch of road; another couple of miles and they'd be back in town. He had to do it now. If the Jag packed up on him he'd dump it and do a runner across the fields.

The road had narrowed to single carriageway. There was a bridge up ahead, over railway lines. Then the road curved away into a wooded area. He could lose himself amongst the trees if he had to. He'd never find a better place. He'd force her on to the verge, send her, head-on, into the pillar at the end of the brick wall that curved over the bridge. Doing sixty, only timber railings, she'd crash down the embankment. She'd never survive it.

Darren pulled out, began to draw alongside. They were closing on the bridge. He eased the Jaguar over, felt a crunch as its length began to chafe against the side of the woman's red Volvo. She glanced towards him, wide-eyed, terror-stricken. He pulled down hard on the wheel. The drumming of metal on metal became deafening and the car began to shudder. Bitch! She was fighting it, trying to turn into him, trying stay on the road. Tyres were screeching. The pillar was looming. He had to force her over. He turned and glared at her. Her hands were gripping the steering wheel, her arms were straining. The bitch! She fucking well wouldn't go over.

The Volvo's side was scraping along the brickwork now. He could hear glass breaking, metal tearing; feel the car bouncing. The vibration suddenly stopped. She'd stood on the brakes. She'd stood on the fucking brakes and he'd left her behind. He careered on, lurching around the bend that curved into the trees. A lorry! Jesus Christ, a lorry! He …

The wind blowing in from the sea was cold. Jennifer buttoned up her grey school coat, it was the only warm coat she had, and tied

162

the belt. Edward was beside her, his laptop in its canvas bag over his arm. They strode past a row of bathing huts, a tiny café, a novelty shop, a place that sold buckets and spades, ice creams and candyfloss. They were all closed.

'I've just got to call at the store and make sure everything's OK,' Edward said.

'The store?' She wished he'd hold her hand.

'Gran sold the amusement arcade when Granddad died.' Edward gestured towards the row of shops. 'These places were built in the gardens of houses on the seafront. Granddad used what was left of the house behind the arcade for storing old games and pinball tables. Gran thought the stuff was going to have rarity value, so she kept the store. She was always going on about having everything valued and sold, but she never got round to it.'

They passed the arcade. Red, blue and green fairground letters spelled out *Henry's House of Fun* along its yellow fascia. Coloured lights flashed, games chimed and pinged and made racing-car noises. A few local teenagers, mostly boys, were playing the machines.

Edward paused by a door set back a little from the pavement. A brass plate, tarnished and discoloured, announced to the world that this was the *Registered Office of Thompson's Amusements Ltd.* He turned a key and heaved the door open, stood aside to let Jennifer enter, then followed her into an open passageway. It ran down the side and turned along the back of the amusement arcade.

The discordant sounds of the gaming machines, fainter now, whispered between brick walls and the grimy windows of the old houses behind the row of shops. There was another door at the bend in the passageway. Edward turned a key in the lock, pushed through and switched on lights. Jennifer followed him inside.

Four bulbs in green coolie-hat shades illuminated a space that had been formed by knocking two large rooms into one. Plaster was crumbling, cobwebs festooned corners, and the cold air was heavy with an odour of dampness and decay. Pinball tables, glass tops reflecting the lights, were standing side by side. Mahogany boxes, with levers that sent metal balls rolling down channels or spinning around spirals, lined the walls. Cranes glinted in glass cases, claws hovered over the dusty remains of cheap prizes.

They threaded their way between the machines, heading towards the back of the room. In a dark corner, a glass case enclosed the head and torso of a doll. Curious, Jennifer stepped towards it. Edward followed her.

She glanced over her shoulder at him. 'What's this?'

'An automaton.'

Closer now, she could see it was a sailor, about as big as a ten-year-old boy and dressed a blue-striped jersey. Jolly Jack Tar was embroidered on the blue ribbon of his white sailor's hat. The clothes were grimy and faded, the face highly coloured, the eyes huge and staring.

Edward crouched down and flicked a switch, then reached up and ran his fingers over the top of the case. He found two old pennies and pushed them into a slot in the base. A mechanism whirred, then the head began to turn from side to side, the torso swayed, the eyes blinked. When the mouth flopped open, the laughter began; a demented, banshee shrieking.

Jennifer shivered. It was sinister. In this gloomy place it was downright scary. She felt an arm circling her waist. She turned. Edward was gazing at her. When the manic laughter stopped, he smiled. He really did look awfully nice when he smiled. 'Don't be afraid,' he said softly, then drew her closer. 'I'm here. Nothing can hurt you while I'm here. OK?'

'I thought it was spooky,' she said. 'The crazy laugh, the crooked teeth in that bright-red mouth, the crafty eyes.'

'It is a bit,' he agreed. 'It seemed different when it was in the arcade.' He gazed down at her for a few heartbeats, then said, 'I've got to go upstairs and check something. Then we'll head back; stop off somewhere for tea. That OK?'

'Perfect,' she said. She felt him squeeze her, hoped he'd kiss her, but he took his arm away and led her through an opening and up a flight of stairs.

Feet clattering, they rounded a landing and entered what had once been a bedroom. Late-afternoon light, grey and watery, filtered in through a grime-streaked window. Jennifer went over and gazed out over rear yards.

Edward slid the laptop from his shoulder. 'They're the backs of the shops on High Street.' He unzipped the canvas bag.

Jennifer turned, perched on the windowsill and looked around the room. A grey metal case was standing on the marble top of an old wash-stand. From a recess just below the maker's name and model number a tiny blue light gleamed steadily. Red and green lights were flickering on and off. Cables descended from the back and snaked along skirtings to a box on the wall behind her legs.

'What does that do?'

'It's a server,' Edward said.

'What's a server?'

'A device that connects computers to the internet.'

She was going to ask him what it was doing here when she saw him frowning at the red and green lights. 'Is something wrong?'

'It's taking traffic. It shouldn't be taking traffic.' He opened the laptop, booted it up, then plugged in a cable to connect it to the server. Fingers tapping on keys suddenly froze. Jennifer heard him gasp, then watched his face turn grey.

'What's wrong, Edward?'

He didn't answer. Mouth hanging open, his shocked eyes went on staring at the laptop screen.

She left the window, crossed dusty boards and peered over his shoulder. She read:

WE KNOW WHO YOU ARE. WE KNOW WHERE YOU ARE.
WE'RE COMING TO GET YOU, YOU THIEVING BASTARDS.
HAVE THE TWENTY MILLION WAITING WHEN WE ARRIVE.

'What does that mean?'

'It means I'm in big trouble. *Really big trouble. Catastrophic trouble.*' He touched keys. Columns of letters and numbers scrolled up the screen. He stared at them with frightened eyes, captured them in the laptop's memory, then shut it down. He jerked a plug from a socket on the wall. The lights on the server faded.

'We've got to go.' He moved over to the window, stared for a moment at the untidy back yards of the shops, then grabbed her hand, led her down to the storeroom and out into the street, locking doors behind them as they went. While they were half-walking, half-running, to the car, he bundled the laptop into its canvas bag.

'What's wrong, Edward? Tell me what's wrong.'

'When we get back to the car.'

They clambered up steps behind the bathing huts, entered the car park, then ran over to his yellow Toyota. Jennifer climbed inside, saw him looking anxiously this way and that before sliding in beside her. They drove off, heading for the road that wound along the coast to Sidmouth.

'You're scaring me, Edward.'

'Scaring you?'

'Your driving. It's so fast and erratic. Pull into a lay-by and tell me what's the matter.'

He did as she asked; switched off the engine and yanked up the brake.

She reached for his hand. Now that he'd had his arm around her, she felt she had licence to. 'Tell me what's happened. Tell me what's upsetting you.'

'I've done a stupid thing, Jennifer. Jesus, I've done such a stupid thing.' He pressed his forehead against the steering wheel and closed his eyes. 'Promise you won't tell anyone?'

'Of course I promise.'

'I've been hacking into banks.'

'Taking money?' Jennifer's voice was shocked.

'No, just hacking in. It's unbelievably difficult. It was a challenge. I wrote a program that could unscramble their encryptions, keep analysing passwords and codes until it penetrated the system. I wanted to see if I could do it. I put a virus in that altered their figures, then put them right. I built in safeguards so they couldn't trace me, but they have. Someone's locked on to me and sent a message back. They've found their way into the server.'

'You said you didn't take any money.'

Edward opened his eyes and looked at her. 'It was just a silly game. I was fooling around, being smart.'

'Then why did the message call you a thief and say you had to have twenty million ready?'

'I don't know. It might not be the bank. But whoever it is, they've traced me. They've—'

'They've sent you a message, Edward. If the bank or whoever it is really did know who and where you are, they'd have contacted you by now. Someone's trying to scare you. Perhaps they're playing games, like you were playing games. I think you should go to the police.'

'Daren't. Hacking into banks is serious stuff. I'd go to prison, probably for years.'

'Then you've got to tell your parents.'

'Dad would go insane. I daren't do that.'

'You've got to do something.'

'They can only get back to the server. There's nothing to trace me on that. The logging's disabled for outgoing data.'

'Logging?'

'Recording all the computers that have accessed it. I modified the software. It only responds to incoming traffic, not my outgoing stuff. I installed my own server so I could control it in that way. And if they've got the means of actually locating the server, they'll find it's registered under a false name: Branwell in Lindon Sands. My name's not mentioned.' He sighed, suddenly realizing something. 'I unplugged it, but I didn't take it out; I should have brought it away with us.'

'Do you want to go back?'

'Not while you're with me. If they meant what they said, someone could be watching the place. I'll wait and see what happens.'

'They got to the server thing. Could they get back to your computer in Cheltenham?'

'Too difficult.'

'It was difficult to hack into banks, but you did it. They could be as clever as you.'

'They're probably cleverer.'

Jennifer squeezed his hand.

'I've been stupid. If this gets out, I'm finished.'

'You've not taken any money. You've not done anything seriously wrong.'

'Someone seems to think I've got their money. Twenty million pounds. They'd lock me up for ever for twenty million pounds.' His voice lowered. 'They might kill me.'

'Go to the police.'

'I daren't.' He took his hand from hers. Calmer now, he started the car, checked the mirrors, then pulled out on to the road. 'I've absolutely no idea what to do. My dad always says, "If in doubt, do nothing," so I think I'll just lie low and wait.'

They skirted Honiton, then joined the M5 and began the journey north to Cheltenham. Jennifer could sense his fear, feel his distress. She didn't know what to say. Small talk seemed out of place, and any mention of computers and programs would do nothing to ease his distress. When they were circling Gloucester, almost home, she remembered something.

'My grandpa tried to contact us after we'd moved to Cheltenham. Mum didn't tell him we were going. It's a bit complicated. I'll tell you about it some other time. Anyway, he hired this private detective, a woman. She found us but she said she wouldn't tell Grandpa where we were. My mum thought she was OK. She left a card with a contact number on. It's in my bedroom. We could talk to her.' It had become 'we'. She was sharing his problems.

Edward risked a glance at her, then looked back at the road. He checked the mirrors. Just lorries behind them, no lingering cars. Jesus, he was scared. 'How could she help?' he asked.

'She's not the police, but surely she'll have experience of these things. She'd know what to do.'

'She wouldn't know about hacking into banks and computers and servers. She'd probably tell me to go to the police.'

'She'd know what to do when people make threats. You could explain the computer part. She might tell you they're just playing games, like you were playing games, and advise you to ignore it.'

'I am trying to ignore it.'

'Only because you don't know what to do.'

Jennifer was right, Edward reflected. He was so scared he couldn't think clearly. He needed someone to advise him, who was calm and detached. He could always ignore the advice if he felt he had to. He had savings, and surely it wouldn't cost all that much to talk to a private detective for an hour?

He glanced at Jennifer. 'Let's try it. When we get home, you find the card and I'll give her a call.'

'Mum … Mum …' Jennifer called up the stairs. There was no answer. Her mother was out. Strange, she was hardly ever out in the evenings. Jennifer glanced at her watch. Not quite seven. Edward was standing in the porch. 'Come in, Edward. I'll go upstairs and see if I can find the card.'

She dashed up to the landing and entered her bedroom. The card was still there, tucked under the base of her reading lamp. As she snatched it up she heard the bell ringing, Edward going to open the door, a male voice saying, 'Good evening, sir. We're trying to locate a Miss Conway. Is she at home?'

Jennifer ran down the stairs. A policeman and a policewoman were looking up at her through the doorway. She felt a rush of alarm.

'Miss Conway?'

Jennifer nodded.

'I'm afraid we have some rather unfortunate news for you, Miss Conway. Your mother was involved in a motoring accident this morning.'

Alarm escalated into mind-numbing panic. She clutched at the newel post. Edward came close and slid his arm around her. 'Is she...?'

'The people at the hospital haven't told us anything. She's been sedated and they're keeping her under observation.'

'She's in hospital?'

'Cheltenham General.'

'I'll take you,' Edward said.

'We could take the young lady, sir. Might be quicker. You could follow and bring her home.'

Dazed, Jennifer walked out of the door.

'Keys,' Edward called after her. 'Give me the keys and I'll lock up.'

She fumbled in her pocket, handed her keys to Edward, then, as an afterthought, pressed the card into his hand. Nothing like this had ever happened to her. Her father had gone away, but her mother had always been there. She suddenly felt desperately frightened and alone.

The policeman waited in the foyer while the policewoman took her up to the ward. 'Will you be all right now, love?'

Jennifer nodded. She might never be all right, ever again.

'Shouldn't be long before your young man arrives. He'll take you home. Anyone to look after you?'

'I'll be fine.' She drew away, eager for information about her mother. Glancing over her shoulder, she said, 'You've been very kind. Edward will make sure I'm all right.'

When she approached the reception desk, one of the nurses looked up.

'My mother's in here: Helen Conway. The police have just brought me.'

'She's sleeping. Tomorrow would be—'

'I want to see her,' Jennifer insisted. Her mouth trembled. Tears began to wet her cheeks.

The nurse rose, took her arm and ushered her into a waiting room.

'She's sleeping, love. She's had a very severe shock.'

'Is she going to die?'

'We're keeping her under observation. She—'

'I want to see her.'

The nurse sighed. 'I'll take you through, but only for a few seconds. And I can't leave you with her.'

They left the waiting room and continued on down the brightly lit corridor. Pausing beside a door, the nurse gave Jennifer a warning look and said softly, 'She mustn't be disturbed,' then led her in.

The room was dark and still. The only bright thing was a monitor screen displaying numbers and moving lines. When Jennifer's eyes adjusted to the gloom, she saw a bag, suspended from a stand, and a pipe connecting it to her mother's wrist.

She felt the nurse's arm slide through hers, felt her leading her over to the bed.

'Mummy,' Jennifer gasped. 'What's happened to you?' Her mother's blond hair was straggly and matted, her blue eyes were buried in puffy folds of blackened flesh, her mouth hidden beneath a hissing plastic mask. Jennifer turned towards the nurse. 'Has she been burned?'

'It's bruising, dear. Very severe bruising.'

Jennifer began to sob. She felt the nurse turning her, steering her back through the door.

'Come back tomorrow morning, love. Ten o'clock. She might be able to speak to you then.'

'The police told me she'd been in a car crash. Is she very badly hurt. Is she—'

'Tomorrow, love. I'll get one of the doctors to talk to you.'

Edward was waiting for her at the desk. He wrapped his arm around her and led her to the lifts. 'Mum said you had to stay with us tonight. She's making up the spare bed.' Doors rumbled open and he helped her inside. 'Is she ... Is your mother very bad?'

Jennifer clung to him, sobbing out her distress, her whole body shaking. He folded his arms around her and held her. He felt utterly inadequate. He had absolutely no idea what to say or do. The message on the server, the bad stuff happening to Jennifer, her sudden dependence on him – his introduction to the world of adult things had left him frightened and confused.

THIRTEEN

Samantha glanced at the dashboard clock. Almost noon. She'd been watching the entrance to the Pond Street Centre for Islamic Studies for more than three hours. Groups of children, men and women, black-robed imams clutching documents, had entered and left. She guessed a sharia court was in progress. She hadn't recognized any of the faces. From her vantage point in front of a newsagent's she could just see an opening to a car park down the side of the place. No cars had arrived or departed.

The door to the building opened. Two women in full burqas, a third in a hijab, stepped out into bright sunlight and headed off down the street. Samantha sighed. She'd watched and waited long enough. Keying the ignition, she checked the mirrors, began to pull away, then let the car roll back. A white Mercedes had just slipped out of the rear yard. When it stopped at the junction with Pond Street, reflections on the windscreen hid the occupants. Samantha waited. Eventually it emerged and swept past. A man she recognized as Virendra Khan was in the front passenger seat, the driver was wearing a white skull cap, a bearded man was riding in the back. She pulled out.

They headed south, curving in front of the Ibis Hotel, bearing left on to London Road, past the railway station, then up the hill. Beyond Victoria Park shops and offices, restaurants and bars gave way to large old houses. The line of cars slowed, then stopped. There was a break in the flow of oncoming traffic and the white

Mercedes turned right through an ornamental gateway. Beyond high walls, Samantha could see tall chimneys and dormer windows rising out of a blue-slate roof. The traffic moved on. As she passed the gates, Samantha glanced down a long driveway towards a red-brick and brown-stone mansion. The ground-floor windows were boarded up and a sold sign had been fastened across a For Sale board.

Samantha made a left turn off the main road and parked in a side street. Bag under her arm, she walked back to the house. The white car was standing beside a short flight of steps that led up to the entrance. The men had disappeared inside.

Bushes and shrubs, dense and overgrown, bordered a neglected lawn. There were no signs of movement beyond the first-floor windows. Samantha entered the gates, began to approach the house along a gap between the vegetation and the high boundary walls, wincing as branches and thorns snatched at her brown, belted coat. Rounding the Mercedes, she climbed the steps and crossed over to the entrance.

One of the heavy doors was ajar. She slid through, into a small vestibule. Glass panels in the inner doors gave her a view of an impressive circular hall. At the far side a central flight of stairs rose to a landing, then divided in two and followed the curve of the walls to the first floor. Sunlight shone through a tall stained-glass window above the landing, enriching the colours of a steamship, a railway locomotive, bales of cotton, sheaves of corn, gears and spanners, all sharply defined by narrow strips of lead. A visual allegory that must have meant something to the original owners of the house.

The inner doors weren't locked. Samantha stepped into the hall and listened. From a distance came the sound of footsteps on bare boards and male voices conversing in Arabic. She tiptoed across an expanse of black-and-white marble, hid in a recess beneath the lower flight of stairs and drew her gun from her bag. While she checked the magazine, she tried to put names to the faces of the driver and the bearded man who'd ridden in the back of the car. Their images were on the disk that Marcus had sent her. Virendra Khan was the one they answered to, he was the leader of the group, but the names of the other two escaped her. She flicked over the safety catch, leaned back against the wall and waited.

The sound of footsteps and voices, advancing and receding, filtered down from the rooms above. Occasional words revealed that they were discussing conversion works, repairs, costs. Eventually their voices became louder and feet began to tread on the stairs.

Samantha pressed herself against the wall. They were directly above her head now. When she heard their shoes shuffling over the marble tiles, she stepped out of the recess, both hands wrapped around the gun, her arms outstretched. They were moving towards the entrance, still discussing things. They hadn't seen her. She squeezed the trigger twice. The bearded man and a man with an attaché-case sagged and fell.

The deafening crashes of the gun merged and echoed around the vast entrance hall. Rigid with shock, Virendra Khan stared down at the bodies. When the echoes had faded, he heard a husky voice whispering his name. He turned, saw a black-haired woman in a brown coat step from the shadows beside the stairs. She was holding a gun in leather-gloved hands. He gazed at her with stricken eyes. Gripped by the nightmare, when he opened his mouth to speak he was unable to make a sound.

'Virendra Khan?' Samantha repeated, stepping closer. 'Perhaps you have so many names you've forgotten who you are today.'

'I am Virendra Khan.' He croaked out the words. Terror was still constricting his throat.

'Remove your coat.'

He stared at her with shocked eyes, his mouth opening and closing but making no sound.

Samantha jerked the gun. 'Take off your coat.'

He did as she asked; allowed it to fall to the floor.

'Now take off your Kameez.'

He suddenly found his voice. 'Why are you doing this? Why are you disrespecting me?'

'Take off your kameez. I won't ask you again.'

He unfastened buttons at wrist and throat, then drew the garment over his head and laid it on top of his coat.

'Shoes,' Samantha demanded.

He crouched down, unlaced his shoes and stepped out of them. He was standing in front of her, dressed only in a vest, socks and baggy white cotton pants now. His brown eyes, huge with terror, were glaring at her.

Keeping him in the sights of the gun, Samantha snapped, 'Walk over to the stairs. Climb three steps, then lean backwards over the rail and let your arms hang down.'

He stumbled and his movements were awkward, but he did as she asked.

Keeping the gun pressed against the back of his head, she clamped a handcuff over a wrist, wrapped the chain around a banister, then captured his other hand. She squeezed the bracelets tight, retrieved her bag, then joined him on the wide stairs.

'Who are you?' he demanded. His back being bent over the handrail, he had to press his chin into his chest in order to see her eyes.

'Just a woman searching for information. Who's Martin Manson?'

'A doctor of divinity. He's a visiting lecturer.'

'They call him Irfam Shehri in Saudi. Why did you invite him here? Is he helping you to recover the money.'

Anger suddenly gripped Virendra. 'How dare you behave like this, killing my brothers, trussing me up like a dog. This is England, a country where the law protects—'

'You're wasting your breath, Khan. I'm not restrained by the law or any human agency. Is Manson helping you search for the money?'

'What money?'

'The thirteen million that went missing before it reached the banks in Pakistan?'

'I work at the Studies Centre, I attend the mosque. What do I know of missing money?'

Samantha stepped forward, tugged at the waistband of his baggy pants, snapped buttons, then dragged the white fabric down to his ankles. 'You lead a cell within a terrorist group, Virendra. What group is it? What's its fancy name? Jihad of the Golden Dawn? The Organization for Preaching and Combat? Tell me what it is?'

'I work at the Centre,' his voice was shaking. 'I organize studies. I engage lecturers.'

'You engage killers, Virendra. Did you call Manson in to kill me?'

'This is ridiculous. He is a learned doctor. He has come to enlighten us.'

'You're pissing me off, Virendra, just like your cab-driver friend, Abdulgader, and the waiter at the bank, little Saeed.'

Samantha took a handkerchief from her bag. When she unfolded it, light glittered on a blade. 'This belonged to Abdulgader.' She brought the knife close to Virendra's face. His eyes squinted when they tried to focus on it. 'I made him give it to me. He was sensible. He told me what I wanted to know before I had to use it. It's sharp, but not too sharp. When it cuts, you'll feel pain. If you wish to remain a complete man, Virendra, you must tell me what I want to know. Now, let's begin again. What's the name of your organization?'

'You're evil,' he screamed. 'Sent by the devil to torment me.'

'You order the killing of innocent men and women and children while they're peacefully going about their business, and you dare to call me evil?'

Samantha stabbed the knife into the handrail, reached into a coat pocket, pulled out a pair of surgical gloves and snapped them on. The sound of their voices was still whispering around the high ceiling. Sunlight, blazing through the stained-glass window, was dappling the chequered floor with patches of brilliant colour.

Retrieving the knife, she slid the blade between his thighs and began to move it towards his groin. 'Now, Virendra,' her husky voice was low and coaxing, her green eyes were searing into his, 'we'll start with the name of your organization and move on from there.'

Samantha parked the white Mercedes in what had once been a stable block at the rear of the house. When she switched off the engine she could hear a phone ringing. Ringing, not bleeping. It wasn't Marcus. She opened her bag, took out her crimson mobile and flicked it open.

'Hullo … Hullo?' The voice had a lingering uncertainty of pitch, like that of a youth who hadn't quite escaped adolescence.

'Who's speaking?'

'Edward Goodwin. I'm sorry I don't know your name. It wasn't on the card. You only wrote your number on the card.'

'What card?'

'The card you left with Mrs Conway. Jennifer gave it to me.'

'Jennifer?'

'Her daughter.'

Samantha remembered. 'You mean Mrs Conway in Cheltenham?'

'That's right.' The voice sounded relieved.

'And why are you calling me, Edward?'

'I'd like to come and see you. I must talk to you.'

'About what?'

'It's too difficult to explain over the phone.'

'Give me a rough idea?'

'I'm being threatened.'

'Go to the police.'

'Can't. It's not the sort of thing I can go to the police about. Can I meet you and talk to you? I'll pay for the time.'

'Does Mrs Conway know you've phoned me?'

'No. She's been hurt. Car accident, yesterday.'

'Is it to do with that?'

'No.'

Samantha made her voice severe. 'You're not wasting my time, are you, Edward?'

'No.' The voice was outraged. 'It's serious.'

'How serious?'

'Twenty million pounds serious.'

Samantha pondered. She had to look over the Centre for Islamic Studies, then contact Marcus. 'Where are you, Edward?'

'Cheltenham.'

'Tomorrow morning,' she offered. 'I could see you in Cheltenham tomorrow morning.'

'Not today?'

'No chance.'

'Where? It has to be somewhere private; somewhere we won't be overheard.'

'Shall I come to your home?' Samantha suggested.

'That's out of the question.'

'What car do you drive?'

'A Toyota Yaris. It's yellow. Registration FD51UHO.'

'There's a car park at the back of High Street. A library backs on to it, and Saint Mary's Church is close by. Be there at eleven, and come alone.' Samantha switched off her mobile.

Beer cans, food wrappers, the treads of a lorry tyre and the remains of a timber pallet were strewn along the bottom of the hedge that enclosed the lay-by. It was late and the road was quiet, just the occasional car swishing past through the rain, a lorry roaring by in a cloud of spray. Samantha clicked open her bag, took out the encrypted phone and keyed in a number.

After a dozen rings she heard a breathless voice gasp, 'Hello?'

'That you, Marcus?'

'Sam! It's after midnight. What's the problem?'

'Just leaving Leicester. I've got information for you.'

'Is it important?'

'Very. I'm driving down to Cheltenham. I think you should meet me there, say about three.'

'Can't we talk over the encrypted phone?'

'I don't think you'd want me to.'

'It's that big?'

'Put it this way, Marcus, If things happen that might happen, you'd feel you'd let the regiment down if you'd not taken this stuff on board.'

'Where do you want to meet?'

'Top of Montpellier, opposite the park. There's a jewellers in a row of shops that's decorated with Greek statues. I'll be parked outside. Don't keep me waiting. I'm bushed.'

Marcus clicked off the phone. 'Sorry about that.'

'Was it Quest?'

'She wants me to meet her in Cheltenham. Two hour's time.'

Loretta Fallon turned on her side and gazed up at him. 'Talk about coitus interruptus. The little bitch must have known.'

Marcus smiled at the face on the pillow. She looked younger with her hair untied, less formidable and very feminine. Her cheeks and the skin around her mouth had been reddened by the stubble on his chin. Her heavy breasts were nestling in the fold of her arm. Brushing a wave of hair from her face, he moved under the duvet, kissed her, then rolled her on to her back and eased a muscular thigh between her legs.

Kissing her again, he whispered, 'You realize Quest's been on the rampage in Leicester and the Universal Caliphate's about to dawn, don't you, ma'am?'

Loretta gave him a louche smile. 'Then you'd better finish what you'd started, hadn't you, Marcus? Before the sharia sex-police kick down the door and cart us off for a whipping.'

*

Bulky in his heavy overcoat, Marcus was suddenly spreading his shoulders across the seats. He'd brought with him into the car the smell of peppermints, old-fashioned shaving soap, and misty night air. As he slammed the door, he said, 'What have you got for me, Sam?'

'New groups have formed. Birmingham, Manchester, Bradford and Leeds; all being organized by people with links to AQAP. For security reasons, they're only loosely affiliated to one another, but some big joint action's being planned for early November.' Samantha took a handwritten sheet from her bag. 'These are the names and locations of the leaders and co-ordinators in the four cities. The names of rank-and-file members are supposed to be on the laptop I gave you when we last met. This information isn't on your disk. You had the Leicester people on the files, but not these. They're new.'

'What about Virendra Khan?'

'He gave me the information. He's dead. So is Arza Mahmood and Habib Alani. Virendra could have been feeding me nonsense, but I don't think so. It was too quick and he was too terrified to dream up lies.' She reached over the seats and brought out a bulging shopping bag. 'The personal papers they were carrying are in here, along with some documents from an attaché-case, mostly about the purchase of a house on London Road. That's where the bodies are. There was fifty-five thousand pounds in the attaché-case. Fifty of it's in the bag. I've kept five for expenses.'

'I authorize your expenses, Sam.'

'I got blood on a Maxmara coat. Are you prepared to authorize five thousand for a coat?'

'Charlotte's never paid more than a couple of hundred pounds for a coat.' He sounded shocked.

'That's just one more reason why I'm glad I'm not married to you, Marcus. I'm keeping the five thou'. I'll let you have a receipt when I do a formal report.'

'Anything in the house on London Road?'

'Too big for me to search. You'll have to put a team in. I hid their car in an old stable block round the back. There were sacks of ammonium nitrate in there, probably a couple of tons. The grounds are big, but they don't need that much fertilizer.'

'What about the Islamic studies centre?'

'Found keys on one of the bodies and looked it over before I drove down. Just books and pamphlets and study guides on the ground floor; classrooms and what looked like a sharia courtroom on the first. There's a workshop down in the cellars. Door's tucked away at the back of a store where they keep cleaning materials. Someone's been using it for making electronic things. Ten five-litre containers of hydrogen peroxide are stored where coal used to be kept. Industrial-strength stuff, not hairdresser's supplies.'

'What time did Virendra Khan and his friends go missing?'

'They left the Centre about noon and they were dead less than an hour later. I waited in Leicester until the place was shut down before I went in. That would be about nine, nine-thirty, yesterday evening. I drove past the big house on London Road on my way out. It was all quiet. No cars outside, no police.'

'I'd better move teams in before dawn. Get in there before they realize something's happening.' He pushed open the door of the car. 'Keep in touch, Sam.'

Detective Chief Inspector Bardeen looked from the rosy-cheeked policewoman to the overweight sergeant. 'Well, what have you got?'

'Car was stolen. Taken from a used-car lot in Hammersmith, day before the accident. Bloke driving it was called Darren Norby. Lives in North London: Barnet. Cocaine in his blood at the time of the accident. His next of kin...' The sergeant glanced at the policewoman.

'Contacted the force in Barnet.' She spoke with a soft Suffolk burr. 'They've notified his mother. Another son's driving her down to identify the body, later this morning.'

The sergeant looked at his notebook. 'Woman in the Volvo

went by the name of Conway: Helen Conway. She called us out about ten days ago. Her estranged husband had paid her a visit and she was scared. She wanted him out of the house.'

'And?' Detective Chief Inspector Bardeen sniffed.

'He went. No trouble. He'd just been released from jail. Manslaughter. Caught his wife in bed with a bloke and killed him. She's scared to death of him.'

'Has she reason to be?'

The sergeant shrugged and looked at the policewoman. 'You did the call with Jack. What did you make of him?'

'He was OK. Calm, reasonable; an educated, well-dressed sort of bloke. When Jack asked him to leave, he did. No trouble. Told his wife he'd phone her about access, then left.'

'Access?'

'He wants to see his daughter.'

Bardeen looked back at the sergeant. 'Did you get any witness statements?'

'Got one from the driver of a car that was following.' He leafed through his notebook. 'A vicar, Canon Rupert Pringle.'

'Rupert Pringle.' Bardeen chuckled. 'There's a name to conjure with.' The sergeant and the policewoman remained stony-faced.

'He said he was certain it was deliberate,' the sergeant went on. 'They were approaching a railway bridge and the man driving the Jaguar tried to force the Volvo on to the verge and down the embankment. Volvo managed to stay on the road, but the Jag pressed it against a brick wall that runs over the bridge. Volvo crashed into a pier about centre span and the Jag continued over the bridge. It was well into the oncoming lane and a lorry hit it, head on. Cab of the lorry rode right over it.'

'What about the woman in the Volvo?'

'Regained consciousness some time yesterday. She's been lucky. Broken ribs, fractured collar bone, very severe bruising. They've still got to do tests, but they don't think there are any internal injuries.'

'What about a statement?'

'Doctor's been holding us off. Alan's taken Jane along on the off-chance. They took the daughter to see her the night of the accident. Daughter's staying with neighbours.'

'And the lorry driver?'

'Poorly. Broken legs, fractured pelvis, internal bleeding. Not got a statement yet. Alan said he'd look in after he's visited the Conway woman.'

Detective Chief Inspector Bardeen tossed his pen on to the desk, sat back in his chair, and hooked an ankle over his knee. 'Do you think the husband's involved?'

The sergeant shrugged. 'Just got out on parole. Would he risk it?'

Bardeen snorted. 'Might be the first thing he'd do.'

'If he was going to sort her, wouldn't he have done it when he found her with the bloke?' the sergeant asked.

'Who knows what he'd have done in a situation like that? Has he been told?'

'Not by us.'

'What's his address?'

The sergeant consulted his notes. 'Elm Trees, Forest Drive, Tanford.'

Bardeen frowned. 'Contact the force there. Ask them to send someone round to tell him; see how he reacts when he finds out she's not dead.'

'It was on local radio and TV yesterday,' the sergeant said. 'He'll probably know. But we can give it a try.'

The policewoman cleared her throat. 'Sir?'

Bardeen favoured her with a scowl.

'Mrs Conway contacted us just before he was released, talking about protection. We got in touch with the people at Tanford then. They sent us stuff from their files.'

Nodding, Bardeen turned to the sergeant. 'Have you got the bloke in the Jag's mobile?'

'They're looking at it now. Bit mangled in the crash.'

'Get in touch with the phone company and ask them to send us a printout of his calls over the past month. No, better make that two months.' He smiled across the cluttered desk. 'That should do it for now. Keep me posted.'

FOURTEEN

Samantha allowed the Ferrari to roll to a stop and glanced around the area of rough concrete. The only yellow car was parked beneath a tree on the far side. Who was this Edward? It could be a ruse to get her here. She clicked open her bag, took out her gun, found the silencer amongst the cosmetics and screwed it on to the muzzle. Long in the barrel and cumbersome now, she laid it on her lap and covered it with her bag before driving closer to the yellow car. She could see a young man's face behind the windscreen. The registration number tallied. Drawing up alongside, cars almost touching, she lowered her sidelight and signalled the youth to do the same. Their faces were close. 'Edward Goodwin?'

He nodded and swallowed. A prominent Adam's apple jerked up and down. 'And you're the private detective?'

'Got it in one, Edward. I'm sorry I'm late.'

'That's OK. I thought perhaps you weren't coming.' He sounded relieved.

Samantha smiled, watched a blush flare on his cheeks and spread down his throat. He seemed to be in awe of her, overwhelmed by this new experience. 'How about I buy you lunch?'

'Jennifer's waiting for me. You told me to come alone, so I left her in a second-hand bookshop. Can we talk here?'

'Remind me, Jennifer is Helen Conway's daughter?'

He nodded.

'She knows about this? We can talk in front of her?'

He nodded again.

'I need lunch, Edward, and Jennifer's been in that bookshop so long she's had time to read half the stock. Collect her and we'll all have lunch. The White Speckled Hen; it's in a village called Bridewell, up in the hills. Do you know it?'

'It's where my parents had their silver wedding do.'

'I'll see you there in twenty minutes.'

Martin Manson keyed numbers into the pad, held the phone to his ear and listened to the ringing tone. He'd been trying for hours now. Whoever had taken the attaché-case must have immobilized the tracker.

He gazed across Victoria Park. A young woman was exercising half a dozen dogs, schoolboys were playing football. Out here everything was so normal, so tranquil, but in echoing halls … The sick rage welled up in him again. Killing Arza and Habib was wretched enough, but what the evil whore had done to Virendra, the gentlest and wisest of men, was beyond all understanding. Tears pricked his eyes. She would pay. If he spent the rest of his life searching for her, she would pay.

He still had books and papers at the Studies Centre, but he dare not collect them. Isghar the Imam had called him at dawn and urged him to leave the town. Police with warrants had entered and begun to search. Filthy kuffar. As Habib used to endlessly repeat, they were like pigs, defecating where they ate and slept, defiling all that they touched. But the black-haired whore, that Daughter of Satan, was an utter abomination. She had to be punished. It had to be made clear to the people who had sent her that they could not treat his brothers in this way.

The low-battery symbol was showing on his phone. He must get it charged. It was vital that he keep trying to reach the tracker. Once again he stabbed angrily at the numbers on the key pad, then lifted the phone to his ear. Just the ringing tone. He prayed that the evil whore hadn't removed the linked phones from the case.

The meal, served at a table close to an open fire, had revived her. Glancing from one pale young face to the other, Samantha said, 'So, Edward, you've been running rings around big city bankers?'

His gaze lowered from big green eyes to breasts beneath a black woollen dress, then jerked down to his cup. He was uncomfortable. He'd never felt more uncomfortable in his life. This woman was weird – gorgeous but weird – the black hair, the fringe, the white teeth behind the scarlet mouth; he'd never seen such a succulent mouth.

'But you didn't take any money?' the husky voice went on.

He shook his head. 'It was just a game; a challenge. It was difficult and I wanted to prove to myself that I could do it. It's the mathematics of programming I'm interested in. I don't know a thing about banking. I've no idea how you'd get serious money out of the system.'

'It would be difficult, removing a large sum of money?'

'I'd have thought it impossible unless you could make the bank think you were the account holder; and even then they should be able to trace it. I mean, you've got to make an electronic deposit somewhere before you can convert it into cash.'

'When did you start getting the threats?'

Edward glanced at Jennifer. 'A couple of days ago?'

She nodded and gave him a reassuring smile.

He turned back to Samantha. 'My parents have a holiday bungalow in Lindon Sands, a tiny seaside place on the south coast. We went there to shut it down for the winter. I keep a server in an old house that's used for storage. We went there before we left so I could check it out. That's when I found there'd been traffic and someone had left a message.'

'Server?'

'It connects computers to the internet. I installed my own so I could control it, disable the logging, stuff like that. If something went wrong, I didn't want trouble coming back to Cheltenham.' He reached into his pocket, pulled out a paper and passed it over the table.

Samantha unfolded it. 'They're saying they want twenty million pounds?'

Edward shrugged. 'Twenty pounds, twenty million pounds; I've no idea what they're talking about.'

'This store; who owns it, what's kept in it?'

'It was my grandparents' until they died. They owned the amusement arcade. It's crammed with old game machines, pinball tables, that sort of stuff.'

'Would there be what they call a Laughing Sailor in there?'

'An automaton? Sure, there's one of those.'

'Jolly Jack Tar on the hatband, paint a bit chipped on the face?'

'That's the one. How did you—'

'You've been using a video of it to mock the bankers.'

He blushed. 'How did you know that?'

She ignored his question. 'You're in big trouble, Edward. Bit like playing around with a ouija board. A merry little game until you summon up the spirits.'

His face had turned grey. 'I'm not sure I know what you mean.'

'Some people, dangerous people, lost a lot of money from one of the banks you were playing games with. They've had people investigating it. They must have managed to trace your server thing, and they've identified you with the theft.'

Jennifer leaned forward. 'Don't you think Edward should go to the police? If these people find out where he lives, it would be worse than anything the police might do.'

'He'd serve time,' Samantha said. 'He'd have a criminal record. And these people haven't found him yet. Can they discover where this server actually is?'

'Not unless they have access to the network provider's records.'

'This server; is it registered under your own name?'

He shook his head. 'George Branwell.'

'Branwell was your grandparents' name?'

'They were called Thompson. I dreamed Branwell up.'

'They're not going to find you, Edward, at least, not quickly. Where is this server now?'

'Still in the house that's been turned into a store. I disconnected it, but I didn't bring it away. God, what a mess. It was just a joke. I never meant to cause all this trouble.'

Jennifer reached over the table and laid her hand on his.

'Do you want me to deal with it?' Samantha asked.

'Would it cost a lot?'

'Don't concern yourself with the cost. You said you devised programmes to hack into the bank. I want you to put everything on marked disks, including the sailor video. And I want you to write a brief description, not too technical, no more than a single typed sheet, explaining what the programmes do, then wipe every trace from your equipment. When I have the disks I can deal with the bankers. Dealing with the people who've been robbed will take a little longer.'

'Should I drive down to Lindon Sands and get the server?' Edward asked.

'It might be better if you don't go near the place for a while. Is it very big?'

'About the same size as a desktop computer. It's in a bedroom in what's left of the house.'

'The wiring to it? Would it be difficult to remove?'

'I unplugged the power lead, but there's a box under the window for the line connection. Tugging on the cable should pull it free.'

'And the Laughing Sailor?'

'In a glass case in the storeroom. Glass case just lifts off. Shouldn't be too difficult to pull the doll from the mechanism.'

'Where is this store?'

While Edward gave directions, he took a bunch of keys from his pocket and began to work two of them free. 'This one's for the door on the street; it's next to the amusement arcade.' He slid a big iron key across the table. 'And this one's for the entrance to the store. It's on the bend in the passageway.' He handed her a key to a cylinder lock. 'Will you be staying overnight in Lindon?'

'Could be.'

'The hotels and bed-and-breakfast places are probably pretty awful.' He removed more keys from the ring. 'These are for the holiday bungalow. Drive west, out of town, along the narrow little road that runs close to the shore. The bungalow's white with a green roof. It's all on its own. You can't miss it. Main switch for the electricity is at the back of the garage.'

Samantha rose, smoothed the skirt of her black dress, then drew on her coat. Virendra's blood still stained it. Before she'd left the hotel she'd tried to sponge it off, then dry the fabric with a hairdryer, but there was still a faint dark patch on the brown. She smiled across at Jennifer. The girl responded with a faint tightening of her lips. Worried and distressed about her mother's accident, she seemed too tired to think, too upset to speak. Samantha linked her arm in hers and they headed out into the sunlit car park.

When Edward walked off towards the cars, Samantha held her back. 'Your mother,' she said. 'How is she?'

Jennifer closed her eyes and began to shake. 'I don't know. They won't tell me much. They're doing brain scans today. Edward's taking me in again this afternoon.' Her eyes blinked open. She was fighting back tears. 'Mummy spoke to me yesterday; well, mumbled something. I think she was trying to tell me not to have anything to do with Daddy.'

'Has he contacted you?'

'Last night. I'm staying at Edward's, but I could hear the phone ringing in our house – it's next door – so I ran round. He said he'd heard about the accident. He wanted to know if I was OK. He gave me his mobile number, told me to ring him if I needed anything or if I wanted to talk.' She brushed blond hair from her eyes. 'It felt really strange, hearing his voice again.'

Samantha took Jennifer's arm and turned her so she could study her face. It was pale and trembling and there were dark shadows around her eyes. 'I think you should follow your mother's advice.'

'Not see Daddy, you mean?'

Samantha nodded.

'People at the police station called the policeman at the hospital this morning and asked him if I was there. They were trying to get Daddy's mobile number.'

'You gave it to them?'

Jennifer shrugged. 'Of course. Can't think why they wanted it. They could call him on the house phone or at his office.' She was suddenly fighting back tears again. 'Do you think it was in case they had to get hold of him quickly, because of Mummy?'

Probably want a record of the calls he's made, Samantha reflected. She gave Jennifer a reassuring smile. 'It's just procedures. They'll be filling in forms.'

Sniffing, Jennifer dabbed away tears with a tiny handkerchief that had rabbits embroidered on it. 'Mummy told you about her and daddy?'

Samantha nodded.

'Marriage seems to be very difficult. Half the girls at school have parents who are divorced. Are you married?'

Surprised by the directness of the question, Samantha said, 'I was. I'm a widow.'

'Were you happy?'

'I thought I was in heaven.'

'How did he die?'

The insensitivity of the young. 'A sniper's bullet; a terrorist. It was a long time ago.'

'But you're still upset. I can tell.'

'I want to kill every terrorist in the world,' Samantha whispered huskily. 'And even that wouldn't compensate for the love they stole from me.'

They joined Edward by the cars. 'I'll communicate with you

through Jennifer,' Samantha said. 'Save you any embarrassment with your parents. Give the disks and the written note to her; tomorrow if you can. That should be the end of it as far as you're concerned. If anyone asks questions, just say you know nothing.'

'Thanks,' Edward said. 'I'm truly grateful.'

Samantha smiled. He was naïve and trusting. Someone older and wiser would have questioned her before involving her in their affairs. But then, he was desperate, and help from any other quarter would have had its consequences.

She slid into the Ferrari, slammed the door and keyed the ignition. Edward wrapped his arm around Jennifer's waist, Jennifer laid her head on his shoulder, and they waved as the low car growled out of the car park.

Samantha lifted the garage door and peered inside. It was cluttered with summer deckchairs, gardening tools, half-used tins of paint. She'd wanted to hide the Ferrari, conceal the fact that the bungalow was occupied, but she was too exhausted to clear a space. It would have to stay on the hard standing. She looked for the electricity meters; saw them, high on the back wall, and went in and switched on the supply.

Her overnight bag was in the boot of the car. She lifted it out. As an afterthought, she grabbed the attaché-case she'd taken from the man who called himself Habib Alani. It still held the five thousand she'd retained from the fifty-five he'd been carrying around: too much to leave in a car, even in this wilderness of sea and sand and muddy pools.

The sailor doll was leering up at her from behind the server. When she was back in Barfield she'd burn the doll and take the server to a waste-disposal site. She dropped the boot lid, secured the car, then climbed steps that rose up a steeply terraced garden and unlocked the front door.

It was cold inside the bungalow. Samantha kept her coat on while she heated a can of soup and made a mug of instant coffee;

black, there was no milk, the fridge had been emptied and its door left ajar. Without switching on the lights, she wandered through the dining room, crossed the hall, and entered a large sitting room where another long window gave her a view over the expanse of mud and reeds and mist-covered pools. Out at sea, the lights of buoys and distant ships were beginning to gleam in the gathering dusk. Only the plaintive cries of seabirds, faint beyond the window, disturbed the silence.

Samantha shivered. The cold, the desolation of the place, suddenly depressed her. She'd been insane to allow Marcus to involve her in this business. And the endless killing – not just over the last few days, but down all the years – was destroying her. In the very act of it, she felt a cathartic release from the all-consuming hatred, but then came disgust and self-loathing. She'd tried to forgive and forget, to move on, but that devious bastard Marcus kept calling her back. And her sessions with Dr Uberman didn't seem to be going anywhere. Perhaps she'd expected too much. She'd had to lie to him to protect herself, and her responses had been so guarded they couldn't have been of any use.

Her eyes were closing. She was exhausted. She'd look over the bedrooms, choose one, then find some pillows and a blanket, take off her dress and shoes, and sleep in the ruined coat. Early in the morning, perhaps before dawn, she'd head north, keep her appointment with Dr Uberman, then drive home. She felt a sudden longing to see Crispin. She missed him. She missed him more than she cared to admit.

Before she found a bed, there was something she had to do. Clicking open her bag, she took out a tiny leather-bound diary, licked a finger and turned its flimsy pages. Eventually she found the notes she'd taken when she'd scrolled the information on Marcus's disk. He'd assured her the surveillance had been painstakingly thorough, that the information was up to date. Grassman – Lawrence, Stuart, Morris: Lawrence was reckoned to be the head of the firm. She perched on an armchair, flicked open her mobile and keyed in his number.

Almost immediately a gruff voice with just a trace of a Birmingham accent growled, 'Who is this?'

'You're a bunch of greedy bastards, Lawrence,' Samantha whispered huskily. 'It was thirteen million and a few thousand that went missing, not twenty million.'

'I said, who is this?' the voice grated.

'Someone calling on behalf of your new business partners.'

'How did you get this number? No one knows this number.'

'I can get any number, Lawrence. I'm almost as smart as your fat friend at the packing warehouse, the man with the computers.'

'Who are you?'

'I've been instructed to arrange a meeting with the Grassman brothers.'

'I didn't ask you what you're trying to do. I asked you who you fucking well think you are. And what would I want to meet anyone for?'

'To get half of the thirteen million back. That's fair, Lawrence. You never lost it; the bank did. And to discuss terms.'

'Terms?'

'For a merger.'

'What would we want a fucking merger for?' His Birmingham accent was strident now.

'It's not what you want, Lawrence. It's what you're going to have to accept. I can tell you're upset, so we'll leave the details for later.' Suddenly remembering the sailor doll, she said, 'I'm going to send you a little present. Shall I address the parcel to that rather nice house you share with the Brazilian woman; or shall I send it to the flat in Rimmington Place, the little love-nest where you have your twice-weekly trysts with Sonya? Bit naughty that, Lawrence, screwing you brother's wife.'

'Who the fuck are you?' There was a hard edge of fear in his voice now.

Samantha laughed huskily. 'Someone who can keep a secret about Sonya. I'll contact you again, in a couple of days, to fix up that meeting.'

Martin Manson's body stiffened. The ringing tone had stopped; the clicking had begun. He'd got through. She must have stored the attaché-case in a car boot or a footwell, somewhere surrounded by metal that had blocked out the signal. He watched the screen on his phone. A network of roads and a stretch of coast-line appeared. He studied the brightly lit display. Sidmouth, Salcombe Regis, Lindon Sands. The red marker was stationary. She'd probably stopped for the night somewhere. He had to act quickly. If she put the case back in her car signals wouldn't reach the mobile phones and he'd lose her again.

He keyed the ignition. Probably best to cut across to Birmingham, travel south on the M5: 150 miles, perhaps a little more. Traffic would be light at this hour, but later he'd have to pinpoint the place where she was staying. He glanced at the dash-board clock. If God willed it, he'd be there well before dawn. He let out the clutch and swept down the service station exit.

FIFTEEN

Her wedding outfit was a disappointment. It had been copied from a photograph in a fashion magazine. Just a tiny bolero jacket over a strapless dress with a short skirt flared out by petticoats, all in white satin. The local seamstress hadn't been able to capture the cheeky style of the haute couture original, but it had been inexpensive. It had been all she could afford.

It was a hot day, even for July. Samantha removed her jacket and wandered out on to the balcony. The hotel had been built near the summit of Mount Carmel and Haifa city, the full sweep of the bay and the sea beyond, were spread out beneath her. The sun burned out of a painfully bright sky. It gleamed on a golden temple dome, glared off distant city walls, made the trees in the Bahai gardens cast dark shadows.

Her new mother-in-law was watching her. Samantha smiled and begged with her eyes. Please be kind to me, for I am a motherless child. Her mother-in-law sipped at her glass, then turned away and began to talk to the rabbi. This slip of a girl, this Gentile, this goy, had stolen her son: her handsome, doctor son. She would never forgive her. How could she forgive her?

Music began to play. Guests were drifting back into the dining room. A hand took hers. It was Ruben. At least he was smiling at her. It was an adoring smile; a smile full of love and happiness and joy. Nothing mattered when Ruben smiled at her like that. She closed her eyes. They were dancing now. He was holding her hand, his arm around her waist. He took her by the wrist and began to turn her. Her feet, in the white satin shoes, weren't nimble enough. She began to fall. His grip tightened. He was still turning her, bringing her face back to his. Her shoulders were cooler now, almost cold. She sensed a strangeness. There was something wrong. The heat, the sound of chattering guests, the lively music, were fading....

Samantha opened her eyes. Two points of light gleamed at her out of the darkness and the cold. She could hear harsh open-mouthed breathing; feel the moist warmth of it on her skin. Her arms were spread wide; her wrists were captured in a fierce grip. Fear lanced through her. Checking an impulse to scream, she snarled, 'Who the hell are you?'

Her captor drew one of her arms down by her side, trapped her wrist beneath his knee, then reached out and switched on the bedside lamp. Dark eyes, cold and menacing, stared down at her. His beard was short, the narrow moustache that curved down to it blurred by stubble. He grabbed her wrist and swung it up to the pillows again. He was kneeling astride her, his legs imprisoning her hips.

'Who are ...' Her mind began to clear. She remembered the striking image Marcus had shown her. It was the man who called himself Manson; the doctor of divinity. She swallowed hard. Her heart was pounding. She had to control her fear. She had to think. Not wise to reveal she knew who he was. That would tell him too much about her.

'You don't need to know who I am.' He spoke English with an American accent, in a voice devoid of emotion. After gazing down at her in silence for a while, he said, 'Why did you murder Arza Mahmood and Habib Alani? Why did you do the things that you did to Virendra Khan? Those men were my brothers.'

'I don't know who you're talking about. I don't know these people.'

'Don't lie to me.' He tightened his grip on her wrists. 'Why did you kill them? What possessed you to do such a depraved thing to Virendra?'

'You're mistaken. I don't—'

His mouth became ugly. 'Stop lying to me. You have Habib's money case. How do you think I found my way to you?'

'What case? I don't know about a case.' She injected a note of anger into her voice. 'And how could a case help you find me?'

'The black attaché-case you stole from him. It held more than fifty thousand pounds. Beneath the lining are two mobile phones. One is connected to the geopositioning system. When the other is activated by a call, it relays back a map showing were it is located. You killed Habib and took the case.' He gripped her hips more tightly between his knees, then released one of her wrists and wrapped a huge hand around her throat. 'No more lies. No more evasions. Tell me who and what you are.'

Samantha's mind raced. More denials would get her a beating. 'The bank hired me to recover money.' Her eyes held his while she stealthily slid her freed hand beneath the pillow.

Sneering, releasing his grip on her throat, he reached behind him on the bed. 'Looking for this?' He held up her gun. 'I took it while you slept.' He ejected the magazine, tossed it across the room, then dropped the gun to the floor. 'Does a woman who recovers money for banks need such a large and powerful weapon?' He suddenly scowled. 'Why did you humiliate Abdulgader? Why did you make him take off his clothes?'

'Abdulgader?'

'The cab-driver you lured into a workshop by the river.'

'He was following me. I hid in the old building but he came inside and found me. He undressed himself because he was going to rape me.'

'And you killed him?'

'What else could I do?'

'You're a liar. What man would remove his clothes to rape a woman in a public place? And Abdulgader would never have defiled himself with a Kafir whore. You made him undress because it was easier for you to search him; it permitted you to see if he had anything strapped to his body. And why did you murder little Rashid Naveed, the brother who served meals to those arrogant pigs at the bank? Why did you murder Tahir Bukhari and Shazad Hussain, the friends who shared his house? You have killed seven of my brothers in as many days.'

'The cab-driver was going to rape me. I don't know anything about the others,' Samantha insisted.

'Liar! Do you take pleasure from humiliating men? And how could you do such an unspeakable thing to Virendra?'

Samantha tried to keep her voice steady, its tone firm. 'I've already told you, I don't know this man you call Virendra,' she insisted.

'You have the attaché-case his friend was carrying.'

'I don't have an attaché-case. If it's in Lindon Sands someone else brought it here.'

He fumbled with buttons, unfastened her coat and pulled it open. 'Such pale flesh,' he muttered. 'Like a corpse, like death.' His gaze flicked back to her face. 'You murdering whore. You sack of filth.'

Heart pounding, mind racing, she stared up at the big head and massive shoulders. This man was heavy and powerfully built, his hands were huge; he was alert and strong and driven by hate. She understood what it was to be driven by hate. It left you without pity, robbed you of all restraint. Struggling with him would be futile. Whatever happened, she had to control her fear and remain calm.

Breathing deeply, she forced her shoulders to relax on the pillow and said, 'You're mistaken about those men. I had to shoot the cab-driver, but I know nothing of the others.' Her voice fell to a whisper. 'What are you going to do with me?'

'Humiliate you, like you humiliated Abdulgader. Mutilate you, just as you mutilated Virendra. I shall avenge them slowly. I shall take pleasure in degrading you and inflicting pain.'

'You don't have the time. My partner's joining me here. We're spending the weekend together. He'll—'

'You're a pathetic liar. No one is coming here. No one will hear your screams. No one will come to your aid. You are going to pay for what you did to my brothers. Tell me your name?'

'Temple; Shirley Temple.'

'And what do you do, Miss Temple? What do you really do.'

'People hire me to investigate things. The bank hired me to recover missing money.'

He tugged straps over her shoulders, slid them down her arms and exposed her breasts. 'And you kill men when you investigate things? You mutilate their bodies? I don't think so, Miss Temple. I think you are employed by the State.' His eyes left hers and drifted down her body. The tempo of his breathing changed; became quick and shallow. He moistened his lips.

Samantha dug her heels into the bed. Slowly, gently, she slid her body along the silk lining of her coat until her shoulders were high on the pillows and her arms were out of the sleeves. Lowering her voice, she made it enticing. 'How could I let that cab-driver man rape me? He was old and fat and ugly.' Lust had hardened Manson's mouth, coarsened his features. His hands slid down from her shoulders and began to fondle her breasts. 'I don't find you ugly,' she whispered huskily. 'With you it would be different. Do you want to kiss me?'

His eyes swept up. 'Kiss you?' he sneered. 'I'd rather kiss a camel's arse.'

'You don't find me attractive? What is it about me that you don't find attractive?'

Samantha knew now what she had to do. It was her only chance of surviving this. Sharon Halevi, her combat instructor at the Shabak, had explained the technique. But it was something you could never practise; something you could only do when the need arose.

Pouting up at him, she smiled and murmured, 'Don't you like

my mouth? Tell me what it is about my face, my body, that you
don't like.' She ran her hand up his arm, eased his jacket over his
shoulders, then pulled on the sleeves.

'Whore,' he breathed. 'You filthy little whore.' He shrugged the
garment off.

'Can I help it if I find you handsome? Women feel desire, too.'
She unfastened his tie, drew it from his collar, then unbuttoned his
shirt. His skin was hot. 'Isn't that better? This doesn't have to be
nasty and unpleasant. Now, kiss me. I'd like you to kiss me.'

Filled with anger and self-loathing at his mounting lust for this
woman, he snarled. 'I wouldn't defile my mouth by touching it to
yours.'

Slowly, gently, Samantha slid an arm around his neck. Sharon
Halevi had stressed the importance of restraining the head.

'If you don't want to kiss my mouth, kiss my breasts. Surely
you'd like to kiss my breasts?' She drew him towards her. She
could feel the warmth of his breath on her skin. It had to be swift;
one quick movement. She wouldn't have a second chance. Raising
her other hand, she caressed his cheek, combed her fingers into his
dark hair, stroked her thumb across his eyebrow and the bridge of
his nose. 'Kiss me,' she whispered. 'I'd like you to.' She imprisoned
his neck in the crook of her arm and drew him closer.

Now. Do it now.

Stabbing her thumb into the corner of his eye, she hooked her
nail into the soft tissue behind it. He reared back, screaming, but
she clung to him, felt a squishy sucking as she gouged the glis-
tening ball from its socket. It seemed surprisingly large in her hand
when she tried to tear it free.

He grabbed her wrist and squeezed until her screams mingled
with his. Releasing the dangling eye, she rolled on to her side,
toppled him off the bed, then fell, sprawling, beside him.

The ornate stem of the bedside lamp was heavy; its glass shade
a cheap Tiffany imitation. She dragged it from the table, let its
weight crash down on Manson's head. Then, grabbing it in both

hands, lifted it and let it drop again, and again, and again. Fragments of glass fell from the shade. The bulb shattered, plunging them into darkness. She kept up the pounding until his screams became moans, then she crawled to the door. Pulling herself to her feet, she switched on the ceiling light. Miraculously, his eye was still attached by a filament of bloody tissue. Wires in the broken bulb of the lamp were pressing against his cheek. She could smell the current burning his flesh; see it making his body shudder.

She stood over him and kicked him. When he made no response, she knelt down, pulled the cable from its socket, tore it from the base of the lamp, then rolled his body over and used it to bind his wrists.

Feeling safer now, she retrieved her gun and searched for the magazine. She found it beneath a chest of drawers and slid it back into the butt.

This was the Goodwins' home. Edward knew she was staying overnight. She couldn't leave a body here. Blood was oozing from the empty eye socket and from lacerations to the head and face. In here the carpet was a mingled brown and terracotta colour that would conceal the staining, but the carpet in the hall was pale green, almost white. She went to the bathroom, took a towel from an airing cupboard, returned and wrapped it around Manson's head and face. His moans were muffled now, his breathing was irregular.

Samantha pulled on her dress, then grabbed the cord binding his wrists and dragged him out of the bedroom and down the hall to the front door. His inert body was heavy; she had to lean forward, balance his weight with hers, in order to keep him moving along the carpet. Kneeling, she patted his hips and thighs, felt coins and keys, then reached into his pockets and turned out the contents. Suddenly remembering, she rose to her feet and crossed over to the kitchen.

When she'd arrived, she'd slid the attaché-case on to a worktop while she heated soup. She clicked it open and peeled back the silk lining. What looked like the inner workings of a pair of mobile phones were taped to the inside of the case. Wires looped down. Pushing aside bundles of bank notes, she tore away more of the silk and exposed a layer of flat grey batteries. After tugging out the wires, she took a knife from a drawer and stabbed at the mobile phones until the circuit boards shattered. Then she carried the case into the hall, scooped up the contents of Manson's pockets and tossed them inside. She retained the keys to his car.

She drew on her coat, pushed her feet into her shoes and switched off the lights. Somehow, Manson had managed to unlatch the front door. Too tired and exhausted to think, she'd not bothered to bolt it before retiring to bed. Even if she had, he'd have found a way in. She dragged him out on to the path. He was arching his back now; straining at the cable that bound his wrists.

She looked down the steeply sloping garden. He'd parked his car, a blue Ford Mondeo, across the drive to block her Ferrari in. Beyond the narrow private road a blanket of mist, white and luminous in the moonlight, was drifting across the marshes. Nearer the horizon the lights of a ship seemed as remote as the stars.

Samantha shivered; pressed her foot into Manson's back and sent him tumbling down the steps. She followed. The hard-standing in front of the garage sloped steeply to the road. She rolled his body down it, opened his car, then climbed into the back and braced herself against the sill of the door while she dragged him inside. Moaning loudly now, he was jerking his arms and trying to break free. She closed the door, knelt on the back seat and drew the gun from her coat. The silencer was in her bag and her bag was in the bungalow. It was an isolated place. She'd take a chance. Pressing the muzzle against his temple, she squeezed the trigger.

There was an overcoat in the boot. She used it to cover the body, then opened suitcases, riffled through shirts and socks and underwear, searched the pockets of slacks and jackets. She found nothing.

Exhausted, but too agitated to rest, Samantha could feel the shock of Manson's assault beginning to numb her mind and chill her body. She daren't succumb to it. There were things she had to do before she could leave this god-forsaken place. Hands shaking, she locked the car and climbed back up the steps to the bungalow. The bloodstained towel was lying on the path. Her assailant's eye was lost amongst the stones.

SIXTEEN

Samantha relaxed on the couch and settled her head on the paper-covered pillow. She felt dishevelled. Her tights were laddered, she hadn't been able to change out of the black dress; hadn't been prepared to take a bath in cold water.

She ran her mind over the events of the past eight hours, trying to think of things she might have missed. The Ford Mondeo was parked on rubble-strewn wasteland to the east of the city. Edward's server and the bloodstained remains of the lamp and the towel were piled on top of Manson's body, along with his clothes. She'd doused them in petrol and left them burning fiercely. By now, everything should be incinerated, the car a blackened shell.

She'd cleaned up the bedroom in the bungalow; moved beach things and bric-à-brac aside and hidden the Ferrari in the garage. Manson's papers, the contents of his pockets and the five thousand pounds, were in the attaché-case. The sailor doll was packed in a box she'd found in the garage, ready to be couriered to Lawrence Grassman – she'd left the box and the attaché-case with Miss Forster in the waiting room. Her gun was in her clutch bag, lying beside her on the couch. Had she overlooked anything? Hopefully not.

God, she was tired. She could hear Dr Uberman rambling on about word association. She must try to pay attention.

'Mother,' the word drifted across the darkened room.

'Father,' she whispered back, too tired to be more inventive.

'Father.'

She yawned. 'Jew.'

'Sister.'

Mother, father, sister? She blinked sleepily. Her family were dead. She ...

Dr Uberman waited for a reply. Her breathing, just audible in the silence, had slowed and deepened. He rose, crept over to the couch and peered down at her. Although not so perfectly groomed today, the pale-complexioned woman lying there was still hauntingly beautiful. She was asleep, and the breasts that shaped the black wool of her dress were gently rising and falling.

He returned to his chair. He'd leave her, wake her near the close of the session and talk to her then. While she slept, he'd read through his notes again, but he didn't expect to find anything that would alter his decision or change the advice he intended to give her.

Presently he glanced at his watch. There was less than fifteen minutes of her time left. He whispered, 'Miss Quest ... Samantha.' He made his voice louder. 'I'd like you to wake now, Samantha.'

He watched her raise herself on to an elbow and eye him sleepily over her shoulder. 'I fell asleep. I'm sorry, Doctor. I—'

'You were obviously tired. I left you to sleep. Sleep can be a wonderful restorative for the mind.'

'We didn't complete the word association; I haven't told you about my dream.'

'There have been developments?' It was irrelevant now, but he couldn't help feeling curious.

'Yes. I last had it two nights ago.'

Enough time remained. He leafed back through his notes and found the page. 'You were wading along a shallow river that was clotted with blood and you'd come upon a huge primordial tree. Its roots, gorged with blood, had entwined around your legs and thighs, holding you safe against the strong current. You were gazing up into a vast canopy of leaves. Did I note everything correctly?'

'Perfectly.' Samantha settled her head into the pillow, then went on, 'I hear a rustling. The leaves are parting. Suddenly I'm gazing up into a painfully bright sky and a voice says, 'Everything has been revealed to you: what you must fear, and what you must do.'

'Is this the voice of a man, or a woman?'

'A man. It is the voice of my husband, Ruben.'

'And what is it that you must fear and do?'

She suddenly grasped the meaning of the dream. 'I've no idea,' she lied.

'And then?'

'And then I wake.'

'You say you last had the dream two nights ago?'

'That is so. And I had the final version of the dream, the one I have just described, every night for two nights before that.'

'But not since?'

'No.'

'Have other dreams replaced the river and tree dream?'

'Yes.'

'Are they similar dreams?'

'Quite different, Doctor. I dream that my husband is making love to me.'

And more than nine years a widow, Dr Uberman mused. The woman was bound by heavy chains. Sighing, he said, 'Although the details of the river and tree dream are somewhat unusual, the theme is not. Dreams where knowledge is revealed and the dreamer is frustrated by ignorance on waking are not uncommon.'

He rose, strode over to the window, released first one blind, then another, until the room was washed by pale and uncertain sunlight. He came over to the couch, took her hand and helped her into a sitting position. When she'd swung her legs to the floor, he sat down beside her. After gazing at her for a moment, he said, 'Samantha, I have given much thought to our conversations, to your responses to the word-associations, to your unfolding dream, and I have come to the conclusion that analysis would be excessively prolonged and achieve little in your case. I feel I should discharge you as a patient.'

'Our sessions are to end?'

He nodded. 'But I have advice for you. Advice I hope you will be able to take, because I think it offers you your only chance of finding the peace of mind you crave.' Reaching for her hand again, he held it in both of his.

Samantha strolled to the end of Harley Street, crossed Marylebone Road and found an empty bench in Regent's Park. Dr Uberman had surprised her. How arrogant she'd been to presume he wouldn't realize she'd contrived many of her answers in the word association tests. But what else could she have done? If she'd allowed herself to fall into the traps he was setting, as she had on that one occasion, she'd have revealed too much. His advice had disturbed her. It was advice she might not be able to take. On reflection, she had to concede the wisdom of it.

The muted roar of traffic surging along Marylebone Road was useful. This small section of the park was deserted now, but people might pass and the constant sound would obscure her words. She opened the encrypted phone and keyed in the number.

'Sam? Where are you?'

'In Regent's Park.'

'Can we meet?'

'No. When I've finished this call I'm going to leave the City. I just wanted to tell you Martin Manson's dead.'

'Christ, not another body. The Chief's having problems with the politicians. She's been trying to persuade them it's sectarian feuding, punishments, settling old scores, stuff like that, but it's wearing thin. And the Met's not being helpful.'

'She shouldn't have too many problems with this one. I put his body and all of his things in the back of a hire car and torched it; there won't be much of him left. I've got his passports, American and Saudi, and some papers. I'll get them to you. I didn't have the chance to question him. Did you do anything with the information I got out of Virendra?'

'Made more than sixty arrests; Birmingham, Leeds, Bradford, some in Leicester. Quite a few British born, a number of them women. The fertilizer stored in Leicester was for bomb-making.'

'Ammonium nitrate and diesel oil; ANFOs?'

'Diesel oil or paraffin. They were going to mix the peroxide stored at the Islamic Studies Centre with acetone to make detonators; we found about a dozen cans of cellulose thinners in an outhouse in the rear yard. They were planning multiple car-bombings, Taliban style; driving in when the pubs and clubs and streets would be crowded, then sending women suicide bombers into the hospitals with the injured. It's all taking quite an ominous turn. How's the bank investigation going?'

'Getting nowhere. I never expected it to.' She yawned. Marcus didn't need to know about Edward's involvement.

'You mentioned a weighty bloke in a computer room at the Coventry warehouse – you thought he might have helped the Grassmans snatch the cash. I had him checked out. He's called Christopher Blessed. Registered sex offender; suspected paedophile. Police have been trying to nail him for years, but he's slippery. Genius with computers.'

'So he could have helped them remove the cash?'

'Or he could be trying to get it back.'

Suddenly overwhelmed by tiredness, she said, 'I'll give the bank thing another week, then I'm going to abandon it.'

'But you'll have lunch with Sir Nigel?'

'Yes, Marcus,' she muttered irritably. 'I'll have lunch with Sir Nigel and report back.'

'And the Grassman brothers and their depot at Loughborough? You'll look the place over?'

'Send someone else in. Let's face it, Marcus, you and Loretta have had more than your money's worth out of the temporary contract.'

'When can we meet? I need to—'

'I'm signing off now, Marcus.'

'Just one more thing, Sam … Sam, you still there?'

She switched off the phone, slid it into her bag and picked up the attaché-case. She had to find a cab-driver who'd take her to the south coast. When she'd collected the Ferrari, she'd head for Cheltenham, check into a hotel, take a bath, change her clothes, and have a meal. Then she'd contact Jennifer Conway and pick up the disks and notes Edward had promised her.

Samantha leafed through a glossy fashion magazine while she waited in the hotel lounge. She'd managed to snatch a few hours' sleep, her bags were packed and loaded in the Ferrari, and her bill was paid. She was wondering whether or not to order tea when she caught sight of Jennifer Conway, her grey topcoat unbuttoned, approaching across the foyer. Automatic glass doors slid open. Jennifer stepped through and glanced around. When she caught sight of Samantha, she strolled over.

Smiling, Samantha gestured towards a chair. 'How are you?'

'Fine.' Jennifer sat down. 'Mother's on the mend, so I'm feeling much better. They're letting her come home tomorrow. Apart from cuts and broken ribs and a fractured collar bone, they can't find anything wrong.'

'Would you like some tea?'

Jennifer shook her head. 'Edward's meeting me.' She opened her leather document case. 'He sent you these.' She handed Samantha a manilla envelope. 'The disks and the notes you asked for. Three sheets of notes: he couldn't get it all on one. Is everything going to be OK now? He won't be arrested or anything, will he?'

Samantha slid the envelope into her bag. 'Tell him to forget it. Tell him he must never mention it to anyone. I've removed the sailor doll and the server. The next time he goes to Lindon Sands, he ought to get rid of the glass case and the mechanism.' She handed Jennifer a package. 'Would you give him that for me. I broke a lamp with a Tiffany shade. That should cover it.' She'd wrapped one of the thousand-pound bundles in brown paper; Edward's folly had earned her a great deal of money.

'The lamp was only a tacky fairground-prize thing. And he thought he was going to have to pay you.'

'Tell him to forget it. As far as he's concerned, it's finished with, and there won't be any come-backs.' Samantha smiled at her. 'Now, tell me how you are: I mean, how you *really* are.'

Sighing, Jennifer managed to return her smile. 'It's all been a bit of an upheaval. Mummy's accident, staying with Edward's parents. His mother's been so kind to me, and Edward's been very supportive.'

'But?'

'But I feel a bit suffocated. I'll be glad when Mummy's home.'

'There's something else, isn't there?' Samantha said softly.

The girl looked down at her hands. 'They've arrested Daddy. He'd been in Cheltenham when he said he'd not. He'd been following me around, trying to catch a glimpse of me. Creepy! I mean, why didn't he just come over and talk to me? And they've got statements from a vicar and a lorry driver saying the crash was deliberate.'

Jennifer glanced up, tried to meet Samantha's searching gaze, but found she couldn't.

'Grandma phoned last night. When she couldn't speak to Mummy, she ranted on at me instead. Said she hoped Mummy was satisfied. She'd destroyed her son's life, destroyed her life, and now Daddy had been arrested and he'd probably be sent to prison again.' She paused and looked up. The big green eyes were still studying her intently. Suddenly deciding to tell this strange woman everything, she went on, 'A letter came in the post this morning. It was addressed to Mummy in Grandma's handwriting. I opened it.'

Samantha took the proffered envelope and withdrew the papers. Jennifer went on, 'Someone's had tests done. They're saying

Daddy's not my real father. I bet Grandma did it to upset Daddy, to turn him against Mummy and me. She always resented us.'

Samantha unfolded the letter. The first page was missing. There was nothing to indicate who it was from or to or when it had been sent. She glanced across at Jennifer.

'What shall I do?'

Samantha folded the papers, slid them inside the envelope and handed them back. 'Nothing for now. Wait until your mother's fully recovered, then give her the letter. She'll tell you what she wants you to know.'

Jennifer gave Samantha a bleak look.

'He'd already gone, love,' Samantha murmured softly. She reached over and squeezed Jennifer's hand. 'How long is it since you've seen him? Four years? Does this make all that big a difference?' She made her voice brighter, trying to distract the girl. 'How do you feel about Edward?'

'He's become quite attentive and he's been very kind, but he's still unbelievably shy. He can't seem to bring himself to kiss me.'

'Do you really want him to?'

Jennifer's nose wrinkled. 'Not really.'

Laughing, they rose and walked through to the lobby. 'Put it all behind you,' Samantha urged. 'Go to university. Make the most of the experience. You're standing on the threshold of a great adventure.'

Jennifer linked her arm through Samantha's as they descended the steps to the street. 'That's more or less what my form mistress told me.'

Samantha pushed at the glass door. It was locked. She peered through. Across a dark foyer light gleamed beyond an opening at the back of the reception desk. She turned, walked the length of the warehouse and rounded the corner at the end. The huge rolling shutter that secured the loading bays had been lowered, but there was a pedestrian door at the top of a flight of concrete steps.

When she climbed up and pressed the handle, it opened. As she'd expected, someone was still inside. She removed her shoes, left them by the door, then walked along one of the loading platforms, moving deeper into the huge metal building.

A light was shining in Christopher Blessed's office. When she'd worked on the packing lines, he'd always lingered on after everyone had left. She could see him now, through the open door, sitting in his shirtsleeves, his great bulk almost filling the tiny space. Marcus had said he was a genius with computers. The Grassman brothers had brought him here and set him up with equipment. If what her companion on the packing lines had told her was correct, he'd arrived shortly after the funds had gone missing from the bank. That being the case, it was unlikely he'd been involved in siphoning money away. He'd probably been investigating the loss for the Grassmans, perhaps trying to effect a recovery. She'd decided to break her journey north, call at the warehouse, persuade him to tell her what he knew about the missing funds.

Samantha descended steps from the loading platform to the warehouse floor. The only illumination came from Blessed's office and some shaded bulbs above the walkway around the mezzanine. The packing lines, the bins and trays containing the various tools, were submerged in shadow.

Sliding her gun from her bag, she moved silently through the labyrinth of racks and roller-topped benches, emerged at the far side, then began to climb up to the mezzanine floor. The metal stairs ended opposite the door to Blessed's office. As she rose up the last few treads, she could seen him, squeezed into his high-backed swivel-chair, peering into a computer monitor. She stepped across the narrow walkway and raised her gun. 'Hullo, Christopher.'

He jerked round, startled. When he saw the black-haired woman dressed in a crimson suit, his body tensed. 'Justyna … Justyna Lukaszewski!' Frightened eyes flickered over her face.

'How's Fred the Feeler? Is he still limping?'

'Foot's turned septic. He's been told he might lose it.' Blessed's voice, thin and high-pitched, wheezed out of the mountain of flesh.

Samantha smiled, then noticed the sailor doll she'd sent to Lawrence Grassman, perched on top of a computer console. 'Where did you get the doll?'

'Someone sent it to one of the Grassman brothers. He thought they were trying to spook him. He dumped it here.'

'Is Lawrence losing his patience with you, Christopher? Is he mad because you've not got his thirteen million back? I suppose it was his idea to ask for twenty?'

'You know about that?'

'I know everything, Christopher. All about you and your sexual preferences; all about the Grassmans.'

His plump hands gripped the arms of his chair. He wetted his lips. 'Lawrence was right,' he whispered. 'You were sent here to work on the packing lines. You were watching us.'

Samantha waved the gun and smiled. 'Have you recovered the thirteen million?'

'It's not going to be recovered. Some very big organization's snatched it. Might be the Government.'

'Might be?'

'More than possible. Whoever did it had access to the codes and passwords at the bank and all the details of the Grassman brothers' account. They were able to set up a bank, registered in the Cayman Islands, to receive the funds, then they got rid of it without leaving a trace after they'd transferred the money some-where. Only a very big organization or a Government department would have the clout and the resources to do that.'

'The Grassman brothers; do they think it might be the Government?'

'They suspected it. Government's been prying into their affairs for years. Do you know about the laughing face?' He gestured towards the sailor doll.

Samantha nodded.

'When we saw that, we decided it couldn't be the Government. They'd sequester the cash, but they wouldn't mock the bank with a laughing face. Then someone made threats and sent the doll to Lawrence. That convinced us it wasn't the Government.'

'The things that were done to take the money: have you got any details?'

'Got a printout of all the moves they made, right up to the Cayman Islands bank that no longer exists.'

Samantha waved the gun. 'Give it to me.'

Metal groaned when he turned his swivel-chair. He reached for a file and plucked out a sheet of paper.

Stepping closer, she said, 'Lay it on the keyboard and put your hands on the desk.'

He did as she asked. Despite the cold, his brow was beaded with sweat and moist patches were creeping across his shirt.

Samantha peered over his shoulder at a list of about a dozen number-and-letter sequences that meant nothing to her.

'That's my best attempt. The trail comes to a dead end at the Cayman Islands bank.'

'Don't turn round. Just pick it up and hand it to me.'

As he passed the document over his shoulder, Samantha glanced at the display screen. Names like Chuck and Baz, Joy Boy and Sensual Sam, identifiers that ensured anonymity, were listed along-side e-mail addresses. What seemed to be subscription details, together with a reference number, were included against each entry. Samantha guessed she was looking at the membership list for Christopher Blessed's paedophile network; when he lingered on after closing time he was dealing with his personal business.

'I've not been here, have I, Christopher?'

He shook his head.

Glancing down, she saw he'd raised plump knees and placed his feet against the bottom drawer of the desk. 'I'm going to leave you, Christopher. Stay where you are for five minutes.'

She flattened herself against a filing cabinet. A heartbeat later he jerked his legs straight and sent the chair careering back. Surprise flared on his face when he brushed past instead of crashing into her, castors rolled out of the door, the chair tipped back and he tumbled, head first, down the stairs.

Samantha stepped on to the decking and peered over the handrail. He was sprawling, motionless, beside a steel column. The up-ended chair was wedged beneath a bench.

Back in the office, she ejected the disk carrying his subscription list and tucked it in her bag; then she slid open drawers and found a plastic lunch box, paper tissues, cartons of orange juice, empty beefburger trays and a box of pens. The filing cabinet was empty. She gathered up some folders stacked at the side of the display screen, grabbed the sailor doll, then went down the stairs.

Christopher Blessed's nose was bleeding, his mouth opening and closing, as if he were trying to speak. Even with the silencer fitted, the thud of the gun seemed loud in the silent warehouse. She slid the weapon back into her bag and ran over to the loading bays. The paedophile ring had lost its coordinator. His successor might not be so clever. The police might be able to identify the people on his membership list. There was a remote chance that the suffering of the innocents would come to an end.

Comfortable again in her shoes, she left the compound and walked out into the deserted industrial estate. Security lights illuminated yards and the blind walls of drab metal buildings. The orange glow of streetlamps punctuated a monotonous ribbon of tarmac that curved towards the motorway. After walking a hundred yards she climbed into the Ferrari, tossed the files and doll on to the passenger seat, then keyed a number into the encrypted phone.

'Marcus?'

'Sam. I'm in a meeting. Can I—'

'No, Marcus. I need to talk now.' She heard men's voices, a door slamming, silence, then:

'What's it about, Sam?' Anger at having been interrupted sounded in his voice.

'You arranged the illicit sequestration of the drug payments, Marcus. You got the dealers and the suppliers agitated, then sent me in to set hares running.'

'Sam, I've no idea—'

'Where's the money, Marcus? I've just been given a printout of the moves your people made. I've been assured no private agency would have the resources to work a scam like that. You arranged it. You wanted to provoke a response.'

'That's sheer fantasy, Sam.'

'Tell me where the money is, Marcus, or Sir Nigel at British and Asian gets a printout listing the steps you took to remove the funds.'

'Your contract might be temporary, Sam, but you're still bound by the Official Secrets Act. You can't—'

'Do you think I give a shit? You've got what you wanted. You've moved in amongst the terrorists. The sequestration was illicit. Pay it back. If you don't tell me how the funds can be recovered, I'll brief Sir Nigel. He can raise it with the politicians. And aren't you supposed to be his friend, Marcus? Don't you drink and dine and smoke cigars with him at that select gentleman's club? He'll feel more betrayed than I do.'

There was an exasperated sigh. 'Look, I've got to get back to the meeting. I'll—'

'Bugger your meeting, Marcus. Now! I want an answer now.'

'Tomorrow,' he said. 'I'll contact you tomorrow.'

'Now, Marcus.'

'I can't do it now, dammit.' The words snarled out of the phone. There was a silence, then a calmer voice said, 'Tomorrow. Tomorrow you'll get a call on this phone, from a woman. When she asks you to identify yourself, say, "Shirley Temple, one of the guardians of Fund 937." Then she'll give you an account number, the name of a bank and a password to access the deposit. You can give that information to Sir Nigel.'

'You treacherous bastard, Marcus.'

'Queen and Country, Sam. There are greater loyalties than the loyalties one has to one's colleagues and one's friends.'

Samantha caught her breath, appalled by the pomposity. 'I'm amazed you have any friends to betray,' she managed to retort. Then, remembering, 'By the way, your paedophile's dead. His body's by the packing bays in the Keen-Bright Tools warehouse in Coventry.' She switched off the phone, dropped it into her bag, then searched for her tiny leather-bound diary. Leafing through it, she found a number, keyed it into her own mobile and listened to the ringing tone. She was about to switch off when a male voice demanded to know who was calling.

'That you, Stuart?'

'Who is this?'

'I think people like me are usually called Well Wishers,' she whispered huskily. 'I just want you to know Lawrence is screwing your lovely little wife; most Tuesday and Thursday afternoons. Takes her to a flat in Rimmington Place.'

After a long silence, a shaky voice said, 'How do you know this?'

'Observation. I live in the building. Don't be hasty, Stuart. Say nothing. Just watch the place tomorrow afternoon, wait half an hour, then follow them in. Belview House; flat 24. You've been spending too much time getting your new club up and running. You've been neglecting affairs on the domestic front.'

Samantha switched off the phone. The Crown Prosecution Service might be too limp-wristed to contemplate arrest and trial. At least she'd sown a little dissent within the Grassman family.

EPILOGUE

Rome could be cold in December. Samantha gathered her furs around her throat and turned into the brightly lit via Napolitano. A sudden feeling of hunger made her recall the lunch she'd had with Sir Nigel Lattimer. He'd been charming and effusively grateful. The chef had excelled himself. She'd given Sir Nigel the Laughing Sailor doll. He'd since told her he'd had the moth-eaten thing mounted in a splendid bronze-framed glass case. Hat tilted rakishly, it now smiled down on the members of the board. British & Asian had recouped its thirteen million. Her million-pound bounty, a trifle dented now, was safe in a Swiss bank account.

She began to ascend worn steps. She was feeling apprehensive. Did she really want to confront herself in this way? The carved door groaned shut behind her. Save for a few old women lighting votive candles and kneeling in prayer, the Baroque church was empty. She saw a woman leave one of the confessionals, walk towards the altar and slide into a pew.

The tapping of Samantha's heels seemed loud as she crossed the aisle and took the woman's place in the dusty booth. Her furs were voluminous; closing the door proved difficult. Kneeling, she glimpsed the white-haired priest through the grille, purple stole around his neck, his back towards her. She took a deep breath. 'Bless me Father, for I have sinned.'

She heard a mumbled prayer.

'It is sixteen years since I last went to confession, and since then I—'

'Sixteen years? May I ask what has brought you back to the sacrament after sixteen years? Forgive me for interrupting you, but I'm curious.'

Samantha pondered. Should she say, 'Because my analyst advised me to?' That might offend him. Anyway, there was more to it than that, and it was all much too complicated to put into words. She had to say something. Closing her eyes, she let her mind range back to her convent school days. Suddenly inspired, she said, 'Because I have offended God's infinite goodness and my sorrow overwhelms me.'

'If you are overwhelmed by sorrow because you have, as you say, offended God's infinite goodness, He has already forgiven you. But we can never be sure of the depth and nature of our sorrow, so make your confession.'

'I have killed many men.'

'How many?'

'I'm not sure, Father. More than a hundred.'

'Why did you kill these men?'

'I was employed by the Government. It was a task assigned to me. They were mostly terrorists and criminals.'

'You serve your country?'

'I have served more than one country.'

'You are a mercenary? You offer your services for hire?'

'No ... Yes. But I did it because ...'

'Because?'

'Because of a craving for justice; because I felt I was protecting the innocent.'

'Do you enjoy the killing?'

'No.'

'Your actions have saved lives?'

'Many lives.'

Samantha heard a sigh, then, 'It seems to me you are like a

soldier, fighting in a war. For a war to be legitimate, it must be pursued with reasonable force, be for a just cause, have some certainty of a good outcome. So far you have told me nothing that violates those principles.'

'I have killed men who weren't terrorists or criminals; innocent agents who became involved.'

'You killed them to preserve your own life?'

'Yes, Father.'

'Only God can judge the right and wrong of this, but I feel that if you continue to live in this way you will be in great moral danger.'

'I have tortured men, Father.'

'Tortured men?'

'I had to learn their secrets. Discovering them saved lives.'

'A good end never justifies an evil means. Were these tortures severe?'

'Humiliating, brutal, painful; always ending in death. I had to act swiftly, Father. I had no time to question them patiently, no time to reflect.'

'That is a grave offence, my child. No matter how beneficial the outcome, no matter how many lives were saved, such actions could never be justified.'

'And I am consumed by hate for the terrorists I kill.'

'You must try to rid yourself of hate. All men deserve our love, no matter what they have done. Is there anyone in your life that you love?'

'A man.'

'You are married to him?'

'No, but we are friends; intimates.'

'You have a carnal relationship?'

'No, Father.'

After a silence, Samantha said, 'I lie to deceive; to conceal my identity. I spend lavishly on clothes and cars.'

'How would the seamstress and the mechanic live if those with money did not buy the things they made?' The old priest sighed, then said, 'If there is nothing else that you wish to confess, I think we have talked enough. There is so much moral ambiguity here, only God can discern the good and the evil in it. I am going to give you absolution. For your penance, say a decade of the rosary; choose from the sorrowful mysteries. Now, make a good act of contrition.'

'Father, the men I tortured and killed, I—'

'Change your employment! You not only endanger your life, you run the risk of damning your immortal soul. And attend mass, daily if you can. And frequent the sacraments.'

'But Father—'

'Enough! I am going to give you absolution. Make a good act of contrition then abandon yourself to the boundless love of God.'

High heels clicking on flagstones, fur coat swirling around her ankles, Samantha strode down the via Lombardia. Tomorrow she and Crispin would try out the new Ferrari Fiorano, drive north to Milan, visit the fashion houses; Crispin could help her choose things from the new collections. Tonight he was out on the town with a gentle-eyed boy he'd met in bar. She'd dine alone, have dinner sent up to her room, then take a bath and retire to bed.

Her analyst had abandoned her to the priest, sent her back to the certainties of childhood. But the years had stolen her innocence, her unquestioning trust, and the old priest's absolution had done little to assuage her guilt. Perhaps she first had to forgive herself.

Samantha pushed through the revolving door, into the opulent foyer of the hotel; she collected her key from the reception desk and crossed over to the lifts.

She was no longer visited by the dream of the stalking man in the culvert and the eyes on the river bed. Since her brush with death at Lindon Sands, it no longer troubled her.

Lift doors rumbled open. Samantha stepped inside and leaned

back against honey-coloured marble. She closed her eyes. She was certain now that her husband had been warning her of the danger she was in; that he'd been trying to reveal the thing she would have to do to escape it. Perhaps one night, when he came to her in her dreams, he would tell her how she might find the peace of mind she craved.